NEXT STOP: TOMORROW

This is a fascinating collection of unusual fiction, written by the outstanding author of stories of the future. Robert A. Heinlein gives free rein to his stimulating imagination in these superb stories about the unexplored realms of the mind and the fascinating possibilities of new worlds ahead.

A security agent of the future seizes the most valuable microfilm in the universe only to find himself engaged in a death battle with sinister forces from another planet. A professor and his students use thought control to enter other worlds. The masterminding forces for good engage in deadly combat with evil powers seeking the conquest of the Earth. A vigorous woman of a future day wages a spirited battle to secure justice for an oppressed worker in a strange world peopled with Martians.

These are exciting and provocative tales by one of the most famous space-age fiction storytellers.

"Robert A. Heinlein stands head and shoulders above most science fiction writers."
—*Springfield Republican*

Other SIGNET Books by Robert A. Heinlein

ASSIGNMENT
IN
ETERNITY

BY

Robert A. Heinlein

A SIGNET BOOK from
NEW AMERICAN LIBRARY
TIMES MIRROR

SIGNET TRADEMARK REG. U.S. PAT. OFF. AND FOREIGN COUNTRIES
REGISTERED TRADEMARK—MARCA REGISTRADA
HECHO EN CHICAGO, U.S.A.

SIGNET, SIGNET CLASSICS, MENTOR AND PLUME BOOKS
are published by The New American Library, Inc.
1301 Avenue of the Americas, New York, New York 10019

PRINTED IN THE UNITED STATES OF AMERICA

Contents

Sprague and Catherine

GULF

THE FIRST-QUARTER ROCKET from Moonbase put him down at Pied-a-Terre. The name he was traveling under began—by foresight—with the letter "A"; he was through port inspection and into the shuttle tube to the city ahead of the throng. Once in the tube car he went to the men's washroom and locked himself in.

Quickly he buckled on the safety belt he found there, snapped its hooks to the wall fixtures, and leaned over awkwardly to remove a razor from his bag. The surge caught him in that position; despite the safety belt he bumped his head—and swore. He straightened up and plugged in the razor. His moustache vanished; he shortened his sideburns, trimmed the corners of his eyebrows, and brushed them up.

He towelled his hair vigorously to remove the oil that had sleeked it down, combed it loosely into a wavy mane. The car was now riding in a smooth, unaccelerated 300 mph; he let himself out of the safety belt without unhooking it from the walls and, working very rapidly, peeled off his moonsuit, took from his bag and put on a tweedy casual outfit suited to outdoors on Earth and quite unsuited to Moon Colony's air-conditioned corridors.

His slippers he replaced with walking shoes from the bag; he stood up. Joel Abner, commercial traveler, had disappeared; in his place was Captain Joseph Gilead, explorer, lecturer, and writer. Of both names he was the sole user; neither was his birth name.

He slashed the moonsuit to ribbons and flushed it down the water closet, added "Joel Abner's" identification card; then peeled a plastic skin off his travel bag and let the bits follow the rest. The bag was now pearl grey and rough, instead of dark brown and smooth. The slippers bothered him; he was afraid they might stop up the car's plumbing. He contented himself with burying them in the waste receptacle.

The acceleration warning sounded as he was doing this; he barely had time to get back into the belt. But, as the car plunged into the solenoid field and surged to a stop, nothing remained of Joel Abner but some unmarked underclothing, very ordinary toilet articles, and nearly two dozen spools of microfilm equally appropriate—until examined—to a commercial traveler or a lecturer-writer. He planned not to let them be examined as long as he was alive.

He waited in the washroom until he was sure of being last man out of the car, then went forward into the next car, left by its exit, and headed for the lift to the ground level.

"New Age Hotel, sir," a voice pleaded near his ear. He felt a hand fumbling at the grip of his travel bag.

He repressed a reflex to defend the bag and looked the speaker over. At first glance he seemed an under-sized adolescent in a smart uniform and a pillbox cap. Further inspection showed premature wrinkles and the features of a man at least forty. The eyes were glazed. A pituitary case, he thought to himself, and on the hop as well. "New Age Hotel," the runner repeated. "Best mechanos in town, chief. There's a discount if you're just down from the moon."

Captain Gilead, when in town as Captain Gilead, always stayed at the old Savoy. But the notion of going to the New Age appealed to him; in that incredibly huge, busy, and ultramodern hostelry he might remain unnoticed until he had had time to do what had to be done.

He disliked mightily the idea of letting go his bag. Nevertheless it would be out of character not to let the runner carry the bag; it would call attention to himself—and the bag. He decided that this unhealthy runt could not outrun him even if he himself were on crutches; it would suffice to keep an eye on the bag.

"Lead on, comrade," he answered heartily, surrendering the bag. There had been no hesitation at all; he had let go the bag even as the hotel runner reached for it.

"Okay, chief." The runner was first man into an empty lift; he went to the back of the car and set the bag down beside him. Gilead placed himself so that his foot rested firmly against his bag and faced forward as other travelers crowded in. The car started.

The lift was jammed; Gilead was subjected to body pressures on every side—but he noticed an additional, unusual, and uncalled-for pressure behind him.

His right hand moved suddenly and clamped down on a skinny wrist and a hand clutching something. Gilead made no further movement, nor did the owner of the hand attempt to draw away or make any objection. They remained so until the car reached the surface. When the passengers had spilled out he reached behind him with his left hand, recovered his bag and dragged the wrist and its owner out of the car.

It was, of course, the runner; the object in his fist was Gilead's wallet. "You durn near lost that, chief," the runner announced with no show of embarrassment. "It was falling out of your pocket."

Gilead liberated the wallet and stuffed it into an inner

pocket. "Fell right through the zipper," he answered cheerfully. "Well, let's find a cop."

The runt tried to pull away. "You got nothing on me!"

Gilead considered the defense. In truth, he had nothing. His wallet was already out of sight. As to witnesses, the other lift passengers were already gone—nor had they seen anything. The lift itself was automatic. He was simply a man in the odd position of detaining another citizen by the wrist. And Gilead himself did not want to talk to the police.

He let go that wrist. "On your way, comrade. We'll call it quits."

The runner did not move. "How about my tip?"

Gilead was beginning to like this rascal. Locating a loose half credit in his change pocket he flipped it at the runner, who grabbed it out of the air but still didn't leave. "I'll take your bag now. Gimme."

"No, thanks, chum. I can find your delightful inn without further help. One side, please."

"Oh, yeah? How about my commission? I gotta carry your bag, else how they gonna know I brung you in? Gimme."

Gilead was delighted with the creature's unabashed insistence. He found a two-credit piece and passed it over. "There's your cumshaw. Now beat it, before I kick your tail up around your shoulders."

"You and who else?"

Gilead chuckled and moved away down the concourse toward the station entrance to the New Age Hotel. His subconscious sentries informed him immediately that the runner had not gone back toward the lift as expected, but was keeping abreast him in the crowd. He considered this. The runner might very well be what he appeared to be, common city riffraff who combined casual thievery with his overt occupation. On the other hand—

He decided to unload. He stepped suddenly off the sidewalk into the entrance of a drugstore and stopped just inside the door to buy a newspaper. While his copy was being printed, he scooped up, apparently as an afterthought, three standard pneumo mailing tubes. As he paid for them he palmed a pad of gummed address labels.

A glance at the mirrored wall showed him that his shadow had hesitated outside but was still watching him. Gilead went on back to the shop's soda fountain and slipped into an unoccupied booth. Although the floor show was going on—a remarkably shapely ecdysiast was working down toward her last string of beads—he drew the booth's curtain.

Shortly the call light over the booth flashed discreetly; he called, "Come in!" A pretty and very young waitress came inside the curtain. Her plastic costume covered without concealing.

9

She glanced around. "Lonely?"

"No, thanks, I'm tired."

"How about a redhead, then? Real cute—"

"I really am tired. Bring me two bottles of beer, unopened, and some pretzels."

"Suit yourself, sport." She left.

With speed he opened the travel bag, selected nine spools of microfilm, and loaded them into the three mailing tubes, the tubes being of the common three-spool size. Gilead then took the filched pad of address labels, addressed the top one to "Raymond Calhoun, P. O. Box 1060, Chicago" and commenced to draw with great care in the rectangle reserved for electric-eye sorter. The address he shaped in arbitrary symbols intended not to be read, but to be scanned automatically. The hand-written address was merely a precaution, in case a robot sorter should reject his hand-drawn symbols as being imperfect and thereby turn the tube over to a human postal clerk for readdressing.

He worked fast, but with the care of an engraver. The waitress returned before he had finished. The call light warned him; he covered the label with his elbow and kept it covered.

She glanced at the mailing tubes as she put down the beer and a bowl of pretzels. "Want me to mail those?"

He had another instant of split-second indecision. When he had stepped out of the tube car he had been reasonably sure, first, that the *persona* of Joel Abner, commercial traveler, had not been penetrated, and, second, that the transition from Abner to Gilead had been accomplished without arousing suspicion. The pocket-picking episode had not alarmed him, but had caused him to reclassify those two propositions from calculated certainties to unproved variables. He had proceeded to test them at once; they were now calculated certainties again—of the opposite sort. Ever since he had spotted his erstwhile porter, the New Age runner, as standing outside this same drugstore his subconscious had been clanging like a burglar alarm.

It was clear not only that he had been spotted but that they were organized with a completeness and shrewdness he had not believed possible.

But it was mathematically probable to the point of certainty that they were not operating through this girl. They had no way of knowing that he would choose to turn aside into this particular drugstore. That she could be used by them he was sure—and she had been out of sight since his first contact with her. But she was clearly not bright enough, despite her alley-cat sophistication, to be approached, subverted, instructed and indoctrinated to the point where she could seize an unexpected opportunity, all in a space of time merely adequate to fetch

10

two bottles of beer. No, this girl was simply after a tip. Therefore she was safe.

But her costume offered no possibility of concealing three mailing tubes, nor would she be safe crossing the concourse to the post office. He had no wish that she be found tomorrow morning dead in a ditch.

"No," he answered immediately. "I have to pass the post office anyway. But it was a kind thought. Here." He gave her a half credit.

"Thanks." She waited and stared meaningfully at the beer. He fumbled again in his change pocket, found only a few bits, reached for his wallet and took out a five-pluton note.

"Take it out of this."

She handed him back three singles and some change. He pushed the change toward her, then waited, frozen, while she picked it up and left. Only then did he hold the wallet closer to his eyes.

It was not his wallet.

He should have noticed it before, he told himself. Even though there had been only a second from the time he had taken it from the runner's clutched fingers until he had concealed it in a front pocket, he should have known it—known it and forced the runner to disgorge, even if he had had to skin him alive.

But why was he sure that it was not his wallet? It was the proper size and shape, the proper weight and feel—real ostrich skin in these days of synthetics. There was the weathered ink stain which had resulted from carrying a leaky stylus in the same pocket. There was a V-shaped scratch on the front which had happened so long ago he did not recall the circumstances.

Yet it was not his wallet.

He opened it again. There was the proper amount of money, there were what seemed to be his Explorers' Club card and his other identity cards, there was a dog-eared flat-photo of a mare he had once owned. Yet the more the evidence showed that it was his, the more certain he became that it was not his. These things were forgeries; they did not *feel* right.

There was one way to find out. He flipped a switch provided by a thoughtful management; the booth became dark. He took out his penknife and carefully slit a seam back of the billfold pocket. He dipped a finger into a secret pocket thus disclosed and felt around; the space was empty—nor in this case had the duplication of his own wallet been quite perfect; the space should have been lined, but his fingers encountered rough leather.

He switched the light back on, put the wallet away, and resumed his interrupted drawing. The loss of the card which should have been in the concealed pocket was annoying, certainly awkward, and conceivably disastrous, but he did not judge that the information on it was jeopardized by the loss of the wallet. The card was quite featureless unless examined by black light; if exposed to visible light—by some one taking the real wallet apart, for example—it had the disconcerting quality of bursting explosively into flame.

He continued to work, his mind busy with the wider problem of why they had taken so much trouble to try to keep him from knowing that his wallet was being stolen—and the still wider and more disconcerting question of why they had bothered with *his* wallet. Finished, he stuffed the remainder of the pad of address labels into a crack between cushions in the booth, palmed the label he had prepared, picked up the bag and the three mailing tubes. One tube he kept separate from the others by a finger.

No attack would take place, he judged, in the drug store. The crowded concourse between himself and the post office he would ordinarily have considered equally safe—but not today. A large crowd of people, he knew, are equal to so many trees as witnesses if the dice were loaded with any sort of a diversion.

He slanted across the bordering slidewalk and headed directly across the middle toward the post office, keeping as far from other people as he could manage. He had become aware of two men converging on him when the expected diversion took place.

It was a blinding light and a loud explosion, followed by screams and startled shouts. The source of the explosion he could imagine; the screams and shouts were doubtless furnished free by the public. Being braced, not for this, but for anything, he refrained even from turning his head.

The two men closed rapidly, as on cue.

Most creatures and almost all humans fight only when pushed. This can lose them decisive advantage. The two men made no aggressive move of any sort, other than to come close to Gilead—nor did they ever attack.

Gilead kicked the first of them in the knee cap, using the side of his foot, a much more certain stroke than with the toe. He swung with his travel bag against the other at the same time, not hurting him but bothering him, spoiling his timing. Gilead followed it with a heavy kick to the man's stomach.

The man whose knee cap he had ruined was on the pavement, but still active—reaching for something, a gun or a knife. Gilead kicked him in the head and stepped over him, continued toward the post office.

Slow march—slow march all the way! He must not give the appearance of running away; he must be the perfect respectable citizen, going about his lawful occasions.

The post office came close, and still no tap on the shoulder, no denouncing shout, no hurrying footsteps. He reached the post office, was inside. The opposition's diversion had worked, perfectly—but for Gilead, not for them.

There was a short queue at the addressing machine. Gilead joined it, took out his stylus and wrote addresses on the tubes while standing. A man joined the queue almost at once; Gilead made no effort to keep him from seeing what address he was writing; it was "Captain Joseph Gilead, the Explorers' Club, New York." When it came his turn to use the symbol printing machine he still made no effort to conceal what keys he was punching—and the symbol address matched the address he had written on each tube.

He worked somewhat awkwardly as the previously prepared gummed label was still concealed in his left palm.

He went from the addressing machine to the mailing receivers; the man who had been behind him in line followed him without pretending to address anything.

Thwonk! and the first tube was away with a muted implosion of compressed air. *Thwonk!* again and the second was gone—and at the same time Gilead grasped the last one in his left hand, sticking the gummed label down firmly over the address he had just printed on it. Without looking at it he made sure by touch that it was in place, all corners sealed, then *thwonk!* it joined its mates.

Gilead turned suddenly and trod heavily on the feet of the man crowded close behind him. "Wups! pardon *me*," he said happily and turned away. He was feeling very cheerful; not only had he turned his dangerous charge over into the care of a mindless, utterly reliable, automatic machine which could not be coerced, bribed, drugged, nor subverted by any other means and in whose complexities the tube would be perfectly hidden until it reached a destination known only to Gilead, but also he had just stepped on the corns of one of the opposition.

On the steps of the post office he paused beside a policeman who was picking his teeth and staring out at a cluster of people and an ambulance in the middle of the concourse. "What's up?" Gilead demanded.

The cop shifted his toothpick. "First some damn fool sets off fireworks," he answered, "then two guys get in a fight and blame near ruin each other."

"My goodness!" Gilead commented and set off diagonally toward the New Age Hotel.

He looked around for his pick-pocket friend in the lobby, did not see him. Gilead strongly doubted if the runt were on the hotel's staff. He signed in as Captain Gilead, ordered a suite appropriate to the *persona* he was wearing, and let himself be conducted to the lift.

13

Gilead encountered the runner coming down just as he and his bellman were about to go up. "Hi, Shorty!" he called out while deciding not to eat anything in this hotel. "How's business?"

The runt looked startled, then passed him without answering, his eyes blank. It was not likely, Gilead considered, that the runt would be used after being detected; therefore some sort of drop box, call station, or headquarters of the opposition was actually inside the hotel. Very well, that would save everybody a lot of useless commuting—and there would be fun for all!

In the meantime he wanted a bath.

In his suite he tipped the bellman who continued to linger.

"Want some company?"

"No, thanks, I'm a hermit."

"Try this then." The bellman inserted Gilead's room key in the stereo panel, fiddled with the controls, the entire wall lighted up and faded away. A svelte blonde creature, backed by a chorus line, seemed about to leap into Gilead's lap. "That's not a tape," the bellman went on, "that's a live transmission direct from the Tivoli. We got the best equipment in town."

"So you have," Gilead agreed, and pulled out his key. The picture blanked; the music stopped. "But I want a bath, so get out—now that you've spent four credits of my money."

The bellman shrugged and left. Gilead threw off his clothes and stepped into the "fresher." Twenty minutes later, shaved from ear to toe, scrubbed, soaked, sprayed, pummeled, rubbed, scented, powdered, and feeling ten years younger, he stepped out. His clothes were gone.

His bag was still there; he looked it over. It seemed okay, itself and contents. There were the proper number of microfilm spools—not that it mattered. Only three of the spools mattered and they were already in the mail. The rest were just shrubbery, copies of his own public lectures. Nevertheless he examined one of them, unspooling a few frames.

It was one of his own lectures all right—but not one he had had with him. It was one of his published transcriptions, available in any large book store. "Pixies everywhere," he remarked and put it back. Such attention to detail was admirable.

"Room service!"

The service panel lighted up. "Yes, sir?"

"My clothes are missing. Chase 'em up for me."

"The valet has them, sir."

"I didn't order valet service. Get 'em back."

The girl's voice and face were replaced, after a slight delay, by those of a man. "It is not necessary to order valet service here, sir. 'A New Age guest receives the best.' "

"Okay, get 'em back—chop, chop! I've got a date with the Queen of Sheba."

"Very good, sir." The image faded.

With wry humor he reviewed his situation. He had already made the possibly fatal error of underestimating his opponent through—he now knew—visualizing that opponent in the unimpressive person of "the runt." Thus he had allowed himself to be diverted; he should have gone anywhere rather than to the New Age, even to the old Savoy, although that hotel, being a known stamping ground of Captain Gilead, was probably as thoroughly booby-trapped by now as this palatial dive.

He must not assume that he had more than a few more minutes to live. Therefore he must use those few minutes to tell his boss the destination of the three important spools of microfilm. Thereafter, if he still were alive, he must replenish his cash to give him facilities for action—the amount of money in "his" wallet, even if it were returned, was useless for any major action. Thirdly, he must report in, close the present assignment, and be assigned to his present antagonists as a case in themselves, quite aside from the matter of the microfilm.

Not that he intended to drop Runt & Company even if not assigned to them. True artists were scarce—nailing him down by such a simple device as stealing his pants! He loved them for it and wanted to see more of them, as violently as possible.

Even as the image on the room service panel faded he was punching the scrambled keys on the room's communicator desk. It was possible—certain—that the scramble code he used would be repeated elsewhere in the hotel and the supposed privacy attained by scrambling thereby breached at once. This did not matter; he would have his boss disconnect and call back with a different scramble from the other end. To be sure, the call code of the station to which he was reporting would thereby be breached, but it was more than worthwhile to expend and discard one relay station to get this message through.

Scramble pattern set up, he coded—not New Washington, but the relay station he had selected. A girl's face showed on the screen. "New Age service, sir. Were you scrambling?"

"Yes."

"I am veree sorree, sir. The scrambling circuits are being repaired. I can scramble for you from the main board."

"No, thanks, I'll call in clear."

"I yam ve-ree sor-ree, sir."

There was one clear-code he could use—to be used only for crash priority. This was crash priority. Very well—

He punched the keys again without scrambling and waited. The same girl's face appeared presently. "I am verree sorree, sir; that code does not reply. May I help you?"

"You might send up a carrier pigeon." He cleared the board.

15

The cold breath on the back of his neck was stronger now; he decided to do what he could to make it awkward to kill him just yet. He reached back into his mind and coded in clear the *Star-Times*.

No answer.

He tried the *Clarion*—again no answer.

No point in beating his head against it; they did not intend to let him talk outside to anyone. He rang for a bellman, sat down in an easy chair, switched it to "shallow massage", and luxuriated happily in the chair's tender embrace. No doubt about it; the New Age *did* have the best mechanos in town —his bath had been wonderful; this chair was superb. Both the recent austerities of Moon Colony and the probability that this would be his last massage added to his pleasure.

The door dilated and a bellman came in—about his own size, Gilead noted. The man's eyebrows went up a fraction of an inch on seeing Gilead's oyster-naked condition. "You want company?"

Gilead stood up and moved toward him. "No, dearie," he said grinning, "I want *you*"—at which he sank three stiffened fingers in the man's solar plexus.

As the man grunted and went down Gilead chopped him in the side of the neck with the edge of his hand.

The shoulders of the jacket were too narrow and the shoes too large; nevertheless two minutes later "Captain Gilead" had followed "Joel Abner" to oblivion and Joe, temporary and free-lance bellman, let himself out of the room. He regretted not being able to leave a tip with his predecessor.

He sauntered past the passengers lifts, firmly misdirected a guest who had stopped him, and found the service elevator. By it was a door to the "quick drop." He opened it, reached out and grasped a waiting pulley belt, and, without stopping to belt himself into it, contenting himself with hanging on, he stepped off the edge. In less time than it would have taken him to parachute the drop he was picking himself up off the cushions in the hotel basement and reflecting that lunar gravitation surely played hob with a man's leg muscles.

He left the drop room and started out in an arbitrary direction, but walking as if he were on business and belonged where he was—any exit would do and he would find one eventually.

He wandered in and out of the enormous pantry, then found the freight door through which the pantry was supplied.

When he was thirty feet from it, it closed and an alarm sounded. He turned back.

He encountered two policemen in one of the many corridors under the giant hotel and attempted to brush on past them. One of them stared at him, then caught his arm. "Captain Gilead—"

Gilead tried to squirm away, but without showing any skill in the attempt. "What's the idea?"

"You are Captain Gilead."

"And you're my Aunt Sadie. Let go of my arm, copper."

The policeman fumbled in his pocket with his other hand, pulled out a notebook. Gilead noted that the other officer had moved a safe ten feet away and had a Markheim gun trained on him.

"You, Captain Gilead," the first officer droned, "are charged on a sworn complaint with uttering a counterfeit five-pluton note at or about thirteen hours this date at the Grand Concourse drugstore in this city. You are cautioned to come peacefully and are advised that you need not speak at this time. Come along."

The charge might or might not have something to it, thought Gilead; he had not examined closely the money in the substituted wallet. He did not mind being booked, now that the microfilm was out of his possession; to be in an ordinary police station with nothing more sinister to cope with than crooked cops and dumb desk sergeants would be easy street compared with Runt & Company searching for him.

On the other hand the situation was too pat, unless the police had arrived close on his heels and found the stripped bellman, gotten his story and started searching.

The second policeman kept his distance and did not lower the Markheim gun. That made other consideration academic. "Okay, I'll go," he protested. "You don't have to twist my arm that way."

They went up to the weather level and out to the street—and not once did the second cop drop his guard. Gilead relaxed and waited. A police car was balanced at the curb. Gilead stopped. "I'll walk," he said. "The nearest station is just around the corner. I want to be booked in my own precinct."

He felt a teeth-chattering chill as the blast from the Markheim hit him; he pitched forward on his face.

He was coming to, but still could not co-ordinate, as they lifted him out of the car. By the time he found himself being half-carried, half-marched down a long corridor he was almost himself again, but with a gap in his memory. He was shoved through a door which clanged behind him. He steadied himself and looked around.

"Greetings, friend," a resonant voice called out. "Drag up a chair by the fire."

Gilead blinked, deliberately slowed himself down, and breathed deeply. His healthy body was fighting off the effects of the Markheim bolt; he was almost himself.

The room was a cell, old-fashioned, almost primitive. The front of the cell and the door were steel bars; the walls were

17

concrete. Its only furniture, a long wooden bench, was occupied by the man who had spoken. He was fiftyish, of ponderous frame, heavy features set in a shrewd, good-natured expression. He was lying back on the bench, head pillowed on his hands, in animal ease. Gilead had seen him before.

"Hello, Dr. Baldwin."

The man sat up with a flowing economy of motion that moved his bulk as little as possible. "I'm not Dr. Baldwin—I'm not Doctor anything, though my name is Baldwin." He stared at Gilead. "But I know you—seen some of your lectures."

Gilead cocked an eyebrow. "A man would seem naked around the Association of Theoretical physicists without a doctor's degree—and you were at their last meeting."

Baldwin chuckled boomingly. "That accounts for it—that has to be my cousin on my father's side, Hartley M.—Stuffy citizen Hartley. I'll have to try to take the curse off the family name, now that I've met you, Captain." He stuck out a huge hand. "Gregory Baldwin, 'Kettle Belly' to my friends. New and used helicopters is as close as I come to theoretical physics. *'Kettle Belly Baldwin, King of the Kopters'*—you must have seen my advertising."

"Now that you mention it, I have."

Baldwin pulled out a card. "Here. If you ever need one, I'll give you a ten percent off for knowing old Hartley. Matter of fact, I can do right well by you in a year-old Curtiss, a family car without a mark on it."

Gilead accepted the card and sat down. "Not at the moment, thanks. You seem to have an odd sort of office, Mr. Baldwin."

Baldwin chuckled again. "In the course of a long life these things happen, Captain. I won't ask you why you are here or what you are doing in that monkey suit. Call me Kettle Belly."

"Okay." Gilead got up and went to the door. Opposite the cell was a blank wall; there was no one in sight. He whistled and shouted—no answer.

"What's itching you, Captain?" Baldwin asked gently.

Gilead turned. His cellmate had dealt a solitaire hand on the bench and was calmly playing.

"I've got to raise the turnkey and send for a lawyer."

"Don't fret about it. Let's play some cards." He reached in a pocket. "I've got a second deck; how about some Russian bank?"

"No, thanks. I've got to get out of here." He shouted again —still no answer.

"Don't waste your lung power, Captain," Baldwin advised him. "They'll come when it suits them and not a second before. I *know*. Come play with me; it passes the time." Baldwin appeared to be shuffling the two decks; Gilead could see that he

18

was actually stacking the cards. The deception amused him; he decided to play—since the truth of Baldwin's advice was so evident.

"If you don't like Russian bank," Kettle Belly went on, "here is a game I learned as a kid." He paused and stared into Gilead's eyes. "It's instructive as well as entertaining, yet it's simple, once you catch on to it." He started dealing out the cards. "It makes a better game with two decks, because the black cards don't mean anything. Just the twenty-six red cards in each deck count—with the heart suit coming first. Each card scores according to its position in that sequence. The ace of hearts is one and the king of hearts counts thirteen; the ace of diamonds is next at fourteen and so on. Savvy?"

"Yes."

"And the blacks don't count. They're blanks . . . spaces. Ready to play?"

"What are the rules?"

"We'll deal out one hand for free; you'll learn faster as you see it. Then, when you've caught on, I'll play you for a half interest in the atomics trust—or ten bits in cash." He resumed dealing, laying the cards out rapidly in columns, five to a row. He paused, finished. "It's my deal, so it's your count. See what you get."

It was evident that Baldwin's stacking had brought the red cards into groups, yet there was no evident advantage to it, nor was the count especially high—nor low. Gilead stared at it, trying to figure out the man's game. The cheating, as cheating seemed too bold to be probable.

Suddenly the cards jumped at him, arranged themselves in a meaningful array. He read:

XTHXY
CANXX
XXXSE
HEARX
XUSXX

The fact that there were only two fives-of-hearts available had affected the spelling but the meaning was clear. Gilead reached for the cards. "I'll try one. I can beat that score." He dipped into the tips belonging to the suit's owner. "Ten bits it is."

Baldwin covered it. Gilead shuffled, making even less attempt to cover up than had Baldwin. He dealt:

WHATS
XXXXX
XYOUR
GAMEX
XXXXX

Baldwin shoved the money toward him and anted again. "Okay, my turn for revenge." He laid out:

19

```
          XXIMX
          XONXX
          YOURX
          XXXXX
          XSIDE
```
"I win again," Gilead announced gleefully. "Ante up."
He grabbed the cards and manipulated them:
```
          YEAHX
          XXXXX
          PROVE
          XXITX
          XXXXX
```
Baldwin counted and said, "You're too smart for me. Gimme
the cards." He produced another ten-bit piece and dealt again:
```
          XXILX
          HELPX
          XXYOU
          XGETX
          OUTXX
```
"I should have cut the cards," Gilead complained, push-
ing the money over. "Let's double the bets." Baldwin grunted
and Gilead dealt again:
```
          XNUTS
          IMXXX
          SAFER
          XXINX
          XGAOL
```
"I broke your luck," Baldwin gloated. "We'll double it
again?"
```
          XUXRX
          XNUTS
          THISX
          NOXXX
          XJAIL
```
The deal shifted:
```
          KEEPX
          XTALK
          INGXX
          XXXXX
          XBUDX
```
Baldwin answered:
```
          THISX
          XXXXX
          XXNEW
          AGEXX
          XHOTL
```
As he stacked the cards again Gilead considered these new
factors. He was prepared to believe that he was hidden some-
where in the New Age Hotel; in fact the counterproposition

that his opponents had permitted two ordinary cops to take him away to a normal city jail was most unlikely—unless they had the jail as fully under control as they quite evidently had the hotel. Nevertheless the point was not proven. As for Baldwin, he might be on Gilead's side; more probably he was planted as an *agent provocateur*—or he might be working for himself.

The permutations added up to six situations, only one of which made it desirable to accept Baldwin's offer for help in a jail break—said situation being the least likely of the six.

Nevertheless, though he considered Baldwin a liar, net, he tentatively decided to accept. A static situation brought him no advantage; a dynamic situation—*any* dynamic situation— he might turn to his advantage. But more data were needed. "These cards are sticky as candy," he complained. "You letting your money ride?"

"Suits." Gilead dealt again:

XXXXX
WHYXX
AMXXX
XXXXI
XHERE

"You have the damnedest luck," Baldwin commented:

FILMS
ESCAP
BFORE
XUXXX
KRACK

Gilead swept up the cards, was about to "shuffle," when Baldwin said, "Oh oh, school's out." Footsteps could be heard in the passage. "Good luck, boy," Baldwin added.

Baldwin knew about the films, but had not used any of the dozen ways to identify himself as part of Gilead's own organization. Therefore he was planted by the opposition, or he was a third factor.

More important, the fact that Baldwin knew about the films proved his assertion that this was not a jail. It followed with bitter certainty that he, Gilead, stood no computable chance of getting out alive. The footsteps approaching the cell could be ticking off the last seconds of his life.

He knew now that he should have found means to report the destination of the films before going to the New Age. But Humpty Dumpty was off the wall, entropy always increases— but the films *must* be delivered.

The footsteps were quite close.

Baldwin might get out alive.

But who was Baldwin?

All the while he was "shuffling" the cards. The action was not final; he had only to give them one true shuffle to destroy

21

the message being set up in them. A spider settled from the ceiling, landed on the other man's hand. Baldwin, instead of knocking it off and crushing it, most carefully reached his arm out toward the wall and encouraged it to lower itself to the floor. "Better stay out of the way, shorty," he said gently, "or one of the big boys is likely to step on you."

The incident, small as it was, determined Gilead's decision —and with it, the fate of a planet. He stood up and handed the stacked deck to Baldwin. "I owe you exactly ten-sixty," he said carefully. "Be sure to remember it—I'll see who our visitors are."

The footsteps had stopped outside the cell door.

There were two of them, dressed neither as police nor as guards; the masquerade was over. One stood well back, covering the maneuver with a Markheim, the other unlocked the door. "Back against the wall, Fatso," he ordered. "Gilead, out you come. And take it easy, or, after we freeze you, I'll knock out your teeth just for fun."

Baldwin shuffled back against the wall; Gilead came out slowly. He watched for any opening but the leader backed away from him without once getting between him and the man with the Markheim. "Ahead of us and take it slow," he was ordered. He complied, helpless under the precautions, unable to run, unable to fight.

Baldwin went back to the bench when they had gone. He dealt out the cards as if playing solitaire, swept them up again, and continued to deal himself solitaire hands. Presently he "shuffled" the cards back to the exact order Gilead had left them in and pocketed them.

The message had read: XTELLXFBSXPOBOXDEBT XXXCHI.

His two guards marched Gilead into a room and locked the door behind him, leaving themselves outside. He found himself in a large window overlooking the city and a reach of the river; balancing it on the left hung a solid portraying a lunar landscape in convincing color and depth. In front of him was a rich but not ostentatious executive desk.

The lower part of his mind took in these details; his attention could be centered only on the person who sat at that desk. She was old but not senile, frail but not helpless. Her eyes were very much alive, her expression serene. Her translucent, well-groomed hands were busy with a frame of embroidery.

On the desk in front of her were two pneumo mailing tubes, a pair of slippers, and some tattered, soiled remnants of cloth and plastic.

She looked up. "How do you do, Captain Gilead?" she said in a thin, sweet soprano suitable for singing hymns.

Gilead bowed. "Well, thank you—and you, Mrs. Keithley?"

"You know me, I see."

22

"Madame would be famous if only for her charities."

"You are kind. Captain, I will not waste your time. I had hoped that we could release you without fuss, but—" She indicated the two tubes in front of her. "—you can see for yourself that we must deal with you further."

"So?"

"Come, now, Captain. You mailed *three* tubes. These two are only dummies, and the third did not reach its apparent destination. It is possible that it was badly addressed and has been rejected by the sorting machines. If so, we shall have it in due course. But it seems much more likely that you found some way to change its address—likely to the point of pragmatic certainty."

"Or possibly I corrupted your servant."

She shook her head slightly. "We examined him quite thoroughly before—"

"Before he died?"

"Please, Captain, let's not change the subject. I must know where you sent that other tube. You cannot be hypnotized by ordinary means; you have an acquired immunity to hypnotic drugs. Your tolerance for pain extends beyond the threshold of unconsciousness. All of these things have already been proved, else you would not be in the job you are in; I shall not put either of us to the inconvenience of proving them again. Yet I must have that tube. What is your price?"

"You assume that I have a price."

She smiled. "If the old saw has any exceptions, history does not record them. Be reasonable, Captain. Despite your admitted immunity to ordinary forms of examination, there are ways of breaking down—of *changing*—a man's character so that he becomes really quite pliant under examination . . . ways that we learned from the commissars. But those ways take time and a woman my age has no time to waste."

Gilead lied convincingly. "It's not your age, ma'am; it is the fact that you know that you must obtain that tube at once or you will never get it." He was hoping—more than that, he was *willing*—that Baldwin would have sense enough to examine the cards for one last message . . . and act on it. If Baldwin failed and he, Gilead, died, the tube would eventually come to rest in a dead-letter office and would in time be destroyed.

"You are probably right. Nevertheless, Captain, I will go ahead with the Mindszenty technique if you insist upon it. What do you say to ten million plutonium credits?"

Gilead believed her first statement. He reviewed in his mind the means by which a man bound hand and foot, or worse, could kill himself unassisted. "Ten million plutons and a knife in my back?" he answered. "Let's be practical."

"Convincing assurance would be given before you need talk."

23

"Even so, it is not my price. After all, you are worth at least five hundred million plutons."

She leaned forward. "I like you, Captain. You are a man of strength. I am an old woman, without heirs. Suppose you became my partner—and my successor?"

"Pie in the sky."

"No, no! I mean it. My age and sex do not permit me actively to serve myself; I must rely on others. Captain, I am very tired of inefficient tools, of men who can let things be spirited away right from under their noses. Imagine! She made a little gesture of exasperation, clutching her hand into a claw. "You and I could go far, Captain. I need you."

"But I do not need you, madame. And I won't have you."

She made no answer, but touched a control on her desk. A door on the left dilated; two men and a girl came in. The girl Gilead recognized as the waitress from the Grand Concourse Drug Store. They had stripped her bare, which seemed to him an unnecessary indignity since her working uniform could not possibly have concealed a weapon.

The girl, once inside, promptly blew her top, protesting, screaming, using language unusual to her age and sex—an hysterical, thalmic outburst of volcanic proportions.

"Quiet, child!"

The girl stopped in midstream, looked with surprise at Mrs. Keithley, and shut up. Nor did she start again, but stood there, looking even younger than she was and somewhat aware of and put off stride by her nakedness. She was covered now with goose flesh, one tear cut a white line down her dust-smeared face, stopped at her lip. She licked at it and sniffled.

"You were out of observation once, Captain," Mrs. Keithley went on, "during which time this person saw you twice. Therefore we will examine her."

Gilead shook his head. "She knows no more than a goldfish. But go ahead—five minutes of hypno will convince you."

"Oh, no, Captain! Hypno is sometimes fallible; if she is a member of your bureau, it is certain to be fallible." She signalled to one of the men attending the girl; he went to a cupboard and opened it. "I am old-fashioned," the old woman went on. "I trust simple mechanical means much more than I do the cleverest of clinical procedures."

Gilead saw the implements that the man was removing from cupboard and started forward. "Stop that!" he commanded. "You can't do that—"

He bumped his nose quite hard.

The man paid him no attention. Mrs. Keithley said, "Forgive me, Captain. I should have told you that this room is not one room, but two. The partition is merely glass, but very special glass—I use the room for difficult interviews. There is no need to hurt yourself by trying to reach us."

24

"Just a moment!"

"Yes, Captain?"

"Your time is already running out. Let the girl and me go free *now*. You are aware that there are several hundred men searching this city for me even now—and that they will not stop until they have taken it apart panel by panel."

"I think not. A man answering your description to the last factor caught the South Africa rocket twenty minutes after you registered at the New Age hotel. He was carrying your very own identifications. He will not reach South Africa, but the manner of his disappearance will point to desertion rather than accident or suicide."

Gilead dropped the matter. "What do you plan to gain by abusing this child? You have all she knows; certainly you do not believe that we could afford to trust in such as she?"

Mrs. Keithley pursed her lips. "Frankly, I do not expect to learn anything from her. I may learn something from you."

"I see."

The leader of the two men looked questioningly at his mistress; she motioned him to go ahead. The girl stared blankly at him, plainly unaware of the uses of the equipment he had gotten out. He and his partner got busy.

Shortly the girl screamed, continued to scream for a few moments in a high adulation. Then it stopped as she fainted.

They roused her and stood her up again. She stood, swaying and staring stupidly at her poor hands, forever damaged even for the futile purposes to which she had been capable of putting them. Blood spread down her wrists and dripped on a plastic tarpaulin, placed there earlier by the second of the two men.

Gilead did nothing and said nothing. Knowing as he did that the tube he was protecting contained matters measured in millions of lives, the problem of the girl, as a problem, did not even arise. It disturbed a deep and very ancient part of his brain, but almost automatically he cut that part off and lived for the time in his forebrain.

Consciously he memorized the faces, skulls, and figures of the two men and filed the data under "personal." Thereafter he unobtrusively gave his attention to the scene out the window. He had been noting it all through the interview but he wanted to give it explicit thought. He recast what he saw in terms of what it would look like had he been able to look squarely out the window and decided that he was on the ninety-first floor of the New Age hotel and approximately one hundred and thirty meters from the north end. He filed this under "professional".

When the girl died, Mrs. Keithley left the room without speaking to him. The men gathered up what was left in the tarpaulin and followed her. Presently the two guards returned and, using the same foolproof methods, took him back to his cell.

As soon as the guards had gone and Kettle Belly was free to leave his position against the wall he came forward and pounded Gilead on the shoulders. "Hi, boy! I'm sure glad to see you—I was scared I would never lay eyes on you again. How was it? Pretty rough?"

"No, they didn't hurt me; they just asked some questions."

"You're lucky. Some of those crazy damn cops play mean when they get you alone in a back room. Did they let you call your lawyer?"

"No."

"Then they ain't through with you. You want to watch it, kid."

Gilead sat down on the bench. "The hell with them. Want to play some more cards?"

"Don't mind if I do. I feel lucky." Baldwin pulled out the double deck, riffled through it. Gilead took them and did the same. Good! they were in the order he had left them in. He ran his thumb across the edges again—yes, even the black nulls were unchanged in sequence; apparently Kettle Belly had simply stuck them in his pocket without examining them, without suspecting that a last message had been written in to them. He felt sure that Baldwin would not have left the message set up if he had read it. Since he found himself still alive, he was much relieved to think this.

He gave the cards one true shuffle, then started stacking them. His first lay-out read:

                XXXXX
                ESCAP
                XXATX
                XXXXX
                XONCE
"Gotcha that time!" Baldwin crowed. "Ante up:"
                DIDXX
                XYOUX
                XXXXX
                XXXXX
                CRACK
"Let it ride," announced Gilead and took the deal:
                XXNOX
                BUTXX
                XXXXX
                XLETS
                XXGOX
"You're too derned lucky to live," complained Baldwin. "Look—we'll leave the bets doubled and double the lay-out. I want a fair chance to get my money back."

His next lay-out read:

```
XXXXX
XTHXN
XXXXX
THXYX
NEEDX
XXXUX
ALIVX
XXXXX
PLAYX
XXXUP
```

"Didn't do you much good, did it?" Gilead commented, took the cards and started arranging them.

"There's something mighty funny about a man that wins all the time," Baldwin grumbled. He watched Gilead narrowly. Suddenly his hand shot out, grabbed Gilead's wrist. "I thought so;" he yelled. "A goddam card sharp—"

Gilead shook his hand off. "Why, you obscene fat slug!"

"Caught you! *Caught you!*" Kettle Belly reclaimed his hold, grabbed the other wrist as well. They struggled and rolled to the floor.

Gilead discovered two things: this awkward, bulky man was an artist at every form of dirty fighting and he could simulate it convincingly without damaging his partner. His nerve holds were an inch off the nerve; his kneeings were to thigh muscle rather than to the crotch.

Baldwin tried for a chancery strangle; Gilead let him take it. The big man settled the flat of his forearm against the point of Gilead's chin rather than against his Adam's apple and proceeded to "strangle" him.

There were running footsteps in the corridor.

Gilead caught a glimpse of the guards as they reached the door. They stopped momentarily; the bell of the Markheim was too big to use through the steel grating, the charge would be screened and grounded. Apparently they did not have pacifier bombs with them, for they hesitated. Then the leader quickly unlocked the door, while the man with the Markheim dropped back to the cover position.

Baldwin ignored them, while continuing his stream of profanity and abuse at Gilead. He let the first man almost reach them before he suddenly said in Gilead's ear, "Close your eyes!" At which he broke just as suddenly.

Gilead sensed an incredibly dazzling flash of light even through his eyelids. Almost on top of it he heard a muffled crack; he opened his eyes and saw that the first man was down, his head twisted at a grotesque angle.

The man with the Markheim was shaking his head; the muzzle of his weapon weaved around. Baldwin was charging him in a waddle, back and knees bent until he was hardly

27

three feet tall. The blinded guard could hear him, let fly a charge in the direction of the noise; it passed over Baldwin.

Baldwin was on him; the two went down. There was another cracking noise of ruptured bone and another dead man. Baldwin stood up, grasping the Markheim, keeping it pointed down the corridor. "How are your eyes, kid?" he called out anxiously.

"They're all right."

"Then come take this chiller." Gilead moved up, took the Markheim. Baldwin ran to the dead end of the corridor where a window looked out over the city. The window did not open; there was no "copter step" beyond it. It was merely a straight drop. He came running back.

Gilead was shuffling possibilities in his mind. Events had moved by Baldwin's plan, not by his. As a result of his visit to Mrs. Keithley's "interview room" he was oriented in space. The corridor ahead and a turn to the left should bring him to the quick-drop shaft. Once in the basement and armed with a Markheim, he felt sure that he could fight his way out—with Baldwin in trail if the man would follow. If not—well, there was too much at stake.

Baldwin was into the cell and out again almost at once. "Come along!" Gilead snapped. A head showed at the bend in the corridor; he let fly at it and the owner of the head passed out on the floor.

"Out of my way, kid!" Baldwin answered. He was carrying the heavy bench on which they had "played" cards. He started up the corridor with it, toward the sealed window, gaining speed remarkably as he went.

His makeshift battering ram struck the window heavily. The plastic bulged, ruptured, and snapped like a soap bubble. The bench went on through, disappeared from sight, while Baldwin teetered on hands and knees, a thousand feet of nothingness under his chin.

"Kid!" he yelled. "Close in! Fall back!"

Gilead backed towards him, firing twice more as he did so. He still did not see how Baldwin planned to get out, but the big man had demonstrated that he had resourcefulness—and resources.

Baldwin was whistling through his fingers and waving. In violation of all city traffic rules a helicopter separated itself from the late afternoon throng, cut through a lane, and approached the window. It hovered just far enough away to keep from fouling its blades. The drive opened the door, a line snaked across and Kettle Belly caught it. With great speed he made it fast to the window's polarizer knob, then grabbed the Markheim. "You first," he snapped. "Hurry!"

Gilead dropped to his knees and grasped the line; the driver immediately increased his tip speed and tilted his rotor; the line tautened. Gilead let it take his weight, then swarmed across it. The driver gave him a hand up while controlling his craft like a highschool horse with his other hand.

The 'copter bucked; Gilead turned and saw Baldwin coming across, a fat spider on a web. As he himself helped the big man in, the driver reached down and cut the line. The ship bucked again and slid away.

There were already men standing in the broken window. "Get lost, Steve!" Baldwin ordered. The driver gave his tip jets another notch and tilted the rotor still more; the 'copter swooped away. He eased it into the traffic stream and inquired, "Where to?"

"Set her for home—and tell the other boys to go home, too. No—you've got your hands full; I'll tell them!" Baldwin crowded up into the other pilot's seat, slipped on phones and settled a quiet-mike over his mouth. The driver adjusted his car to the traffic, set up a combination on his pilot, then settled back and opened a picture magazine.

Shortly Baldwin took off the phones and came back to the passenger compartment. "Takes a lot of 'copters to be sure you have one cruising by when you need it," he said conversationally. "Fortunately, I've got a lot of 'em. Oh, by the way, this is Steve Halliday. Steve, meet Joe—Joe, what is your last name?"

"Greene," answered Gilead.

"Howdy," said the driver and let his eyes go back to his magazine.

Gilead considered the situation. He was not sure that it had been improved. Kettle Belly, whatever he was, was more than a used 'copter dealer—*and* he knew about the films. This boy Steve looked like a harmless young extrovert but, then, Kettle Belly himself looked like a lunk. He considered trying to overpower both of them, remembered Kettle Belly's virtuosity in rough-and-tumble fighting, and decided against it. Perhaps Kettle Belly really was on his side, completely and utterly. He heard rumors that the Department used more than one echelon of operatives and he had no way of being sure that he himself was at the top level.

"Kettle Belly," he went on, "could you set me down at the airport first? I'm in one hell of a hurry."

Baldwin looked him over. "Sure, if you say so. But I thought you would want to swap those duds? You're as conspicuous as a preacher at a stag party. And how are you fixed for cash?"

With his fingers Gilead counted the change that had come with the suit. A man without cash had one arm in a sling. "How long would it take?"

"Ten minutes extra, maybe."

Gilead thought again about Kettle Belly's fighting ability and decided that there was no way for a fish in water to get any wetter. "Okay." He settled back and relaxed completely.

Presently he turned again to Baldwin. "By the way, how did you manage to sneak in that dazzle bomb?"

Kettle Belly chuckled. "I'm a large man, Joe; there's an awful lot of me to search." He laughed again. "You'd be amazed at where I had that hidden."

Gilead changed the subject. "How did you happen to be there in the first place?"

Baldwin sobered. "That's a long and complicated story. Come back some day when you're not in such a rush and I'll tell you all about it."

"I'll do that—soon."

"Good. Maybe I can sell you that used Curtiss at the same time."

The pilot alarm sounded; the driver put down his magazine and settled the craft on the roof of Baldwin's establishment.

Baldwin was as good as his word. He took Gilead to his office, sent for clothes—which showed up with great speed—and handed Gilead a wad of bills suitable to stuff a pillow. "You can mail it back," he said.

"I'll bring it back in person," promised Gilead.

"Good. Be careful out on the street. Some of our friends are sure to be around."

"I'll be careful." He left, as casually as if he had called there on business, but feeling less sure of himself than usual. Baldwin himself remained a mystery and, in his business, Gilead could not afford mysteries.

There was a public phone booth in the lobby of Baldwin's building. Gilead went in, scrambled, then coded a different relay station from the one he had attempted to use before. He gave his booth's code and instructed the operator to scramble back. In a matter of minutes he was talking to his chief in New Washington.

"Joe! Where the hell have you been?"

"Later, boss—get this." In departmental oral code as an added precaution, he told his chief that the films were in post office box 1060, Chicago, and insisted that they be picked up by a major force at once.

His chief turned away from the view plate, then returned, "Okay, it's done. Now what happened to you?"

"Later, boss, later. I think I've got some friends outside who are anxious to rassle with me. Keep me here and I may get a hole in my head."

"Okay—but head right back here. I want a full report; I'll wait here for you."

"Right." He switched off.

He left the booth light-heartedly, with the feeling of satisfaction that comes from a hard job successfully finished. He rather hoped that some of his "friends" would show up; he felt like kicking somebody who needed kicking.

But they disappointed him. He boarded the transcontinental rocket without alarms and slept all the way to New Washington.

He reached the Federal Bureau of Security by one of many concealed routes and went to his boss's office. After scan and voice check he was let in. Bonn looked up and scowled.

Gilead ignored the expression; Bonn usually scowled. "Agent Joseph Briggs, three-four-oh-nine-seven-two, reporting back from assignment, sir," he said evenly.

Bonn switched a desk control to "recording" and another to "covert." "You are, eh? Why, thumb-fingered idiot! how do you dare to show your face around here?"

"Easy now, boss—what's the trouble?"

Bonn fumed incoherently for a time, then said, "Briggs, twelve star men covered that pick up—and the box was empty. Post office box ten-sixty, Chicago, indeed! Where are those films? Was it a cover up? Have you got them with you?"

Gilead-Briggs restrained his surprise. "No. I mailed them at the Grand Concourse post office to the address you just named." He added, "The machine may have kicked them out; I was forced to letter by hand the machine symbols."

Bonn looked suddenly hopeful. He touched another control and said, "Carruthers! On that Briggs matter: Check the rejection stations for that routing." He thought and then added, "Then try a rejection sequence on the assumption that the first symbol was acceptable to the machine but mistaken. Also for each of the other symbols; run them simultaneously—crash priority for all agents and staff. After that try combinations of symbols taken two at a time, then three at a time, and so on." He switched off.

"The total of that series you just set up is every postal address in the continent," Briggs suggested mildly. "It can't be done."

"It's got to be done! Man, have you any idea of the *importance* of those films you were guarding?"

"Yes. The director at Moon Base told me what I was carrying."

"You don't act as if you did. You've lost the most valuable thing this or any other government can possess—the absolute weapon. Yet you stand there blinking at me as if you had mislaid a pack of cigarettes."

"Weapon?" objected Briggs. "I wouldn't call the nova effect that, unless you class suicide as a weapon. And I don't concede that I've lost it. As an agent acting alone and charged primarily with keeping it out of the hands of others, I used the best means available in an emergency to protect it. That is well

31

within the limits of my authority. I was spotted, by some means—"

"You shouldn't have been spotted!"

"Granted. But I was. I was unsupported and my estimate of the situation did not include a probability of staying alive. Therefore I had to protect my charge by some means which did not depend on my staying alive."

"But you *did* stay alive—you're here."

"Not my doing nor yours, I assure you. I should have been covered. It was your order, you will remember, that I act alone."

Bonn looked sullen. "That was necessary."

"So? In any case, I don't see what all the shooting is about. Either the films show up, or they are lost and will be destroyed as unclaimed mail. So I go back to the Moon and get another set of prints."

Bonn chewed his lip. "You can't do that."

"Why not?"

Bonn hesitated a long time. "There were just two sets. You had the originals, which were to be placed in a vault in the Archives—and the others were to be destroyed at once when the originals were known to be secure."

"Yes? What's the hitch?"

"You don't see the importance of the procedure. Every working paper, every file, every record was destroyed when these films were made. Every technician, every assistant, received hypno. The intention was not only to protect the results of the research but to wipe out the very fact that the research had taken place. There aren't a dozen people in the system who even know of the existence of the nova effect."

Briggs had his own opinions on this point, based on recent experience, but he kept still about them. Bonn went on, "The Secretary has been after me steadily to let him know when the originals were secured. He has been quite insistent, quite critical. When you called in, I told him that the films were safe and that he would have them in a few minutes."

"Well?"

"Don't you see, you fool—he gave the order at once to destroy the other copies."

Briggs whistled. "Jumped the gun, didn't he?"

"That's not the way he'll figure it—mind you, the President was pressuring *him*. He'll say that *I* jumped the gun."

"And so you did."

"No, *you* jumped the gun. You told me the films were in that box."

"Hardly. I said I had sent them there."

"No, you didn't."

"Get out the tape and play it back."

32

"There is no tape—by the President's own order no records are kept on this operation."

"So? Then why are you recording now?"

"Because," Bonn answered sharply, "some one is going to pay for this and it is not going to be me."

"Meaning," Briggs said slowly, "that it is going to be me."

"I didn't say that. It might be the Secretary."

"If his head rolls, so will yours. No, both of you are figuring on using me. Before you plan on that, hadn't you better hear my report? It might affect your plans. I've got news for you, boss."

Bonn drummed the desk. "Go ahead. It had better be good."

In a passionless monotone Briggs recited all events as recorded by sharp memory from receipt of the films on the Moon to the present moment. Bonn listened impatiently.

Finished, Briggs waited. Bonn got up and strode around the room. Finally he stopped and said, "Briggs, I never heard such a fantastic pack of lies in my life. A fat man who plays cards! A wallet that wasn't your wallet—your clothes stolen! And Mrs. Keithley—Mrs. *Keithley!* Don't you know that she is one of the strongest supporters of the Administration?"

Briggs said nothing. Bonn went on, "Now I'll tell you what actually did happen. Up to the time you grounded at Pied-a-Terre your report is correct, but—"

"How do you know?"

"Because you were covered, naturally. You don't think I would trust this to one man, do you?"

"Why didn't you tell me? I could have hollered for help and saved all this."

Bonn brushed it aside. "You engaged a runner, dismissed him, went in that drugstore, came out and went to the post office. There was no fight in the concourse for the simple reason that no one was following you. At the post office you mailed three tubes, one of which may or may not have contained the films. You went from there to the New Age hotel, left it twenty minutes later and caught the transrocket for Cape Town. You—"

"Just a moment," objected Briggs. "How could I have done that and still be here now?"

"Eh?" For a moment Bonn seemed stumped. "That's just a detail; you were positively identified. For that matter, it would have been a far, far better thing for you if you had stayed on that rocket. In fact—" The bureau chief got a far-away look in his eyes. "—you'll be better off for the time being if we assume officially that you did stay on that rocket. You are in a bad spot, Briggs, a very bad spot. You did not muff this assignment—you sold out!"

Briggs looked at him levelly. "You are preferring charges?"

"Not just now. That is why it is best to assume that you stayed on that rocket—until matters settle down, clarify."

Briggs did not need a graph to show him what solution would come out when "matters clarified." He took from a pocket a memo pad, scribbled on it briefly, and handed it to Bonn.

It read: "I resign my appointment effective immediately." He had added signature, thumbprint, date, and hour.

"So long, boss," he added. He turned slightly, as if to go.

Bonn yelled, "Stop! Briggs, you are under arrest." He reached toward his desk.

Briggs cuffed him in the windpipe, added one to the pit of Bonn's stomach. He slowed down then and carefully made sure that Bonn would remain out for a satisfactory period. Examination of Bonn's desk produced a knockout kit; he added a two-hour hypodermic, placing it inconspicuously beside a mole near the man's backbone. He wiped the needle, restored everything to its proper place, removed the current record from the desk and wiped the tape of all mention of himself, including door check. He left the desk set to "covert" and "do not disturb" and left by another of the concealed routes to the Bureau.

He went to the rocket port, bought a ticket, unreserved, for the first ship to Chicago. There was twenty minutes to wait; he made a couple of minor purchases from clerks rather than from machines, letting his face be seen. When the Chicago ship was called he crowded forward with the rest.

At the inner gate, just short of the weighing-in platform, he became part of the crowd present to see passengers off, rather than a passenger himself. He waved at some one in the line leaving the weighing station beyond the gate, smiled, called out a good-by, and let the crowd carry him back from the gate as it closed. He peeled off from the crowd at the men's washroom. When he came out there were several hasty but effective changes in his appearance.

More important, his manner was different.

A short, illicit transaction in a saloon near a hiring hall provided the work card he needed; fifty-five minutes later he was headed across country as Jack Gillespie, loader and helper-driver on a diesel freighter.

Could his addressing of the pneumo tube have been bad enough to cause the automatic postal machines to reject it? He let the picture of the label, as it had been when he had completed it, build in his mind until it was as sharp as the countryside flowing past him. No, his lettering of the symbols had been perfect and correct; the machines would accept it.

Could the machine have kicked out the tube for another cause, say a turned-up edge of the gummed label? Yes, but the written label was sufficient to enable a postal clerk to get

34

it back in the groove. One such delay did not exceed ten minutes, even during the rush hour. Even with five such delays the tube would have reached Chicago more than one hour before he reported to Bonn by phone.

Suppose the gummed label had peeled off entirely; in such case the tube would have gone to the same destination as the two cover-up tubes.

In which case Mrs. Keithley would have gotten it, since she had been able to intercept or receive the other two.

Therefore the tube had reached the Chicago post office box.

Therefore Kettle Belly *had* read the message in the stacked cards, had given instructions to some one in Chicago, had done so while at the helicopter's radio. After an event, "possible" and "true" are equivalent ideas, whereas "probable" becomes a measure of one's ignorance. To call a conclusion "improbable" *after the event* was self-confusing amphigory.

Therefore Kettle Belly Baldwin had the films—a conclusion he had reached in Bonn's office.

Two hundred miles from New Washington he worked up an argument with the top driver and got himself fired. From a local booth in the town where he dropped he scrambled through to Baldwin's business office. "Tell him I'm a man who owes him money."

Shortly the big man's face built up on the screen. "Hi, kid! How's tricks?"

"I'm fired."

"I thought you would be."

"Worse than that—I'm wanted."

"Naturally."

"I'd like to talk with you."

"Swell. Where are you?"

Gilead told him.

"You're clean?"

"For a few hours, at least."

"Go to the local air port. Steve will pick you up."

Steve did so, nodded a greeting, jumped his craft into the air, set his pilot, and went back to his reading. When the ship settled down on course, Gilead noted it and asked, "Where are we going?"

"The boss's ranch. Didn't he tell you?"

"No." Gilead knew it was possible that he was being taken for a one-way ride. True, Baldwin had enabled him to escape an otherwise pragmatically certain death—it was certain that Mrs. Keithley had not intended to let him stay alive longer that suited her uses, else she would not have had the girl killed in his presence. Until he had arrived at Bonn's office, he had assumed that Baldwin had saved him because he knew something that Baldwin most urgently wanted to know—whereas

35

now it looked as if Baldwin had saved him for altruistic reasons.

Gilead conceded the existence in this world of altruistic reasons, but was inclined not to treat them as "least hypothesis" until all other possible hypotheses had been eliminated; Baldwin might have had his own reasons for wishing him to live long enough to report to New Washington and nevertheless be pleased to wipe him out now that he was a wanted man whose demise would cause no comment.

Baldwin might even be a partner in these dark matters of Mrs. Keithley. In some ways that was the simplest explanation though it left other factors unexplained. In any case Baldwin was a key actor—and he had the films. The risk was necessary.

Gilead did not worry about it. The factors known to him were chalked up on the blackboard of his mind, there to remain until enough variables become constants to permit a solution by logic. The ride was very pleasant.

Steve put him down on the lawn of a large rambling ranch house, introduced him to a motherly old party named Mrs. Garver, and took off. "Make yourself at home, Joe," she told him. "Your room is the last one in the east wing—shower across from it. Supper in ten minutes."

He thanked her and took the suggestion, getting back to the living room with a minue or two to spare. Several others, a dozen or more of both sexes, were there. The place seemed to be a sort of a dude ranch—not entirely dude, as he had seen Herefords on the spread as Steve and he were landing.

The other guests seemed to take his arrival as a matter of course. No one asked why he was there. One of the women introduced herself as Thalia Wagner and then took him around the group. Ma Garver came in swinging a dinner bell as this was going on and they all filed into a long, low dining room. Gilead could not remember when he had had so good a meal in such amusing company.

After eleven hours of sleep, his first real rest in several days, he came fully, suddenly awake at a group of sounds his subconscious could not immediately classify and refused to discount. He opened his eyes, swept the room with them, and was at once out of bed, crouching on the side away from the door.

There were hurrying footsteps moving past his bedroom door. There were two voices, one male, one female, outside the door; the female was Thalia Wagner, the man he could not place.

Male: "tsɨmaeq?"
Female: "nø!"
Male: "zʊlntsɨ."
Female: "ɨpbit' New Jersey."

These are not precisely the sounds that Gilead heard, first because of the limitations of phonetic symbols, and second

36

because his ears were not used to the sounds. Hearing is a function of the brain, not of the ear; his brain, sophisticated as it was, nevertheless insisted on forcing the sounds that reached his ears into familiar pockets rather than stop to create new ones.

Thalia Wagner identified, he relaxed and stood up. Thalia was part of the unknown situation he accepted in coming here; a stranger known to her he must accept also. The new unknowns, including the odd language, he filed under "pending" and put aside.

The clothes he had had were gone, but his money—Baldwin's money, rather—was where his clothes had been and with it his work card as Jack Gillespie and his few personal articles. By them some one had laid out a fresh pair of walking shorts and new sneakers, in his size.

He noted, with almost shocking surprise, that some one had been able to serve him thus without waking him.

He put on his shorts and shoes and went out. Thalia and her companion had left while he dressed. No one was about and he found the dining room empty, but three places were set, including his own of supper, and hot dishes and facilities were on the sideboard. He selected baked ham and hot rolls, fried four eggs, poured coffee. Twenty minutes later, warmly replenished and still alone, he stepped out on the veranda.

It was a beautiful day. He was drinking it in and eyeing with friendly interest a desert lark when a young woman came around the side of the house. She was dressed much as he was, allowing for difference in sex, and she was comely, though not annoyingly so. "Good morning," he said.

She stopped, put her hands on her hips, and looked him up and down. "Well!" she said. "Why doesn't somebody tell me these things?"

Then she added, "Are you married?"

"No."

"I'm shopping around. Object: matrimony. Let's get acquainted."

"I'm a hard man to marry. I've been avoiding it for years."

"They're all hard to marry," she said bitterly. "There's a new colt down at the corral. Come on."

They went. The colt's name was War Conqueror of Baldwin; hers was Gail. After proper protocol with mare and son they left. "Unless you have pressing engagements," said Gail, "now is a salubrious time to go swimming."

"If salubrious means what I think it does, yes."

The spot was shaded by cottonwoods, the bottom was sandy; for a while he felt like a boy again, with all such matters as lies and nova effects and death and violence away in some improbable, remote dimension. After a long while he pulled himself up on the bank and said, "Gail, what does 'tsumaeq' mean?"

"Come again?" she answered. "I had water in my ear."

He repeated all of the conversation he had heard. She looked incredulous, then laughed. "You didn't hear that, Joe, you just didn't." She added, "You got the 'New Jersey' part right."

"But I did."

"Say it again."

He did so, more carefully, and giving a fair imitation of the speakers' accents.

Gail chortled. "I got the gist of it that time. That Thalia; someday some strong man is going to wring her neck."

"But what does it mean?"

Gail gave him a long, sidewise look. "If you ever find out, I really will marry you, in spite of your protests."

Some one was whisting from the hill top. "Joe! Joe Greene —the boss wants you."

"Gotta go," he said to Gail. "G'bye."

"See you later," she corrected him.

Baldwin was waiting in a study as comfortable as himself. "Hi, Joe," he greeted him. "Grab a seatful of chair. They been treating you right?"

"Yes, indeed. Do you always set as good a table as I've enjoyed so far?"

Baldwin patted his middle. "How do you think I came by my nickname?"

"Kettle Belly, I'd like a lot of explanations."

"Joe, I'm right sorry you lost your job. If I'd had my druthers, it wouldn't have been the way it was."

"Are you working with Mrs. Keithley?"

"No. I'm against her."

"I'd like to believe that, but I've no reason to—yet. What were you doing where I found you?"

"They had grabbed me—Mrs. Keithley and her boys."

"They just happened to grab you—and just happened to stuff you in the same cell with me—and you just happened to know about the films I was supposed to be guarding—and you just happened to have a double deck of cards in your pocket? Now, really!"

"If I hadn't had the cards, we would have found some other way to talk," Kettle Belly said mildly. "Wouldn't we, now?"

"Yes. Granted."

"I didn't mean to suggest that the set up was an accident. We had you covered from Moon Base; when you were grabbed —or rather as soon as you let them suck you into the New Age, I saw to it that they grabbed me too; I figured I might have a chance to lend you a hand, once I was inside." He added, "I kinda let them think that I was an FBS man, too."

"I see. Then it was just luck that they locked us up together."

"Not luck," Kettle Belly objected. "Luck is a bonus that follows careful planning—it's never free. There was a computable probability that they would put us together in hopes of finding out what they wanted to know. We hit the jackpot because we paid for the chance. If we hadn't, I would have had to crush out of that cell and look for you—but I had to be inside to do it."

"Who is Mrs. Keithley?"

"Other than what she is publicly, I take it. She is the queen bee—or the black widow—of a gang. 'Gang' is a poor word—power group, maybe. One of several such groups, more or less tied together where their interests don't cross. Between them they divvy up the country for whatever they want like two cats splitting a gopher."

Gilead nodded; he knew what Baldwin meant, though he had not known that the enormously respected Mrs. Keithley was in such matters—not until his nose had been rubbed in the fact. "And what are you, Kettle Belly?"

"Now, Joe—I like you and I'm truly sorry you're in a jam. You led wrong a couple of times and I was obliged to trump, as the stakes were high. See here, I feel that I owe you something; what do you say to this: we'll fix you up with a brand-new personality, vacuum tight—even new fingerprints if you want them. Pick any spot on the globe you like and any occupation; we'll supply all the money you need to start over—or money enough to retire and play with the cuties the rest of your life. What do you say?"

"No." There was no hesitation.

"You've no close relatives, no intimate friends. Think about it. I can't put you back in your job; this is the best I can do."

"I've thought about it. The devil with the job, I want to finish my case! you're the key to it."

"Reconsider, Joe. This is your chance to get out of affairs of state and lead a normal, happy life."

" 'Happy', he says!"

"Well, safe, anyhow. If you insist on going further your life expectancy becomes extremely problematical."

"I don't recall ever having tried to play safe."

"You're the doctor. Joe. In that case—" A speaker on Baldwin's desk uttered: "œnɪe ʀ ɦøg rylp."

Baldwin answered, "nʊ," and sauntered quickly to the fireplace. An early-morning fire still smouldered in it. He grasped the mantel piece, pulled it toward him. The entire masonry assembly, hearth, mantel, and grate, came toward him, leaving an arch in the wall. "Duck down stairs, Joe," he said. "It's a raid."

"A real priest's hole!"

"Yeah, corny, ain't it? This joint has more bolt holes than a rabbit's nest—and booby-trapped, too. Too many gadgets, if you ask me." He went back to his desk, opened a drawer, removed three film spools and dropped them in a pocket.

Gilead was about to go down the staircase; seeing the spools, he stopped. "Go ahead, Joe," Baldwin said urgently. "You're covered and outnumbered. With this raid showing up we wouldn't have time to fiddle; we'ud just have to kill you."

They stopped in a room well underground, another study much like the one above, though lacking sunlight and view. Baldwin said something in the odd language to the mike on the desk, was answered. Gilead experimented with the idea that the lingo might be reversed English, discarded the notion.

"As I was saying," Baldwin went on, "if you are dead set on knowing all the answers—"

"Just a moment. What about this raid?"

"Just the government boys. They won't be rough and not too thorough. Ma Garver can handle them. We won't have to hurt anybody as long as they don't use penetration radar."

Gilead smiled wryly at the disparagement of his own former service. "And if they do?"

"That gimmick over there squeals like a pig, if it's touched by penetration frequencies. Even then we're safe against anything short of an A-bomb. They won't do that; they want the films, not a hole in the ground. Which reminds me—here, catch."

Gilead found himself suddenly in possession of the films which were at the root of the matter. He unspooled a few frames and made certain that they were indeed the right films. He sat still and considered how he might get off this limb and back to the ground without dropping the eggs. The speaker again uttered something; Baldwin did not answer it but said, "We won't be down here long."

"Bonn seems to have decided to check my report." Some of his—former—comrades were upstairs. If he did Baldwin in, could he locate the inside control for the door?

"Bonn is a poor sort. He'll check me—but not too thoroughly; I'm rich. He won't check Mrs. Keithley at all; she's too rich. He thinks with his political ambitions instead of his head. His late predecessor was a better man—he was one of us."

Gilead's tentative plans underwent an abrupt reversal. His oath had been to a government; his personal loyalty had been given to his former boss. "Prove that last remark and I shall be much interested."

"No, you'll come to learn that it's true—if you still insist on knowing the answers. Through checking those films, Joe? Toss 'em back."

Gilead did not do so. "I suppose you have made copies in any case?"

"Wasn't necessary; I looked at them. Don't get ideas, Joe; you're washed up with the FBS, even if you brought the films

40

and my head back on a platter. You slugged your boss—remember?"

Gilead remembered that he had not told Baldwin so. He began to believe that Baldwin did have men inside the FBS, whether his late bureau chief had been one of them or not.

"I would at least be allowed to resign with a clear record. I know Bonn—officially he would be happy to forget it." He was simply stalling for time, waiting for Baldwin to offer an opening.

"Chuck them back, Joe. I don't want to rassle. One of us might get killed—both of us, if you won the first round. You can't prove your case, because I can prove I was home teasing the cat. I sold 'copters to two very respectable citizens at the exact time you would claim I was somewhere else." He listened again to the speaker, answered it in the same gibberish.

Gilead's mind evaluated his own tactical situation to the same answer that Baldwin had expressed. Not being given to wishful thinking he at once tossed the films to Baldwin.

"Thanks, Joe." He went to a small oubliette set in the wall, switched it to full power, put the films in the hopper, waited a few seconds, and switched it off. "Good riddance to bad rubbish."

Gilead permitted his eyebrows to climb. "Kettle Belly, you've managed to surprise me."

"How?"

"I thought you **wanted** to keep the nova effect as a means to power."

"Nuts! Scalping a man is a hell of a poor way to cure him of dandruff. Joe, how much do you know about the nova effect?"

"Not much. I know it's a sort of atom bomb powerful enough to scare the pants off anybody who gets to thinking about it."

"It's not a bomb. It's not a weapon. It's a means of destroying a planet and everything on it completely—by turning that planet into a nova. If that's a weapon, military or political, then I'm Samson and you're Delilah."

"But I'm not Samson," he went on, "and I don't propose to pull down the Temple—nor let anybody else do so. There are moral lice around who would do just that, if anybody tried to keep them from having their own way. Mrs. Keithley is one such. Your boy friend Bonn is another such, if only he had the guts and the savvy—which he ain't. I'm bent on frustrating such people. What do you know about ballistics, Joe?"

"Grammar school stuff."

"Inexcusable ignorance." The speaker sounded again; he answered it without breaking his flow. "The problem of three bodies still lacks a neat general solution, but there are several special solutions—the asteroids that chase Jupiter in Jupiter's

41

own orbit at the sixty degree position, for example. And there's the straight-line solution—you've heard of the asteroid 'Earth-Anti'?"

"That's the chunk of rock that is always on the other side of the Sun, where we never see it."

"That's right—only it ain't there any more. It's been no-vaed."

Gilead, normally immune to surprise, had been subjected to one too many. "Huh? I thought this nova effect was theory?"

"Nope. If you had had time to scan through the films you would have seen pictures of it. It's a plutonium, lithium, and heavy water deal, with some flourishes we won't discuss. It adds up to the match that can set afire a world. It did—a little world flared up and was gone.

"Nobody saw it happen. No one on Earth *could* see it, for it was behind the Sun. It couldn't have been seen from Moon Colony; the Sun still blanked it off from there—visualize the geometry. All that ever saw it were a battery of cameras in a robot ship. All who knew about it were the scientists who rigged it—and *all* of them were with us, except the director. If *he* had been, too, you would never have been in this mix up."

"Dr. Finnley?"

"Yep. A nice guy, but a mind like a pretzel. A 'political' scientist, second-rate ability. He doesn't matter; our boys will ride herd on him until he's pensioned off. But we couldn't keep him from reporting and sending the films down. So I had to grab 'em and destroy them."

"Why didn't you simply save them? All other considerations aside, they are unique in science."

"The human race doesn't need that bit of science, not this millenium. I saved all that mattered, Joe—in my head."

"You *are* your cousin Hartley, aren't you?"

"Of course. But I'm also Kettle Belly Baldwin, and several other guys."

"You can be Lady Godiva, for all of me."

"As Hartley, I was entitled to those films, Joe. It was my project. I instigated it, through my boys."

"I never credited Finnley with it. I'm not a physicist, but he obviously isn't up to it."

"Sure, sure. I was attempting to prove that an artificial nova could not be created; the political—the *racial*—importance of establishing the point is obvious. It backfired on me—so we had to go into emergency action."

"Perhaps you should have left well enough alone."

"No. It's better to know the worst; now we can be alert for it, divert research away from it." The speaker growled again; Baldwin went on, "There may be a divine destiny, Joe, unlikely as it seems, that makes really dangerous secrets too difficult

42

to be broached until intelligence reaches the point where it can cope with them—*if* said intelligence has the will and the good intentions. Ma Garver says to come up now."

They headed for the stairs. "I'm surprised that you leave it up to an old gal like Ma to take charge during an emergency."

"She's competent, I assure you. But I *was* running things— you heard me."

"Oh."

They settled down again in the above-surface study. "I give you one more chance to back out, Joe. It doesn't matter that you know all about the films, since they are gone and you can't prove anything—but beyond that—you realize that if you come in with us, are told what is going on, you will be killed deader than a duck at the first suspicious move?"

Gilead did; he knew in fact that he was already beyond the point of no return. With the destruction of the films went his last chance of rehabilitating his former main *persona*. This gave him no worry; the matter was done. He had become aware that from the time he had admitted that he understood the first message this man had offered him concealed in a double deck of cards he had no longer been a free actor, his moves had been constrained by moves made by Baldwin. Yet there was no help for it; his future lay here or nowhere.

"I know it; go ahead."

"I know what your mental reservations are, Joe; you are simply accepting risk; not promising loyalty."

"Yes—but why are you considering taking a chance on me?"

Baldwin was more serious in manner than he usually allowed himself to be. "You're an able man, Joe. You have the savvy and the moral courage to do what is reasonable in an odd situation rather than what is conventional."

"That's why you want me?"

"Partly that. Partly because I like the way you catch on to a new card game." He grinned. "And even partly because Gail likes the way you behave with a colt."

"Gail? What's she got to do with it?"

"She reported on you to me about five minutes ago, during the raid."

"Hmm—go ahead."

"You've been warned." For a moment Baldwin looked almost sheepish. "I want you to take what I say next at its face value, Joe—don't laugh."

"Okay."

"You asked what I was. I'm sort of the executive secretary of this branch of an organization of supermen."

"I thought so."

"Eh? How long have you known?"

43

"Things added up. The card game, your reaction time. I knew it when you destroyed the films."

"Joe, what is a superman?"

Gilead did not answer.

"Very well, let's chuck the term," Baldwin went on. "It's been overused and misused and beat up until it has mostly comic connotations. I used it for shock value and I didn't shock you. The term 'supermen' has come to have a fairy tale meaning, conjuring up pictures of x-ray eyes, odd sense organs, double hearts, uncuttable skin, steel muscles—an adolescent's dream of the dragon-killing hero. Tripe, of course. Joe, what is a *man*? What is man that makes him more than an animal? Settle that and we'll take a crack at defining a superman—or New Man, *homo novis,* who must displace *homo sapiens*—is displacing him—because he is better able to survive than is homo sap. I'm not trying to define myself, I'll leave it up to my associates and the inexorable processes of time as to whether or not I am a superman, a member of the new species of man —same test to apply to you."

"*Me?*"

"You. You show disturbing symptoms of being *homo novis,* Joe, in a sloppy, ignorant, untrained fashion. Not likely, but you just might be one of the breed. Now—what is man? What is the one thing he can do better than animals which is so strong a survival factor that it outweighs all the things that animals of one sort or another can do much better than he can?"

"He can think."

"I fed you that answer; no prize for it. Okay, you pass yourself off a man; let's see you do something. What is the one possible conceivable factor—or factors, if you prefer—which the hypothetical superman could have, by mutation or magic or any means, and which could be added to this advantage which man already has and which has enabled him to dominate this planet against the unceasing opposition of a million other species of fauna? Some factor that would make the domination of man by his successor, as inevitable as your domination over a hound dog? Think, Joe. What is the *necessary* direction of evolution to the next dominant species?"

Gilead engaged in contemplation for what was for him a long time. There were so many lovely attributes that a man might have: to be able to see both like a telescope and microscope, to see the insides of things, to see throughout the spectrum, to have hearing of the same order, to be immune to disease, to grow a new arm or leg, to fly through the air without bothering with silly gadgets like helicopters or jets, to walk unharmed the ocean bottom, to work without tiring—

Yet the eagle could fly and he was nearly extinct, even though his eyesight was better than man's. A dog has better smell and hearing; seals swim better, balance better, and furthermore can store oxygen. Rats can survive where men would starve or die of hardship; they are smart and pesky hard to kill. Rats could—

Wait! Could tougher, smarter rats displace man? No, it just wasn't in them; too small a brain.

"To be able to think better," Gilead answered almost instantly.

"Hand the man a cigar! Supermen are superthinkers; anything else is a side issue. I'll allow the possibility of super-somethings which might exterminate or dominate mankind other than by outsmarting him in his own racket—thought. But I deny that it is possible for a *man* to conceive in discrete terms what such a super-something would be or how this something would win out. New Man will beat out homo sap in homo sap's own specialty—rational thought, the ability to recognize data, store them, integrate them, evaluate correctly the result, and arrive at a correct decision. That is how man got to be champion; the creature who can do it better is the coming champion. Sure, there are other survival factors, good health, good sense organs, fast reflexes, but they aren't even comparable, as the long, rough history of mankind has proved over and over—Marat in his bath, Roosevelt in his wheelchair, Caesar with his epilepsy and his bad stomach, Nelson with one eye and one arm, blind Milton; when the chips are down it's *brain* that wins, not the body's tools."

"Stop a moment," said Gilead. "How about E.S.P.?"

Baldwin shrugged. "I'm not sneering at extra-sensory perception any more than I would at exceptional eyesight—E.S.P. is not in the same league with the ability to think correctly. E.S.P. is a grab bag name for the means other than the known sense organs by which the brain may gather data—but the trick that pays off with first prize is to make use of that data, to *reason* about it. If you would like a telepathic hook up to Shanghai, I can arrange it; we've got operators at both ends —but you can get whatever data you might happen to need from Shanghai by phone with less trouble, less chance of a bad connection, and less danger of somebody listening in. Telepaths can't pick up a radio message; it's not the same wave band."

"What wave band is it?"

"Later, later. You've got a lot to learn."

"I wasn't thinking especially of telepathy. I was thinking of all parapsychological phenomena."

"Same reasoning. Apportation would be nice, if telekinetics had gotten that far—which it ain't. But a pick-up truck moves things handily enough. Television in the hands of an intelligent man counts for more than clairvoyance in a moron. Quit wasting my time, Joe."

"Sorry."

"We defined thinking as integrating data and arriving at correct answers. Look around you. Most people do that stunt just well enough to get to the corner store and back without breaking a leg. If the average man thinks at all, he does silly things like generalizing from a single datum. He uses one-valued logics. If he is exceptionally bright, he may use two-valued, 'either-or' logic to arrive at his wrong answers. If he is hungry, hurt, or personally interested in the answer, he can't use any sort of logic and will discard an observed fact as blithely as he will stake his life on a piece of wishful thinking. He uses the technical miracles created by superior men without wonder nor surprise, as a kitten accepts a bowl of milk. Far from aspiring to higher reasoning, he is not even aware that higher reasoning exists. He classes his own mental process as being of the same sort as the genius of an Einstein. Man is not a rational animal; he is a rationalizing animal.

"For explanations of a universe that confuses him he seizes onto numerology, astrology, hysterical religions, and other fancy ways to go crazy. Having accepted such glorified nonsense, facts make no impression on him, even if at the cost of his own life. Joe, one of the hardest things to believe is the abysmal depth of human stupidity.

"That is why there is always room at the top, why a man with just a *leetle* more on the ball can so easily become governor, millionaire, or college president—and why homo sap is sure to be displaced by New Man, because there is so much room for improvement and evolution never stops.

"Here and there among ordinary men is a rare individual who really thinks, can and does use logic in at least one field —he's often as stupid as the rest outside his study or laboratory —but he can think, if he's not disturbed or sick or frightened. This rare individual is responsible for *all* the progress made by the race; the others reluctantly adopt his results. Much as the ordinary man dislikes and distrusts and persecutes the process of thinking he is forced to accept the results occasionally, because thinking is efficient compared with his own maunderings. He may still plant his corn in the dark of the Moon but he will plant better corn developed by better men than he.

"Still rarer is the man who thinks habitually, who applies reason, rather than habit pattern, to all his activity. Unless he masques himself, his is a dangerous life; he is regarded as queer, untrustworthy, subversive of public morals; he is a pink monkey among brown monkeys—a fatal mistake. Unless the pink monkey can dye himself brown before he is caught.

"The brown monkey's instinct to kill is correct; such men are dangerous to all monkey customs.

"Rarest of all is the man who can and does reason at all times, quickly, accurately, inclusively, despite hope or fear or bodily distress, without egocentric bias or thalmic disturbance,

46

with correct memory, with clear distinction between fact, assumption, and non-fact. Such men exist, Joe; they are 'New Man'—human in all respects, indistinguishable in appearance or under the scalpel from homo sap, yet as unlike him in action as the Sun is unlike a single candle."

Gilead said, "Are you that sort?"

"You will continue to form your own opinions."

"And you think I may be, too?"

"Could be. I'll have more data in a few days."

Gilead laughed until the tears came. "Kettle Belly, if I'm the future hope of the race, they had better send in the second team quick. Sure I'm brighter than most of the jerks I run into, but, as you say, the competition isn't stiff. But I haven't any sublime aspirations. I've got as lecherous an eye as the next man. I enjoy wasting time over a glass of beer. I just don't *feel* like a superman."

"Speaking of beer, let's have some." Baldwin got up and obtained two cans of the brew. "Remember that Mowgli felt like a wolf. Being a New Man does not divorce you from human sympathies and pleasures. There have been New Men all through history; I doubt if most of them suspected that their difference entitled them to call themselves a different breed. Then they went ahead and bred with the daughters of men, diffusing their talents through the racial organism, preventing them from effectuating until chance brought the genetic factors together again."

"Then I take it that New Man is not a special mutation?"

"Huh? Who isn't a mutation, Joe? All of us are a collection of millions of mutations. Around the globe hundreds of mutations have taken place in our human germ plasm while we have been sitting here. No, homo novis didn't come about because great grandfather stood too close to a cyclotron; homo novis was not even a separate breed until he became aware of himself, organized, and decided to hang on to what his genes had handed him. You could mix New Man back into the race today and lose him; he's merely a variation becoming a species. A million years from now is another matter; I venture to predict that New Man, of that year and model, won't be able to interbreed with homo sap—no viable offspring."

"You don't expect present man—homo sapiens—to disappear?"

"Not necessarily. The dog adapted to man. Probably more dogs now than in umpteen B. C.—and better fed."

"And man would be New Man's dog."

"Again not necessarily. Consider the cat."

"The idea is to skim the cream of the race's germ plasm and keep it biologically separate until the two races are permanently distinct. You chaps sound like a bunch of stinkers, Kettle Belly."

47

"Monkey talk."

"Perhaps. The new race would necessarily run things—"

"Do you expect New Man to decide grave matters by counting common man's runny noses?"

"No, that was my point. Postulating such a new race, the result is inevitable. Kettle Belly, I confess to a monkey prejudice in favor of democracy, human dignity, and freedom. It goes beyond logic; it is the kind of a world I like. In my job I have jungled with the outcasts of society, shared their slumgullion. Stupid they may be, bad they are not—I have no wish to see them become domestic animals."

For the first time the big man showed concern. His *persona* as "King of the Kopters", master merchandiser, slipped away; he sat in brooding majesty, a lonely and unhappy figure. "I know, Joe. They are of us; their little dignities, their nobilities, are not lessened by their sorry state. Yet it must be."

"Why? New Man will come—granted. But why hurry the process?"

"Ask yourself." He swept a hand toward the oubliette. "Ten minutes ago you and I saved this planet, all our race. It's the hour of the knife. Some one must be on guard if the race is to live; there is no one but us. To guard effectively we New Men must be organized, must never fumble any crisis like this —and must increase our numbers. We are few now, Joe; as the crises increase, we must increase to meet them. Eventually —and it's a dead race with time—we must take over and make certain that baby never plays with matches."

He stopped and brooded. "I confess to that same effection for democracy, Joe. But it's like yearning for the Santa Claus you believed in as a child. For a hundred and fifty years or so democracy, or something like it, could flourish safely. The issues were such as to be settled without disaster by the votes of common men, befogged and ignorant as they were. But now, if the race is simply to stay alive, political decisions depend on real knowledge of such things as nuclear physics, planetary ecology, genetic theory, even system mechanics. They aren't up to it, Joe. With goodness and more will than they possess less than one in a thousand could stay awake over one page of nuclear physics; they can't learn what they must know."

Gilead brushed it aside. "It's up to us to brief them. Their hearts are all right; tell them the score—they'll come down with the right answers."

"No, Joe. We've tried it; it does not work. As you say, most of them are good, the way a dog can be noble and good. Yet there are bad ones—Mrs. Keithley and company and more like her. Reason is poor propaganda when opposed by the yammering, unceasing lies of shrewd and evil and self-serving men. The little man has no way to judge and the shoddy lies are packaged more attractively. There is no way to offer color to

48

a colorblind man, nor is there any way for us to give the man of imperfect brain the canny skill to distinguish a lie from a truth.

"No, Joe. The gulf between us and them is narrow, but it is very deep. We cannot close it."

"I wish," said Gilead, "that you wouldn't class me with your 'New Man'; I feel more at home on the other side."

"You will decide for yourself which side you are on, as each of us has done."

Gilead forced a change in subject. Ordinarily immune to thalamic disturbance this issue upset him; his brain followed Baldwin's argument and assured him that it was true; his inclinations fought it. He was confronted with the sharpest of all tragedy; two equally noble and valid rights, utterly opposed. "What do you people do, aside from stealing films?"

"Mmm—many things." Baldwin relaxed, looked again like a jovial sharp businessman. "Where a push here and a touch there will keep things from going to pot, we apply the pressure, by many and devious means. And we scout for suitable material and bring it into the fold when we can—we've had our eye on you for ten years."

"So?"

"Yep. That is a prime enterprise. Through public data we eliminate all but about one tenth of one per cent; that thousandth individual we watch. And then there are our horticultural societies." He grinned.

"Finish your joke."

"We weed people."

"Sorry, I'm slow today."

"Joe, didn't you ever feel a yen to wipe out some evil, obscene, rotten jerk who infected everything he touched, yet was immune to legal action? We treat them as cancers; we excise them from the body social. We keep a 'Better Dead' list; when a man is clearly morally bankrupt we close his account at the first opportunity."

Gilead smiled. "If you were sure what you were doing, it could be fun."

"We are always sure, though our methods would be no good in a monkey law court. Take Mrs. Keithley—is there doubt in your mind?"

"None."

"Why don't you have her indicted? Don't bother to answer. For example, two weeks from tonight there will be giant powwow of the new, rejuvenated, bigger-and-better-than-ever Ku Klux Klan on a mountain top down Carolina way. When the fun is at its height, when they are mouthing obscenities, working each other up to the pogrom spirit, an act of God is going to wipe out the whole kit and kaboodle. Very sad."

"Could I get in on that?"

"You aren't even a cadet as yet." Baldwin went on. "There is the project to increase our numbers, but that is a thousand-year program; you'd need a perpetual calendar to check it. More important is keeping matches away from baby. Joe, it's been eighty-five years since we beheaded the last commissar: have you wondered why so little basic progress in science has been made in that time?"

"Eh? There have been a lot of changes."

"Minor adaptations—some spectacular, almost none of them basic. Of course there was very little progress made under communism; a totalitarian political religion is incompatible with free investigation. Let me digress: the communist inter-regnum was responsible for the New Men getting together and organizing. Most New Men are scientists, for obvious reasons. When the commissars started ruling on natural laws by political criteria—Lysenko-ism and similar nonsense—it did not sit well; a lot of us went underground.

"I'll skip the details. It brought us together, gave us practice in underground activity, and gave a backlog of new research, carried out underground. Some of it was obviously dangerous; we decided to hang onto it for a while. Since then such secret knowledge has grown, for we never give out an item until it has been scrutinized for social hazards. Since much of it *is* dangerous and since very few indeed outside our organization are capable of real original thinking, basic science has been almost at a—public!—standstill.

"We hadn't expected to have to do it that way. We helped to see to it that the new constitution was liberal and—we thought—workable. But the new Republic turned out to be an even poorer thing than the old. The evil ethic of communism had corrupted, even after the form was gone. We held off. Now we know that we must hold off until we can revise the whole society."

"Kettle Belly," Joe said slowly, "you speak as if you had been on the spot. How old are you?"

"I'll tell you when you are the age I am now. A man has lived long enough when he no longer longs to live. I ain't there yet. Joe, I must have your answer, or this must be continued in our next."

"You had it at the beginning—but, see here, Kettle Belly, there is one job I want promised to me."

"Which is?"

"I want to kill Mrs. Keithley."

"Keep your pants on. When you're trained, and if she's still alive then, you'll be used for that purpose—"

"Thanks!"

"—provided you are the proper tool for it." Baldwin turned toward the mike, called out, "Gail!" and added one word in the strange tongue.

Gail showed up promptly. "Joe," said Baldwin, "when this young lady gets through with you, you will be able to sing, whistle, chew gum, play chess, hold your breath, and fly a kite simultaneously—and all this while riding a bicycle under water. Take him, sis, he's all yours."

Gail rubbed her hands. "Oh, boy!"

"First we must teach you to see and to hear, then to remember, then to speak, and then to think."

Joe looked at her. "What's this I'm doing with my mouth at this moment?"

"It's not talking, it's a sort of grunting. Furthermore English is not structurally suited to thinking. Shut up and listen."

In their underground classroom Gail had available several types of apparatus to record and manipulate light and sound. She commenced throwing groups of figures on a screen, in flashes. "What was it, Joe?"

"nine-six-oh-seven-two—That was as far as I got."

"It was up there a full thousandth of a second. Why did you get only the left hand side of the group?"

"That's all the farther I had read."

"Look at *all* of it. Don't make an effort of will; just look at it." She flashed another number.

Joe's memory was naturally good; his intelligence was high —just how high he did not yet know. Unconvinced that the drill was useful, he relaxed and played along. Soon he was beginning to grasp a nine-digit array as a single *gestalt;* Gail reduced the flash time.

"What is this magic lantern gimmick?" he inquired.

"It's a Renshaw tachistoscope. Back to work."

Around World War II Dr. Samuel Renshaw at the Ohio State University was proving that most people are about one-fifth efficient in using their capacities to see, hear, taste, feel and remember. His research was swallowed in the morass of communist pseudoscience that obtained after World War III, but, after his death, his findings were preserved underground. Gail did not expose Gilead to the odd language he had heard until he had been rather thoroughly Renshawed.

However, from the time of his interview with Baldwin the other persons at the ranch used it in his presence. Sometimes someone—usually Ma Garver—would translate, sometimes not. He was flattered to feel accepted, but gravelled to know that it was at the lowest cadetship. He was a child among adults.

Gail started teaching him to hear by speaking to him single words from the odd language, requiring him to repeat them back. "No, Joe. Watch." This time when she spoke the word it appeared on the screen in sound analysis, by a means basically like one long used to show the deaf-and-dumb their speech mistakes. "Now you try it."

He did, the two arrays hung side by side. "How's that, teacher?" he said triumphantly.

"Terrible, by several decimal places. You held the final guttural too long—" She pointed. "—the middle vowel was formed with your tongue too high and you pitched it too low and you failed to let the pitch rise. And six other things. You couldn't possibly have been understood. I heard what you said, but it was gibberish. Try again. And don't call me 'teacher'."

"Yes, ma'am," he answered solemnly.

She shifted the controls; he tried again. This time his analysis array was laid down on top of hers; where the two matched, they cancelled. Where they did not match, his errors stood out in contrasting colors. The screen looked like a sun burst.

"Try again, Joe." She repeated the word without letting it affect the display.

"Confound it, if you would tell me what the words mean instead of treating me the way Milton treated his daughters about Latin, I could remember them easier."

She shrugged. "I can't, Joe. You must learn to hear and to speak first. Speedtalk is a flexible language; the same word is not likely to recur. This practice word means: 'The far horizons draw no nearer.' That's not much help, is it?"

The definition seemed improbable, but he was learning not to doubt her. He was not used to women who were always two jumps ahead of him. He ordinarily felt sorry for the poor little helpless cuddly creatures; this one he often wanted to slug. He wondered if this response were what the romancers meant by "love"; he decided that it couldn't be.

"Try again, Joe." Speedtalk was a structurally different speech from any the race had ever used. Long before, Ogden and Richards had shown that eight hundred and fifty words were sufficient vocabulary to express anything that could be expressed by "normal" human vocabularies, with the aid of a handful of special words—a hundred odd—for each special field, such as horse racing or ballistics. About the same time phoneticians had analyzed all human tongues into about a hundred-odd sounds, represented by the letters of a general phonetic alphabet.

On these two propositions Speedtalk was based.

To be sure, the phonetic alphabet was much less in number than the words in Basic English. But the letters representing sound in the phonetic alphabet were each capable of variation several different ways—length, stress, pitch, rising, falling. The more trained an ear was the larger the number of possible variations; there was no limit to variations, but, without much refinement of accepted phonetic practice, it was possible to establish a one-to-one relationship with Basic English so that *one phonetic symbol* was equivalent to an entire word in a "normal" language, one Speedtalk word was equal to an entire sentence. The language consequently was learned by letter units rather than by word units—but each word was spoken and listened to as a single structured gestalt.

But Speedtalk was not "shorthand" Basic English. "Normal" languages, having their roots in days of superstition and ignorance, have in them inherently and unescapably wrong structures of mistaken ideas about the universe. One can think logically in English only by extreme effort, so bad it is as a mental tool. For example, the verb "to be" in English has twenty-one distinct meanings, *every single one of which is false-to-fact*.

A symbolic structure, invented instead of accepted without question, can be made similar in structure to the real-world to which it refers. The structure of Speedtalk did *not* contain the hidden errors of English; it was structured as much like the real world as the New Men could make it. For example, it did not contain the unreal distinction between nouns and verbs found in most other languages. The world—the continuum known to science and including all human activity—does not contain "noun things" and "verb things"; it contains space-time events and relationships between them. The advantage for achieving truth, or something more nearly like truth, was similar to the advantage of keeping account books in Arabic numerals rather than Roman.

All other languages made scientific, multi-valued logic almost impossible to achieve; in Speedtalk it was as difficult *not* to be logical. Compare the pellucid Boolean logic with the obscurities of the Aristotelean logic it supplanted.

Paradoxes are verbal, do not exist in the real world—and Speedtalk did not have such built into it. Who shaves the Spanish Barber? Answer: follow him around and see. In the syntax of Speedtalk the paradox of the Spanish Barber could not even be expressed, save as a self-evident error.

But Joe Greene-Gilead-Briggs could not learn it until he had learned to hear, by learning to speak. He slaved away; the screen continued to remain lighted with his errors.

Came finally a time when Joe's pronunciation of a sentence-word blanked out Gail's sample; the screen turned dark. He felt more triumph over that than anything he could remember.

His delight was short. By a circuit Gail had thoughtfully added somedays earlier the machine answered with a flourish of trumpets, loud applause, and then added in a cooing voice, "Mama's *good* boy!"

He turned to her. "Woman, you spoke of matrimony. If you ever do manage to marry me, I'll beat you."

"I haven't made up my mind about you yet," she answered evenly. "Now try this word, Joe—"

Baldwin showed up that evening, called him aside. "Joe! C'mere. Listen, lover boy, you keep your animal nature out of your work, or I'll have to find you a new teacher."

"But—"

"You heard me. Take her swimming, take her riding, after hours you are on your own. Work time—strictly business. I've got plans for you; I want you to get smarted up."

"She complained about me?"

"Don't be silly. It's my business to know what's going on."

"Hmm. Kettle Belly, what is this shopping-for-a-husband she kids about? Is she serious, or is it just intended to rattle me?"

"Ask her. Not that it matters, as you won't have any choice if she means it. She has the calm persistence of the law of gravitation."

"Ouch! I had had the impression that the 'New Men' did not bother with marriage and such like, as you put it, 'monkey customs.'"

"Some do, some don't. Me, I've been married quite a piece, but I mind a mousy little member of our lodge who had had nine kids by nine fathers—all wonderful genius-plus kids. On the other hand I can point out one with eleven kids—Thalia Wagner—who has never so much as looked at another man. Geniuses make their own rules in such matters, Joe; they always have. Here are some established statistical facts about genius, as shown by Armatoe's work—"

He ticked them off. "Geniuses are usually long lived. They are not modest, not honestly so. They have infinite capacity for taking pains. They are emotionally indifferent to accepted codes of morals—they make their own rules. You seem to have the stigmata, by the way."

"Thanks for nothing. Maybe I should have a new teacher, is there is anyone else available who can do it."

"*Any* of us can do it, just as anybody handy teaches a baby to talk. She's actually a biochemist, when she has time for it."

"When she has time?"

"Be careful of that kid, son. Her real profession is the same as yours—honorable hatchet man. She's killed upwards of three hundred people." Kettle Belly grinned. "If you want to switch teachers, just drop me a wink."

Gilead-Greene hastily changed the subject. "You were speaking of work for me: how about Mrs. Keithley? Is she still alive?"

"Yes, blast her."

"Remember, I've got dibs on her."

"You may have to go to the Moon to get her. She's reported to be building a vacation home there. Old age seems to be telling on her; you had better get on with your home work if you want a crack at her." Moon Colony even then was a center of geriatrics for the rich. The low gravity was easy on their hearts, made them feel young—and possibly extended their lives.

"Okay, I will."

Instead of asking for a new teacher Joe took a highly polished apple to their next session. Gail ate it, leaving him very little core, and put him harder to work than ever. While perfecting his hearing and pronunciation, she started him on the basic thousand-letter vocabulary by forcing him to start to talk simple three and four-letter sentences, and by answering him in different word-sentences using the same phonetic letters. Some of the vowel and consonant sequences were very difficult to pronounce.

Master them he did. He had been used to doing most things easier than could those around him; now he was in very fast company. He stretched himself and began to achieve part of his own large latent capacity. When he began to catch some of the dinner-table conversation and to reply in simple Speedtalk—being forbidden by Gail to answer in English—she started him on the ancillary vocabularies.

An economical language cannot be limited to a thousand words; although almost every idea can be expressed somehow in a short vocabulary, higher orders of abstraction are convenient. For technical words Speedtalk employed an open expansion of sixty of the thousand-odd phonetic letters. They were the letters ordinarily used as numerals; by preceding a number with a letter used for no other purpose, the symbol was designated as having a word value.

New Men numbered to the base sixty—three times four times five, a convenient, easily factored system, most economical, i. e., the symbol "100" identified the number described in English as thirty-six hundred—yet permitting quick, in-the-head translation from common notation to Speedtalk figures and vice versa.

By using these figures, each prefaced by the indicator—a voiceless Welsh or Burmese "1"—a pool of 215,999 words (one less than the cube of sixty) were available for specialized meaning without using more than four letters including the indicator. Most of them could be pronounced as one syllable. These had not the stark simplicity of basic Speedtalk; nevertheless words such as "ichthyophagous" and "constitutionality" were thus compressed to monosyllables. Such shortcuts can best be appreciated by anyone who has heard a long speech in Cantonese translated into a short speech in English. Yet English is not the most terse of "normal" languages—and expanded Speedtalk is many times more economical than the briefest of "normal" tongues.

By adding one more letter (sixty to the fourth power) just short of thirteen *million* words could be added if needed— and most of them could still be pronounced as one syllable.

When Joe discovered that Gail expected him to learn a couple of hundred thousand new words in a matter of days, he balked. "Damn it, Fancy Pants, I am not a superman. I'm in here by mistake."

"Your opinion is worthless; I think you can do it. Now listen."

"Suppose I flunk; does that put me safely off your list of possible victims?"

"If you flunk, I wouldn't have you on toast. Instead I'd tear your head off and stuff it down your throat. But you won't flunk; I *know*. However," she added, "I'm not sure you would be a satisfactory husband; you argue too much."

He made a brief and bitter remark in Speedtalk; she answered with one word which described his shortcomings in detail. They got to work.

Joe was mistaken; he learned the expanded vocabulary as fast as he heard it. He had a latent eidetic memory; the Renshawing process now enabled him to use it fully. And his mental processes, always fast, had become faster than he knew.

The ability to learn Speedtalk at all is proof of supernormal intelligence; the *use* of it by such intelligence renders that mind efficient. Even before World War II Alfred Korzybski had shown that human thought was performed, when done efficiently, only in symbols; the notion of "pure" thought, free of abstracted speech symbols, was merely fantasy. The brain was so constructed as to work without symbols only on the animal level; to speak of "reasoning" without symbols was to speak nonsense.

Speedtalk did not merely speed up communication—by its structures it made thought more logical; by its economy it made thought processes enormously faster, since it takes almost as long to *think* a word as it does to speak it.

Korzybski's monumental work went fallow during the communist interregnum; *Das Kapital* is a childish piece of work, when analyzed by semantics, so the politburo suppressed semantics—and replaced it by *ersatz* under the same name, as Lysenkoism replaced the science of genetics.

Having Speedtalk to help him learn *more* Speedtalk, Joe learned very rapidly. The Renshawing had continued; he was now able to grasp a gestalt or configuration in many senses at once, grasp it, remember it, reason about it with great speed.

Living time is not calendar time; a man's life is the thought that flows through his brain. Any man capable of learning Speedtalk had an association time at least three times as fast as an ordinary man. Speedtalk itself enabled him to manipulate symbols approximately seven times as fast as English symbols could be manipulated. Seven times three is twenty-one; a new man had an *effective* life time of at least *sixteen hundred years*, reckoned in flow of ideas.

They had time to become encyclopedic synthesists, something denied any ordinary man by the straitjacket of his sort of time.

When Joe had learned to talk, to read and write and cipher, Gail turned him over to others for his real education. But before she checked him out she played him several dirty tricks.

For three days she forbade him to eat. When it was evident that he could think and keep his temper despite low blood-sugar count, despite hunger reflex, she added sleeplessness and pain—intense, long, continued, and varied pain. She tried subtly to goad him into irrational action; he remained bedrock steady, his mind clicking away at any assigned task as dependably as an electronic computer.

"Who's not a superman?" she asked at the end of their last session.

"Yes, teacher."

"Come her, lug." She grabbed him by the ears, kissed him soundly. "So long." He did not see her again for many weeks.

His tutor in E.S.P. was an ineffectual-looking little man who had taken the protective coloration of the name Weems. Joe was not very good at producing E.S.P. phenomena. Clairvoyance he did not appear to have. He was better at precognition, but he did not improve with practice. He was best at telekinesis; he could have made a soft living with dice. But, as Kettle Belly had pointed out, from affecting the roll of dice to moving tons of freight was quite a gap—and one possibly not worth bridging.

"It may have other uses, however," Weems had said softly, lapsing into English. "Consider what might be done if one could influence the probability that a neutron would reach a particular nucleus—or change the statistical probability in a mass."

Gilead let it ride; it was an outrageous thought.

At telepathy he was erratic to exasperation. He called the Rhine cards once without a miss, then had poor scores for three weeks. More highly structured communication seemed quite beyond him, until one day without apparent cause but during an attempt to call the cards by telepathy, he found himself hooked in with Weems for all of ten seconds—time enough for a thousand words by Speedtalk standards.

—it comes out as speech!

—why not? thought is speech.

—how do we do it?

—if we knew it would not be so unreliable. as it is, some can do it by volition, some by accident, and some never seem to be able to do it. we do know this: while thought may not be of the physical world in any fashion we can now define and manipulate, it is similar to events in continuum in its quantal nature. You are now studying the extension of the quantuum

57

concept to all features of the continuum, you know the chronon, the mensum, and the viton, as quanta, as well as the action units of quanta such as the photon. The continuum has not only structure but texture in all its features. The least unit of thought we term the psychon.

—define it. put salt on its tail.

—some day, some day. I can tell you this; the fastest possible rate of thought is one psychon per chronon; this is a basic, universal constant.

—how close do we come to that?

—less than sixty-to-the-minus-third-power of the possibility.

—! ! ! ! ! !

—better creatures than ourselves will follow us. We pick pebbles at a boundless ocean.

—what can we do to improve it?

—gather our pebbles with serene minds.

Gilead paused for a long split second of thought. *—can psychons be destroyed?*

—vitons may be transferred. psychons are—

The connection was suddenly destroyed. "As I was saying," Weems went on quietly, "psychons are as yet beyond our comprehension in many respects. Theory indicates that they may not be destroyed, that thought, like action, is persistent. Whether or not such theory, if true, means that personal identity is also persistent must remain an open question. See the daily papers—a few hundred years from now—or a few hundred thousand." He stood up.

"I'm anxious to try tomorrow's session, Doc," Gilead-Greene almost bubbled. "Maybe—"

"I'm finished with you."

"But, Doctor Weems that connection was clear as a phone hook-up. Perhaps tomorrow—"

"We have established that your talent is erratic. We have no way to train it to dependability. Time is too short to waste, mine and yours." Lapsing suddenly into English, he added, "No."

Gilead left.

During his training in other fields Joe was exposed to many things best described as impressive gadgets. There was an integrating pantograph, a factory-in-a-box, which the New Men planned to turn over to ordinary men as soon as the social system was no longer dominated by economic wolves. It could and did reproduce almost any prototype placed on its stage, requiring thereto only materials and power. Its power came from a little nucleonics motor the size of Joe's thumb; its theory played hob with conventional notions of entropy. One put in "sausage"; one got out "pig".

Latent in it was the shape of an economic system as different from the current one as the assembly-line economy differed

58

from the family-shop system—and in such a system lay possibilities of human freedom and dignity missing for centuries, if they had ever existed.

In the mean time New Men rarely bought more than one of anything—a pattern. Or they made a pattern.

Another useful but hardly wonderful gadget was a dictaphone-typewriter-printing-press combination. The machine's analysers recognized each of the thousand-odd phonetic symbols; there was a typebar for each sound. It produced one or many copies. Much of Gilead's education came from pages printed by this gadget, saving the precious time of others.

The arrangement, classification, and accessibility of knowledge remains in all ages the most pressing problem. With the New Men, complete and organized memory licked most of the problem and rendered record keeping, most reading and writing—and most especially the time-destroying trouble of rereading—unnecessary. The autoscriber gadget, combined with a "librarian" machine that could "hear" that portion of Speedtalk built into it as a filing system, covered most of the rest of the problem. New Men were not cluttered with endless bits of paper. They *never* wrote memoranda.

The area under the ranch was crowded with technological wonders, all newer than next week. Incredibly tiny manipulators for micrurgy of all sorts, surgical, chemical, biological manipulation, oddities of cybernetics only less complex than the human brain—the list is too long to describe. Joe did not study all of them; an encyclopedic synthesist is concerned with structured shapes of knowledge; he cannot, even with Speedtalk, study details in every field.

Early in his education, when it was clear that he had had the potential to finish the course, plastic surgery was started to give him a new identity and basic appearance. His height was reduced by three inches; his skull was somewhat changed; his complexion was permanently darkened. Gail picked the facial appearance he was given; he did not object. He rather liked it; it seemed to fit his new inner personality.

With a new face, a new brain, and a new outlook, he was almost in fact a new man. Before he had been a natural genius; now he was a *trained* genius.

"Joe, how about some riding?"

"Suits."

"I want to give War Conqueror some gentle exercise. He's responding to the saddle; I don't want him to forget."

"Right with you."

Kettle Belly and Gilead-Greene rode out from the ranch buildings. Baldwin let the young horse settle to a walk and began to talk. "I figure you are about ready for work son."

Even in Speedtalk Kettle Belly's speech retained his own flavor.

"I suppose so, but I still have those mental reservations."

"Not sure we are on the side of the angels?"

"I'm sure you mean to be. It's evident that the organization selects for good will and humane intentions quite as carefully as for ability. I wasn't sure at one time—"

"Yes?"

"That candidate who came here about six months ago, the one who broke his neck in a riding accident."

"Oh, yes! Very sad."

"Very opportune, you mean, Kettle Belly."

"Damn it, Joe, if a bad apple gets in this far, we can't let him out." Baldwin reverted to English for swearing purposes; he maintained that it had "more juice."

"I know it. That's why I'm sure about the quality of our people."

"So it's 'our people' now?"

"Yes. But I'm not sure we are on the right track."

"What's your notion of the right track?"

"We should come out of hiding and teach the ordinary man what he can learn of what we know. He could learn a lot of it and could use it. Properly briefed and trained, he could run his affairs pretty well. He would gladly kick out the no-goods who ride on his shoulders, if only he knew how. We could show him. That would be more to the point than this business of spot assassination, now and then, here and there—mind you, I don't object to killing any man who merits killing; I simply say it's inefficient. No doubt we would have to continue to guard against such crises as the one that brought you and me together but, in the main, people could run their own affairs if we would just stop pretending that we are so scared we can't mix with people, come out of our hole, and lend a hand."

Baldwin reined up. "Don't say that I don't mix with the common people, Joe; I sell used 'copters for a living. You can't get any commoner. And don't imply that my heart is not with them. We are not like them, but we are tied to them by the strongest bond of all, for we are all, each every one, sickening with the same certainly fatal disease—we are alive.

"As for our killings, you don't understand the principles of assassination as a political weapon. Read—" He named a Speedtalk library designation. "If I were knocked off, our organization wouldn't even hiccup, but organizations for bad purposes are different. They are personal empires; if you pick the time and the method, you can destroy such an organization by killing one man—the parts that remain will be almost harmless until assimilated by another leader—then you kill *him*.

60

It is not inefficient; it's quite efficient, if planned with the brain and not with the emotions.

"As for keeping ourselves separate, we are about like the U-235 in U-238, not effective unless separated out. There have been potential New Men in every generation, but they were spread too thin.

"As for keeping our existence secret, it is utterly necessary if we are to survive and increase. There is nothing so danger-out as being the Chosen People—and in the minority. One group was persecuted for two thousand years merely for making the claim."

He again shifted to English to swear. "Damn it, Joe, face up to it. This world is run the way my great aunt Susie flies a 'copter. Speedtalk or no Speedtalk, common man *can't* learn to cope with modern problems. No use to talk about the un-used potential of his brain, he has not got the *will* to learn what he would have to know. We can't fit him out with new genes, so we have to lead him by the hand to keep him from killing himself—and us. We can give him personal liberty, we can give him autonomy in most things, we can give him a great measure of personal dignity—and we will, because we believe that individual freedom, at all levels, is the direction of evolution, of maximum survival value. But we can't let him fiddle with issues of racial life and death; he ain't up to it.

"No help for it. Each shape of society develops its own ethic. We are shaping this the way we are inexorably forced to, by the logic of events. We *think* we are shaping it toward survival."

"Are we?" mused Greene-Gilead.

"Remains to be seen. Survivors survive. We'll know—Wup! Meeting's adjourned."

The radio on Baldwin's pommel was shrilling his personal emergency call. He listened, then spoke one sharp word in Speedtalk. "Back to the house, Joe!" He wheeled and was away. Joe's mount came of less selected stock; he was forced to follow.

Baldwin sent for Joe soon after he got back. Joe went in; Gail was already there.

Baldwin's face was without expression. He said in English, "I've work for you, Joe, work you won't have any doubt about. Mrs. Keithley."

"Good."

"Not good." Baldwin shifted to Speedtalk. "We have been caught flat-footed. Either the second set of films was never destroyed, or there was a third set. We do not know; the man who could tell us is dead. But Mrs. Keithley obtained a set and has been using them.

"This is the situation. The 'fuse' of the nova effect has been installed in the New Age hotel. It has been sealed off and can be triggered only by radio signal from the Moon—her signal. The 'fuse' has been rigged so that any attempt to break in, as long as the firing circuit is still armed, will trigger it and set it off. Even an attempt to examine it by penetration wavelengths will set it off. Speaking as a physicist, it is my considered opinion that *no* plan for tackling the 'nova' fuse bomb itself will work unless the arming circuit is first broken on the Moon and that no attempt should be made to get at fuse before then, because of extreme danger to the entire planet.

"The arming circuit and the radio relay to the Earthside trigger is located on the Moon in a building inside her private dome. The triggering control she keeps with her. From the same control she can disarm the arming circuit temporarily; it is a combination dead-man switch and time-clock arrangement. It can be set to disarm for a maximum of twelve hours, to let her sleep, or possibly to permit her to order rearrangements. Unless it is switched off any attempt to enter the building in which the arming circuit is housed will also trigger the 'Nova' bomb circuit. While it is disarmed, the housing on the Moon may be broached by force but this will set off alarms which will warn her to rearm and then to trigger at once. The set up is such that the following sequence of events must take place:

"First, she must be killed, and the circuit disarmed.

"Second, the building housing the arming circuit and radio relay to the trigger must be broken open and the circuits destroyed *before* the time clock can rearm and trigger. This must be done with speed, not only because of guards, but because her surviving lieutenants will attempt to seize power by possessing themselves of the controls.

"Third, as soon as word is received on Earth that the arming circuit is destroyed, the New Age will be attacked in force and the 'Nova' bomb destroyed.

"Fourth, as soon as the bomb is destroyed, a general round up must be made of all persons technically capable of setting up the 'Nova' effect from plans. This alert must be maintained until it is certain that no plans remain in existence, including the third set of films, and further established by hypno that no competent person possesses sufficient knowledge to set it up without plans. This alert may compromise our secret status; the risk must be taken.

"Any questions?"

"Kettle Belly," said Joe, "Doesn't she know that if the Earth becomes a Nova, the Moon will be swallowed up in the disaster?"

"Crater walls shield her dome from line-of-sight with Earth; apparently she believes she is safe. Evil is essentially stupid, Joe; despite her brilliance, she believes what she wishes to believe. Or it may be that she is willing to risk her own death against the tempting prize of absolute power. Her plan is to proclaim power with some pious nonsense about being high priestess of peace—a euphemism for Empress of Earth. It is a typical paranoid deviation; the proof of the craziness lies in the fact that the physical arrangements make it certain— if we do not intervene—that Earth will be destroyed automatically a few hours after her death; a thing that could happen any time—and a compelling reason for all speed. No one has ever quite managed to conquer all of Earth, not even the commissars. Apparently she wishes not only to conquer it, but wants to destroy it after she is gone, lest anyone else ever manage to do so again. Any more questions?"

He went on, "The plan is this:

"You two will go to the Moon to become domestic servants to Mr. and Mrs. Alexander Copley, a rich, elderly couple living at the Elysian Rest Homes, Moon Colony. They are of us. Shortly they will decide to return to Earth; you two will decide to remain, you like it. You will advertise, offering to work for anyone who will post your return bond. About this time Mrs. Keithley will have lost through circumstances that will be arranged, two or more of her servants; she will probably hire you, since domestic service is the scarcest commodity on the Moon. If not, a variation will be arranged for you.

"When you are inside her dome, you'll maneuver yourselves into positions to carry out your assignments. When both of you are so placed, you will carry out procedures one and two with speed.

"A person named McGinty, already inside her dome, will help you in communication. He is not one of us but is our agent, a telepath. His ability does not extend past that. Your communication hook up will probably be, Gail to McGinty by telepathy, McGinty to Joe by concealed radio."

Joe glanced at Gail; it was the first that he had known that she was a telepath. Baldwin went on, "Gail will kill Mrs. Keithley; Joe will break into the housing and destroy the circuits. Are you ready to go?"

Joe was about to suggest swapping the assignments when Gail answered, "Ready;" he echoed her.

"Good. Joe, you will carry your assumed I.Q. at about 85, Gail at 95; she will appear to be the dominant member of a married couple—" Gail grinned at Joe. "—but you, Joe, will be in charge. Your personalities and histories are now being made up and will be ready with your identifications. Let me say again that the greatest of speed is necessary; government security forces here may attempt a fool-hardy attack on the New Age hotel. We shall prevent or delay such efforts, but act with speed. Good luck."

Operation Black Widow, first phase, went off as planned.

63

Eleven days later Joe and Gail were inside Mrs. Keithley's dome on the moon and sharing a room in the servants' quarters. Gail glanced around when first they entered it and said in Speedtalk, "Now you'll have to marry me; I'm compromised."

"Shut that up, idiot! Some one might hear you."

"Pooh! They'd just think I had asthma. Don't you think it's noble of me, Joe, to sacrifice my girlish reputation for home and country?"

"What reputation?"

"Come closer so I can slug you."

Even the servants' quarter were luxurious. The dome was a sybarite's dream. The floor of it was gardened in real beauty save where Mrs. Keithley's mansion stood. Opposite it, across a little lake—certainly the only lake on the Moon—was the building housing the circuits; it was disguised as a little Doric Grecian shrine.

The dome itself was edge-lighted fifteen hours out of each twenty-four, shutting out the black sky and the harsh stars. At "night" the lighting was gradually withdrawn.

McGinty was a gardener and obviously enjoyed his work. Gail established contact with him, got out of him what little he knew. Joe left him alone save for contacts in character.

There was a staff of over two hundred, having its own social hierarchy, from engineers for dome and equipment, Mrs. Keithley's private pilot, and so on down to gardeners' helpers. Joe and Gail were midway, being inside servants. Gail made herself popular as the harmlessly flirtatious but always helpful and sympathetic wife of a meek and older husband. She had been a beauty parlor operator, so it seemed, before she "married" and had great skill in massaging aching backs and stiff necks, relieving headaches and inducing sleep. She was always ready to demonstrate.

Her duties as a maid had not yet brought her into close contact with their employer. Joe, however, had acquired the job of removing all potted plants to the "outdoors" during "night"; Mrs. Keithley, according to Mr. James, the butler, believed that plants should be outdoors at "night." Joe was thus in a position to get outside the house when the dome was dark; he had already reached the point where the night guard at the Grecian temple would sometimes get Joe to "jigger" for him while the guard snatched a forbidden cigarette.

McGinty had been able to supply one more important fact: in addition to the guard at the temple building, and the locks and armor plate of the building itself, the arming circuit was booby-trapped. Even if it were inoperative as an arming circuit for the 'Nova' bomb on Earth, it itself would blow up if tampered with. Gail and Joe discussed it in their room, Gail sitting on his lap like an affectionate wife, her lips close to his

64

left ear. "Perhaps you could wreck it from the door, without exposing yourself."

"I've got to be sure. There is certainly some way of switching that gimmick off. She has to provide for possible repairs or replacements."

"Where would it be?"

"Just one place that matches the pattern of the rest of her planning. Right under her hand, along with the disarming switch and the trigger switch." He rubbed his other ear; it contained his short-range radio hook-up to McGinty and itched almost constantly.

"Hmm—then there's just one thing to be done; I'll have to wring it out of her before I kill her."

"We'll see."

Just before dinner the following "evening" she found him in their room. "It worked, Joe, it worked!"

"What worked?"

"She fell for the bait. She heard from her secretary about my skill as a masseuse; I was ordered up for a demonstration this afternoon. Now I am under strict instructions to come to her tonight and rub her to sleep."

"It's tonight, then."

McGinty waited in his room, behind a locked door. Joe stalled in the back hall, spinning out endlessly a dull tale to Mr. James.

A voice in his ear said, "She's in *her* room now."

"—and that's how my brother got married to two women at once," Joe concluded. "Sheer bad luck. I better get these plants outside before the missus happens to ask about 'em."

"I suppose you had. Goodnight."

"Goodnight, Mr. James." He picked up two of the pots and waddled out."

He put them down outside and heard, "She says she's started to massage. She's spotted the radio switching unit; it's on the belt that the old gal keeps at her bedside table when she's not wearing it."

"Tell her to kill her and grab it."

"She says she wants to make her tell how to unswitch the booby-trap gimmick first."

"Tell her not to delay."

Suddenly, inside his head, clear and sweet as a bell as if they were her own spoken tones, he heard her. *—Joe, I can hear you. can you hear me?*

—yes, yes! Aloud he added, "*Stand by the phones anyhow, Mac.*"

—it won't be long. I have her in intense pain; she'll crack soon.

65

—hurt her plenty! He began to run toward the temple building. *—Gail, are you still shopping for a husband?*

—I've found him.

—marry me and I'll beat you every Saturday night.

—the man who can beat me hasn't been born.

—I'd like to try. He slowed down before he came near the guard's station. "Hi, Jim!"

—it's a deal.

"Well, if it taint Joey boy! Got a match?"

"Here." He reached out a hand—then, as the guard fell, he eased him to the ground and made sure that he would stay out. *—Gail! It's got to be now!*

The voice in his head came back in great consternation: *—Joe! She was too tough, she wouldn't crack. She's dead!*

—good! get that belt, break the arming circuit, then see what else you find. I'm going to break in.

He went toward the door of the temple.

—it's disarmed, Joe. I could spot it; it has a time set on it. I can't tell about the others; they aren't marked and they all look alike.

He took from his pocket a small item provided by Baldwin's careful planning. *—twist them all from where they are to the other way. You'll probably hit it.*

—oh, Joe, I hope so!

He had placed the item against the lock; the metal around it turned red and now was melting away. An alarm clanged somewhere.

Gail's voice came again in his head; there was urgency in it but no fear: *—Joe! they're beating on the door. I'm trapped.*

—McGinty! be our witness! He went on: *—I, Joseph, take thee, Gail, to be my lawfully wedded wife—*

He was answered in tranquil rhythm: *—I, Gail, take thee, Joseph, to be my lawfully wedded husband—*

—to have and to hold, he went on.

to have and to hold, my beloved!

—for better, for worse—

*—for better, for worse—*Her voice in his head was singing. . .*—till death do us part. I've got it open, darling; I am going in.*

—till death do us part! They are breaking down the bedroom door, Joseph my dearest.

—hang on! I'm almost through here.

—they have broken it down, Joe. They are coming toward me. Good-bye my darling! I am very happy. Abruptly her "voice" stopped.

He was facing the box that housed the disarming circuit, alarms clanging in his ears; he took from his pocket another gadget and tried it.

The blast that shattered the box caught him full in the chest. The letters on the metal marker read:

TO THE MEMORY OF
MR. AND MRS. JOSEPH GREENE
WHO, NEAR THIS SPOT,
DIED FOR ALL THEIR FELLOW MEN

THE END

ELSEWHEN

Excerpt from the *Evening* STANDARD:

SOUGHT SAVANT EVADES POLICE

City Hall Scandal Looms

Professor Arthur Frost, wanted for questioning in connection
with the mysterious disappearance from his home of five of his
students, escaped today from under the noses of a squad of police
sent to arrest him. Police Sergeant Izowski claimed that Frost
disappeared from the interior of the Black Maria under conditions
which leave the police puzzled. District Attorney Karnes labeled
Izowski's story as preposterous and promised the fullest possible
investigation.

"But, Chief, I didn't leave him alone for a second!"

"Nuts!" answered the Chief of Police. "You claim you put
Frost in the Wagon, stopped with one foot on the tailboard
to write in your notebook, and when you looked up he was
gone. D'yuh expect the Grand Jury to believe that? D'yuh
expect *me* to believe that?"

"Honest, Chief," persisted Izowski, "I just stopped to write
down—"

"Write down what?"

"Something he said. I said to him, 'Look, Doc, why don't
you tell us where you hid 'em? You know we're bound to
dig 'em up in time.' And he just gives me a funny faraway
look, and says, 'Time—ah, time . . . yes, you could dig them
up, in Time.' I thought it was an important admission and
stops to write it down. But I was standing in the only door he
could use to get out of the Wagon. You know, I ain't little;
I kinda fill up a door."

"That's all you do," commented the Chief bitterly. "Izowski,
you were either drunk, or crazy—or somebody got to you.
The way you tell it, it's impossible!"

Izowski was honest, nor was he drunk, nor crazy.

Four days earlier Doctor Frost's class in speculative meta-
physics had met as usual for their Friday evening seminar at
the professor's home. Frost was saying, "And why not? Why
shouldn't time be a fifth as well as a fourth dimension?"

Howard Jenkins, hard-headed engineering student, answered, "No harm in speculating, I suppose, but the question is meaningless."

"Why?" Frost's tones were deceptively mild.

"No question is meaningless," interrupted Helen Fisher.

"Oh, yeah? How high is up?"

"Let him answer," meditated Frost.

"I will," agreed Jenkins. "Human beings are constituted to perceive three spatial dimensions and one time dimension. Whether there are more of either is meaningless to us for there is no possible way for us to know—*ever*. Such speculation is a harmless waste of time."

"So?" said Frost. "Ever run across J. W. Dunne's theory of serial universe with serial time? And he's an engineer, like yourself. And don't forget Ouspensky. He regarded time as multi-dimensional."

"Just a second, Professor," put in Robert Monroe. "I've seen their writings—but I still think Jenkins offered a legitimate objection. How can the question mean anything to us if we aren't built to perceive more dimensions? It's like in mathematics—you can invent any mathematics you like, on any set of axioms, but unless it can be used to describe some sort of phenomena, it's just so much hot air."

"Fairly put," conceded Frost. "I'll give a fair answer. Scientific belief is based on observation, either one's own or that of a competent observer. I believe in a two-dimensional time because I have actually observed it."

The clock ticked on for several seconds.

Jenkins said, "But that is impossible, Professor. You aren't built to observe two time dimensions."

"Easy, there . . ." answered Frost. "I am built to perceive them *one at a time*—and so are you. I'll tell you about it, but before I do so, I must explain the theory of time I was forced to evolve in order to account for my experience. Most people think of time as a track that they run on from birth to death as inexorably as a train follows its rails—they feel instinctively that time follows a straight line, the past lying behind, the future lying in front. Now I have reason to believe—to know— that time is analagous to a surface rather than a line, and a rolling hilly surface at that. Think of this track we follow over the surface of time as a winding road cut through hills. Every little way the road branches and the branches follow side canyons. At these branches the crucial decisions of your life take place. You can turn right or left into entirely different futures. Occasionally there is a switchback where one can scramble up or down a bank and skip over a few thousand or million years—if you don't have your eyes so fixed on the road that you miss the short cut.

"Once in a while another road crosses yours. Neither its

past nor its future has any connection whatsoever with the world we know. If you happened to take that turn you might find yourself on another planet in another space-time with nothing left of you or your world but the continuity of your ego.

"Or, if you have the necessary intellectual strength and courage, you may leave the roads, or paths of high probability, and strike out over the hills of possible time, cutting through the roads as you come to them, following them for a little way, even following them backwards, with the past *ahead* of you, and the future *behind* you. Or you might roam around the hilltops doing nothing but the extremely improbable. I can not imagine what that would be like—perhaps a bit like Alice-through-the-Looking-Glass.

"Now as to my evidence— When I was eighteen I had a decision to make. My father suffered financial reverses and I decided to quit college. Eventually I went into business for myself, and, to make a long story short, in nineteen-fifty-eight I was convicted of fraud and went to prison."

Martha Ross interrupted. "Nineteen-fifty-eight, Doctor? You mean forty-eight?"

"No, Miss Ross. I am speaking of events that did not take place on this time track."

"Oh!" She looked blank, then muttered, "With the Lord all things are possible."

"While in prison I had time to regret my mistakes. I realized that I had never been cut out for a business career, and I earnestly wished that I had stayed in school many years before. Prison has a peculiar effect on a man's mind. I drifted further and further away from reality, and lived more and more in an introspective world of my own. One night, in a way not then clear to me, my ego left my cell, went back along the time track, and I awoke in my room at my college fraternity house.

"This time I was wiser— Instead of leaving school, I found part-time work, graduated, continued as a graduate fellow, and eventually arrived where you now see me." He paused and glanced around.

"Doctor," asked young Monroe, "can you give us any idea as to how the stunt was done?"

"Yes, I can," Frost assented. "I worked on that problem for many years, trying to recapture the conditions. Recently I have succeeded and have made several excursions into possibility."

Up to this time the third woman, Estelle Martin, had made no comment, although she had listened with close attention. Now she leaned forward and spoke in an intense whisper.

"Tell us how, Professor Frost!"

"The means is simple. The key lies in convincing the sub-conscious mind that it can be done—"

"Then the Berkeleian idealism is proved!"

70

"In a way, Miss Martin. To one who believes in Bishop Berkeley's philosophy the infinite possibilities of two-dimensional time offer proof that the mind creates its own world, but a Spencerian determinist, such as good friend Howard Jenkins, would never leave the road of maximum probability. To him the world would be mechanistic and real. An orthodox free-will Christian, such as Miss Ross, would have her choice of several of the side roads, but would probably remain in a physical environment similar to Howard's.

"I have perfected a technique which will enable others to travel about in the pattern of times as I have done. I have the apparatus ready and any who wish can try it. That is the real reason why these Friday evening meetings have been held in my home—so that when the time came you all might try it, if you wished." He got up and went to a cabinet at the end of the room.

"You mean we could go tonight, Doctor?"

"Yes, indeed. The process is one of hypnotism and suggestion. Neither are necessary, but that is the quickest way of teaching the sub-conscious to break out of its groove and go where it pleases. I use a revolving ball to tire the conscious mind into hypnosis. During that period the subject listens to a recording which suggests the time-road to be followed, whereupon he does. It is as simple as that. Do any of you care to try it?"

"Is it likely to be dangerous, Doctor?"

He shrugged his shoulders. "The process isn't—just a deep sleep and a phonograph record. But the world of the time track you visit will be as real as the world of this time track. You are all over twenty-one. I am not urging you, I am merely offering you the opportunity."

Monroe stood up. "I'm going, Doctor."

"Good! Sit here and use these earphones. Anyone else?"

"Count me in." It was Helen Fisher.

Estelle Martin joined them. Howard Jenkins went hastily to her side. "Are you going to try this business?"

"Most certainly."

He turned to Frost. "I'm in, Doc."

Martha Ross finally joined the others. Frost seated them where they could wear the ear-phones and then asked,

"You will remember the different types of things you could do; branch off into a different world, skip over into the past or the future, or cut straight through the maze of probable tracks on a path of extreme improbability. I have records for all of those."

Monroe was first again. "I'll take a right angle turn and a brand new world."

Estelle did not hesitate. "I want to— How did you put it? —climb up a bank to a higher road somewhere in the future."

71

"I'll try that, too." It was Jenkins.

"I'll take the remote-possibilities track," put in Helen Fisher.

"That takes care of everybody but Miss Ross," commented the professor. "I'm afraid you will have to take a branch path in probability. Does that suit you?"

She nodded. "I was going to ask for it."

"That's fine. All of these records contain the suggestion for you to return to this room two hours from now, figured along this time track. Put on your ear-phones. The records run thirty minutes. I'll start them and the ball together."

He swung a glittering many-faceted sphere from a hook in the ceiling, started it whirling, and turned a small spotlight on it. Then he turned off the other lights, and started all the records by throwing a master switch. The scintillating ball twirled round and round, slowed and reversed and twirled back again. Doctor Frost turned his eyes away to keep from being fascinated by it. Presently he slipped out into the hall for a smoke. Half an hour passed and there came the single note of a gong. He hurried back and switched on the light.

Four of the five had disappeared.

The remaining figure was Howard Jenkins, who opened his eyes and blinked at the light. "Well, Doctor, I guess it didn't work."

The Doctor raised his eyebrows. "No? Look around you."

The younger man glanced about him. "Where are the others?"

"Where? Anywhere," replied Frost, with a shrug, "and any*when*."

Jenkins jerked off his ear-phones and jumped to his feet. "Doctor, *what have you done to Estelle?*"

Frost gently disengaged a hand from his sleeve. "I haven't done anything, Howard. She's out on another time track."

"But I meant to go with her!"

"And I tried to send you with her."

"But why didn't I go?"

"I can't say—probably the suggestion wasn't strong enough to overcome your skepticism. But don't be alarmed, son— We expect her back in a couple of hours, you know."

"Don't be alarmed! —that's easy to say. I didn't want her to try this damn fool stunt in the first place, but I knew I couldn't change her mind, so I wanted to go along to look out for her—she's so impractical! But see here, Doc—where are their bodies? I thought we would just stay here in the room in a trance."

"Apparently you didn't understand me. These other time tracks are real, as real as this one we are in. Their whole beings have gone off on other tracks, as if they had turned down a side street."

"But that's impossible—it contradicts the law of the conservation of energy!"

"You must recognize a fact when you see one— they are gone. Besides, it doesn't contradict the law; it simply extends it to include the total universe."

Jenkins rubbed a hand over his face. "I suppose so. But in that case, anything can happen to her—she could even be *killed* out there. And I can't do a damn thing about it. Oh, I wish we had never seen this damned seminar!"

The professor placed an arm around his shoulders. "Since you can't help her, why not calm down? Besides, you have no reason to believe that she is in any danger. Why borrow trouble? Let's go out to the kitchen and open a bottle of beer while we wait for them." He gently urged him toward the door.

After a couple of beers and a few cigarettes, Jenkins was somewhat calmed down. The professor made conversation.

"How did you happen to sign up for this course, Howard?"

"It was the only course I could take with Estelle."

"I thought so. I let you take it for reasons of my own. I knew you weren't interested in speculative philosophy, but I thought that your hard-headed materialism would hold down some of the loose thinking that is likely to go on in such a class. You've been a help to me. Take Helen Fisher for example. She is prone to reason brilliantly from insufficient data. You help to keep her down to earth."

"To be frank, Doctor Frost, I could never see the need for all this high-falutin discussion. I like facts."

"But you engineers are as bad as metaphysicians—you ignore any fact that you can't weigh in scales. If you can't bite it, it's not real. You believe in a mechanistic, deterministic universe, and ignore the facts of human consciousness, human will, and human freedom of choice—facts that you have directly experienced."

"But those things can be explained in terms of reflexes."

The professor spread his hands. "You sound just like Martha Ross—she can explain anything in terms of Bible-belt fundamentalism. Why don't both of you admit that there a few things you don't understand?" He paused and cocked his head. "Did you hear something?"

"I think I did."

"Let's check. It's early, but perhaps one of them is back."

They hurried to the study, where they were confronted by an incredible and awe-inspiring sight.

Floating in the air near the fireplace was a figure robed in white and shining with a soft mother-of-pearl radiance. While they stood hesitant at the door, the figure turned its face to them and they saw that it had the face of Martha Ross, cleansed and purified to an unhuman majesty. Then it spoke.

"Peace be unto you, my brothers." A wave of peace and

lovingkindness flowed over them like a mother's blessing. The figure approached them, and they saw, curving from its shoulders, the long, white, sweeping wings of a classical angel. Frost cursed under his breath in a dispassionate monotone.

"Do not be afraid. I have come back, as you asked me to. To explain and to help you."

The Doctor found his voice. "Are you Martha Ross?"

"I answer to that name."

"What happened after you put on the ear-phones?"

"Nothing. I slept for a while. When I woke, I went home."

"Nothing else? How do you explain your appearance?"

"My appearance is what you earthly children expect of the Lord's Redeemed. In the course of time I served as a missionary in South America. There it was required of me that I give up my mortal life in the service of the Lord. And so I entered the Eternal City."

"You went to Heaven?"

"These many eons I have sat at the foot of the Golden Throne and sung hosannas to His name."

Jenkins interrupted them. "Tell me, Martha—or Saint Martha—*Where is Estelle?* Have you seen her?"

The figure turned slowly and faced him. "Fear not."

"But tell me where she is!"

"It is not needful."

"That's no help," he answered bitterly.

"I will help you. Listen to me; Love the Lord thy God with all thy heart, and Love thy neighbor as thyself. That is all you need to know."

Howard remained silent, at a loss for an answer, but unsatisfied. Presently the figure spoke again. "I must go. God's blessing on you." It flickered and was gone.

The professor touched the young man's arm. "Let's get some fresh air." He led Jenkins, mute and unresisting, out into the garden. They walked for some minutes in silence. Finally Howard asked a question,

"Did we see an angel in there?"

"I think so, Howard."

"But that's insane!"

"There are millions of people who wouldn't think so—unusual certainly, but not insane."

"But it's contrary to all modern beliefs—Heaven—Hell—a personal God—Resurrection. Everything I've believed in must be wrong, or I've gone screwy."

"Not necessarily—not even probably. I doubt very much if you will ever see Heaven or Hell. You'll follow a time track in accordance with your nature."

"But she seemed *real*."

"She *was* real. I suspect that the conventional hereafter is real to any one who believes in it whole-heartedly, as Martha

74

evidently did, but I expect you to follow a pattern in accordance with the beliefs of an agnostic—except in one respect; when you die, you won't die all over, no matter how intensely you may claim to expect to. *It is an emotional impossibility for any man to believe in his own death.* That sort of self-annihilation can't be done. You'll have a hereafter, but it will be one appropriate to a materialist."

But Howard was not listening. He pulled at his under lip and frowned. "Say, doc, why wouldn't Martha tell me what happened to Estelle? That was a dirty trick."

"I doubt if she knew, my boy. Martha followed a time track only slightly different from that we are in; Estelle chose to explore one far in the past, or in the distant future. For all practical purposes, each is non-existent to the other."

They heard a call from the house, a clear contralto voice, "Doctor! Doctor Frost!"

Jenkins whirled around. "That's Estelle!" They ran back into the house, the Doctor endeavoring manfully to keep up.

But it was not Estelle. Standing in the hallway was Helen Fisher, her sweater torn and dirty, her stockings missing, and a barely-healed scar puckering one cheek. Frost stopped and surveyed her. "Are you all right, child?" he demanded.

She grinned boyishly. "I'm okay. You should see the other guy."

"Tell us about it."

"In a minute. How about a cup of coffee for the prodigal? And I wouldn't turn up my nose at scrambled eggs and some —lots—of toast. Meals are inclined to be irregular where I've been."

"Yes, indeed. Right away," answered Frost, "but where *have* you been?"

"Let a gal eat, please," she begged. "I won't hold out on you. What is Howard looking so sour about?"

The professor whispered an explanation. She gave Jenkins a compassionate glance. "Oh, she hasn't? I thought I'd be the last man in; I was away so long. What day is this?"

Frost glanced at his wrist watch. "You're right on time; it's just eleven o'clock."

"The hell you say! Oh, excuse me, Doctor. 'Curiouser and curiouser,' said Alice.' All in a couple of hours. Just for the record, I was gone several weeks at least."

When her third cup of coffee had washed down the last of the toast, she began:

"When I woke up I was falling upstairs—through a nightmare, several nightmares. Don't ask me to describe *that*— nobody could. That went on for a week, maybe, then things started to come into focus. I don't know in just what order things happened, but when I first started to notice clearly I was standing in a little barren valley. It was cold, and the air

75

was thin and acrid. It burned my throat. There were two suns in the sky, one big and reddish, the other smaller and too bright to look at."

"Two suns!" exclaimed Howard. "That's not possible—binary stars don't have planets."

She looked at him. "Have it your own way—I was *there*. Just as I was taking this all in, something whizzed overhead and I ducked. That was the last I saw of *that* place.

"I slowed down next back on earth—at least it looked like it—and in a city. It was a big and complicated city. I was in trafficway with a lot of fast-moving traffic. I stepped out and tried to flag one of the vehicles—a long crawling caterpillar thing with about fifty wheels—when I caught sight of what was driving it and dodged back in a hurry. It wasn't a man and it wasn't an animal either—not one I've ever seen or heard of. It wasn't a bird, or a fish, nor an insect. The god that thought up the inhabitants of that city doesn't deserve worship. I don't know what they were, but they crawled and they crept and they *stank*. Ugh!"

"I slunk around holes in that place," she continued, "for a couple of weeks before I recovered the trick of jumping the time track. I was desperate, for I thought that the suggestion to return to now hadn't worked. I couldn't find much to eat and I was light-headed part of the time. I drank out of what I suspect was their drainage system, but there was nobody to ask and I didn't want to know. I was thirsty."

"Did you see any human beings?"

"I'm not sure. I saw some shapes that might have been men squatting in a circle down in the tunnels under the city, but something frightened them, and they scurried away before I could get close enough to look."

"What else happened there?"

"Nothing. I found the trick again that same night and got away from there as fast as I could. I am afraid I lost the scientific spirit, Professor—I didn't care how the other half lived.

"This time I had better luck. I was on earth again, but in pleasant rolling hills, like the Blue Ridge Mountains. It was summer, and very lovely. I found a little stream and took off my clothes and bathed. It was wonderful. After I had found some ripe berries, I lay down in the sun and went to sleep.

"I woke wide awake with a start. Someone was bending over me. It was a man, but no beauty. He was a Neanderthal. I should have run, but I tried to grab my clothes first, so he grabbed me. I was led back into camp, a Sabine woman, with my new spring sports outfit tucked fetchingly under one arm.

"I wasn't so bad off. It was the Old Man who had found me, and he seemed to regard me as a strange pet, about on a par with the dogs that snarled around the bone heap, rather than as a member of his harem. I fed well enough, if you

76

aren't fussy—I wasn't fussy after living in the bowels of that awful city.

"The Neanderthal isn't a bad fellow at heart, rather good-natured, although inclined to play rough. That's how I got this." She fingered the scar on her cheek. "I had about decided to stay a while and study them, when one day I made a mistake. It was a chilly morning, and I put on my clothes for the first time since I had arrived. One of the young bucks saw me, and I guess it aroused his romantic nature. The Old Man was away at the time and there was no one to stop him.

"He grabbed me before I knew what was happening and tried to show his affection. Have you ever been nuzzled by a cave man, Howard? They have halitosis, not to mention B.O. I was too startled to concentrate on the time trick, or else I would have slipped right out into space-time and left him clutching air."

Doctor Frost was aghast. "Dear God, child! What did you do?"

"I finally showed him a jiu jitsu trick I learned in Phys. Ed. II, then I ran like hell and skinned up a tree. I counted up to a hundred and tried to be calm. Pretty soon I was shooting upstairs in a nightmare again and very happy to be doing it."

"Then you came back here?"

"Not by a whole lot—worse luck! I landed in this present all right, and apparently along this time dimension, but there was plenty that was wrong about it. I was standing on the south side of Forty-second street in New York. I knew where I was for the first thing I noticed was the big lighted letters that chase around the TIMES building and spell out news flashes. It was running backwards. I was trying to figure out 'DETROIT BEAT TO HITS NINE GET YANKEES' when I saw two cops close to me running as hard as they could—backwards, away from me." Doctor Frost smothered an ejaculation. "What did you say?"

"Reversed entropy—you entered the track backwards—your time arrow was pointing backwards."

"I figured that out, when I had time to think about it. Just then I was too busy. I was in a clearing in the crowd, but the ring of people was closing in on me, all running backwards. The cops disappeared in the crowd, and the crowd ran right up to me, stopped, and started to scream. Just as that happened, the traffic lights changed, cars charged out from both directions, driving backwards. It was too much for little Helen. I fainted.

"Following that I seemed to slant through a lot of places—"

"Just a second," Howard interrupted, "just what happened before that? I thought I savvied entropy, but that got me licked."

"Well," explained Frost, "The easiest way to explain it is

to say that she was travelling backwards in time. Her future was their past, and vice versa. I'm glad she got out in a hurry. I'm not sure that human metabolism can be maintained in such conditions."

"Hmm— Go ahead, Helen."

"This slanting through the axes would have been startling, if I hadn't been emotionally exhausted. I sat back and watched it, like a movie. I think Salvador Dali wrote the script. I saw landscapes heave and shift like a stormy sea. People melted into plants—I think my own body changed at times, but I can't be sure. Once I found myself in a place that was all *insides*, instead of outsides. Some of the things we'll skip—I don't believe them myself.

"Then I slowed down in a place that must have had an extra spatial dimension. Everything looked three dimensional to me, but they changed their shapes when I *thought* about them. I found I could look inside solid objects simply by wanting to. When I tired of prying into the intimate secrets of rocks and plants, I took a look at myself, and it worked just as well. I know more about anatomy and physiology now than an M.D. It's fun to watch your heart beat—kind o'cute.

"But my appendix was swollen and inflamed. I found I could reach in and touch it—it was tender. I've had trouble with it so I decided to perform an emergency operation. I nipped it off with my nails. It didn't hurt at all, bled a couple of drops and closed right up."

"Good Heavens, child! You might have gotten peritonitis and died."

"I don't think so. I believe that ultra-violet was pouring all through me and killing the bugs. I had a fever for a while, but I think what caused it was a bad case of internal sunburn.

"I forgot to mention that I couldn't walk around in this place, for I couldn't seem to touch anything but myself. I sliced right through anything I tried to get a purchase on. Pretty soon I quit trying and relaxed. It was comfortable and I went into a warm happy dope, like a hibernating bear.

"After a long time—a long, long time, I went sound asleep and came to in your big easy-chair. That's all."

Helen answered Howard's anxious inquiries by telling him that she had seen nothing of Estelle. "But why don't you calm down and wait? She isn't really overdue."

They were interrupted by the opening of the door from the hallway. A short wiry figure in a hooded brown tunic and tight brown breeches strode into the room.

"Where's Doctor Frost? Oh—Doctor, I need help!"

It was Monroe, but changed almost beyond recognition. He had been short and slender before, but was now barely five feet tall, and stocky, with powerful shoulder muscles. The

78

brown costume with its peaked hood, or helmet, gave him a strong resemblance to the popular notion of gnome.

Frost hurried to him. "What is it, Robert? How can I help?"

"This first." Monroe hunched forward for inspection of his left upper arm. The fabric was tattered and charred, exposing an ugly burn. "He just grazed me, but it had better be fixed, if I am to save the arm."

Frost examined it without touching it. "We must rush you to a hospital."

"No time. I've got to get back. They need me—and the help I can bring."

The Doctor shook his head. "You've got to have treatment, Bob. Even if there is strong need for you to go back wherever you have been, you are in a different time track now. Time lost here isn't necessarily lost there."

Monroe cut him short. "I think this world and my world have connected time rates. I must hurry."

Helen Fisher placed herself between them. "Let me see that arm, Bob. Hm—pretty nasty, but I think I can fix it. Professor, put a kettle on the fire with about a cup of water in it. As soon as it boils, chuck in a handful of tea leaves."

She rummaged through the kitchen cutlery drawer, found a pair of shears, and did a neat job of cutting away the sleeve and cleaning the burned flesh for dressing. Monroe talked as she worked.

"Howard, I want you to do me a favor. Get a pencil and paper and take down a list. I want a flock of things to take back—all of them things that you can pick up at the fraternity house. You'll have to go for me—I'd be thrown out with my present appearance— What's the matter? Don't you want to?"

Helen hurriedly explained Howard's preoccupation. He listened sympathetically. "Oh! Say, that's tough lines, old man." His brow wrinkled. "But look— You can't do Estelle any good by waiting here, and I really do need your help for the next half hour. Will you do it?"

Jenkins reluctantly agreed. Monroe continued,

"Fine! I do appreciate it. Go to my room first and gather up my reference books on math—also my slide rule. You'll find an India-paper radio manual, too. I want that. And I want your twenty-inch log-log duplex slide rule, as well. You can have my Rabelais and the *Droll Stories*. I want your *Marks' Mechanical Engineers' Handbook*, and any other technical reference books that you have and I haven't. Take anything you like in exchange.

"Then go up to Stinky Beanfield's room, and get his *Military Engineer's Handbook*, his *Chemical Warfare*, and his texts on ballistics and ordnance. Yes, and *Miller's Chemistry of Explosives*, if he has one. If not, pick up one from some other of the R.O.T.C. boys; it's important." Helen was deftly applying a poultice to his arm. He winced as the tea leaves, still warm, touched his seared flesh, but went ahead.

"Stinky keeps his service automatic in his upper bureau drawer. Swipe it, or talk him out of it. Bring as much ammunition as you can find—I'll write out a bill of sale for my car for you to leave for him. Now get going. I'll tell Doc all about it, and he can tell you later. Here. Take my car." He fumbled at his thigh, then looked annoyed. "Cripes! I don't have my keys."

Helen came to the rescue. "Take mine. The keys are in my bag on the hall table."

Howard got up. "OK, I'll do my damndest. If I get flung in the can, bring me cigarettes." He went out.

Helen put the finishing touches on the bandages. "There! I think that will do. How does it feel?"

He flexed his arm cautiously. "Okay. It's a neat job, kid. It takes the sting out."

"I believe it will heal if you keep tannin solution on it. Can you get tea leaves where you are going?"

"Yes, and tannic acid, too. I'll be all right. Now you deserve an explanation. Professor, do you have a cigaret on you? I could use some of that coffee, too."

"Surely, Robert." Frost hastened to serve him.

Monroe accepted a light and began,

"It's all pretty cock-eyed. When I came out of the sleep, I found myself, dressed as I am now and looking as I now look, marching down a long, deep fosse. I was one of a column of threes in a military detachment. The odd part about it is that I felt perfectly natural. I knew where I was and why I was there—and who I was. I don't mean Robert Monroe; my name over there is Igor." Monroe pronounced the gutteral deep in his throat and trilled the "r." "I hadn't forgotten Monroe; it was more as if I had suddenly remembered him. I had *one* identity and *two* pasts. It was something like waking up from a clearly remembered dream, only the dream was perfectly real. I *knew* Monroe was real, just as I knew Igor was real.

"My world is much like earth; a bit smaller, but much the same surface gravity. Men like myself are the dominant race, and we are about as civilized as you folks, but our culture has followed a difficult course. We live underground about half the time. Our homes are there and a lot of our industry. You see it's warm underground in our world, and not entirely dark. There is a mild radioactivity; it doesn't harm us.

"Nevertheless we are a surface-evolved race, and can't be healthy nor happy if we stay underground all the time. Now there is a war on and we've been driven underground for eight or nine months. The war is going against us. As it stands

80

now, we have lost control of the surface and my race is being reduced to the status of hunted vermin.

"You see, we aren't fighting human beings. I don't know just what it is we are fighting—maybe beings from outer space. We don't know. They attacked us several places at once from great flying rings the like of which we had never seen. They burned us down without warning. Many of us escaped underground where they haven't followed us. They don't operate at night either—seem to need sunlight to be active. So it's a stalemate—or was until they started gassing our tunnels.

"We've never captured one and consequently don't know what makes them tick. We examined a ring that crashed, but didn't learn much. There was nothing inside that even vaguely resembled animal life, nor was there anything to support animal life. I mean there were no food supplies, nor sanitary arrangements. Opinion is divided between the idea that the one we examined was remotely controlled and the idea that the enemy are some sort of non-protoplasmic intelligence, perhaps force patterns, or something equally odd.

"Our principal weapon is a beam which creates a stasis in the ether, and freezes 'em solid. Or rather it should, but it will destroy all life and prevent molar action—but the rings are simply put temporarily out of control. Unless we can keep a beam on a ring right to the moment it crashes, it recovers and gets away. Then its pals come and burn out our position.

"We've had better luck with mining their surface camps, and blowing them up at night. We're accomplished sappers, of course. But we need better weapons. That's what I sent Howard after. I've got two ideas. If the enemy are simply some sort of intelligent force patterns, or something like that, radio may be the answer. We might be able to fill up the ether with static and jam them right out of existence. If they are too tough for that, perhaps some good old-fashioned anti-aircraft fire might make them say 'Uncle.' In any case there is a lot of technology here that we don't have, and which may have the answer. I wish I had time to pass on some of our stuff in return for what I'm taking with me."

"You are determined to go back, Robert?"

"Certainly. It's where I belong. I've no family here. I don't know how to make you see it, Doc, but those are my people—that is my world. I suppose if conditions were reversed, I'd feel differently."

"I see," said Helen, "you're fighting for the wife and kids."

He turned a weary face toward her. "Not exactly. I'm a bachelor over there, but I do have a family to think about; my sister is in command of the attack unit I'm in. Oh, yes, the women are in it—they're little and tough, like you, Helen."

She touched his arm lightly. "How did you pick up this?"

"That burn? You remember we were on the march. We were retreating down that ditch from a surface raid. I thought we had made good our escape when all of a sudden a ring swooped down on us. Most of the detachment scattered, but I'm a junior technician armed with the stasis ray. I tried to get my equipment unlimbered to fight back, but I was burned down before I could finish. Luckily it barely grazed me. Several of the others were fried. I don't know yet whether or not Sis got hers. That's one of the reasons why I'm in a hurry.

"One of the other techs who wasn't hit got his gear set up and covered our retreat. I was dragged underground and taken to a dressing station. The medicos were about to work on me when I passed out and came to in the Professor's study."

The doorbell rang and the Professor got up to answer it. Helen and Robert followed him. It was Howard, bearing spoils.

"Did you get everything?" Robert asked anxiously.

"I think so. Stinky was in, but I managed to borrow his books. The gun was harder, but I telephoned a friend of mine and had him call back and ask for Stinky. While he was out of the room, I lifted it. Now I'm a criminal—government property, too."

"You're a pal, Howard. After you hear the explanation, you'll agree that it was worth doing. Won't he, Helen?"

"Absolutely!"

"Well, I hope you're right," he answered dubiously. "I brought along something else, just in case. Here it is." He handed Robert a book.

"*Aerodynamics and Principles of Aircraft Construction,*" Robert read aloud. "My God, yes! Thanks, Howard."

In a few minutes, Monroe had his belongings assembled and fastened to his person. He had announced that he was ready when the Professor checked him:

"One moment, Robert. How do you know that these books will go with you?"

"Why not? That's why I'm fastening them to me."

"Did your earthly clothing go through the first time?"

"Noo—" His brow furrowed. "Good grief, Doc, what can I do? I couldn't possibly memorize what I need to know."

"I don't know, Son. Let's think about it a bit." He broke off and stared at the ceiling. Helen touched his hand.

"Perhaps I can help, Professor."

"In what way, Helen?"

"Apparently I don't metamorphize when I change time tracks. I had the same clothes with me everywhere I went. Why couldn't I ferry this stuff over for Bob?"

"Hm, perhaps you could."

"No, I couldn't let you do that," interposed Monroe. "You might get killed or badly hurt."

"I'll chance it."

"I've got an idea," put in Jenkins. "Couldn't Doctor Frost set his instructions so that Helen would go over and come right back? How about it, Doc?"

"Mmm, yes, perhaps." But Helen held up a hand.

"No good. The boodle might come bouncing back with me. I'll go over without any return instructions. I like the sound of this world of Bob's anyway. I may stay there. Cut out the chivalry, Bob. One of the things I liked about your world was the notion of treating men and women alike. Get unstuck from that stuff and start hanging it on me. I'm going."

She looked like a Christmas tree when the dozen-odd books had been tied to various parts of her solid little figure, the automatic pistol strapped on, and the two slide rules, one long and one short, stuck in the pistol belt.

Howard fondled the large slide rule before he fastened it on. "Take good care of this slipstick, Bob," he said, "I gave up smoking for six months to pay for it."

Frost seated the two side by side on the sofa in the study. Helen slipped a hand into Bob's. When the shining ball had been made to spin, Frost motioned for Jenkins to leave, closed the door after him and switched out the light. Then he started repeating hypnotic suggestions in a monotone.

Ten minutes later he felt a slight swish of air and ceased. He snapped the light switch. The sofa was empty, even of books.

Frost and Jenkins kept an uneasy vigil while awaiting Estelle's return. Jenkins wandered nervously around the study, examining objects that didn't interest him and smoking countless cigarets. The Professor sat quietly in his easy chair, simulating a freedom from anxiety that he did not feel. They conversed in desultory fashion.

"One thing I don't see," observed Jenkins, "is why in the world Helen could go a dozen places and not change, and Bob goes just one place and comes back almost unrecognizable—shorter, heavier, decked out in outlandish clothes. What happened to his ordinary clothes anyhow? How do you explain those things, Professor?"

"Eh? I don't explain them—I merely observe them. I think perhaps he changed, while Helen didn't, because Helen was just a visitor to the places she went to, whereas Monroe belonged over there—as witness he fitted into the pattern of that world. Perhaps the Great Architect intended for him to cross over."

"Huh? Good heavens, Doctor, surely you don't believe in divine predestination!"

"Perhaps not in those terms. But, Howard, you mechanistic skeptics make me tired. Your naive ability to believe that things 'jest growed' approaches childishness. According to you a fortuitous accident of entropy produced Beethoven's Ninth Symphony."

"I think that's unfair, Doctor. You certainly don't expect a man to believe in things that run contrary to his good sense without offering him any reasonable explanation."

Frost snorted. "I certainly do—if he has observed it with his own eyes and ears, or gets it from a source known to be credible. A fact doesn't have to be understood to be true. Sure, any reasonable mind wants explanations, but it's silly to reject facts that don't fit your philosophy.

"Now these events tonight, which you are so anxious to rationalize in orthodox terms, furnish a clue to a lot of things that scientists have been rejecting because they couldn't explain them. Have you ever heard the tale of the man who walked around the horses? No? Around 1810 Benjamin Bathurst, British Ambassador to Austria, arrived in his carriage at an inn in Perleberg, Germany. He had his valet and secretary with him. They drove into the lighted courtyard of the inn. Bathurst got out, and, in the presence of bystanders and his two attaches, walked around the horses. He hasn't been seen since."

"What happened?"

"Nobody knows. I think he was preoccupied and inadvertently wandered into another time track. But there are literally hundreds of similar cases, way too many to laugh off. The two-time-dimensions theory accounts for most of them. But I suspect that there are other as-yet-undreamed-of natural principles operating in some of the rejected cases."

Howard stopped pacing and pulled at his lower lip. "Maybe so, Doctor. I'm too upset to think. Look here—it's one o'clock. Oughtn't she to be back by now?"

"I'm afraid so, Son."

"You mean she's not coming back."

"It doesn't look like it."

The younger man gave a broken cry and collapsed on the sofa. His shoulders heaved. Presently he calmed down a little. Frost saw his lips move and suspected that he was praying. Then he showed a drawn face to the Doctor.

"Isn't there *anything* we can do?"

"That's hard to answer, Howard. We don't know where she's gone; all we do know is that she left here under hypnotic suggestion to cross over into some other loop of the past or future."

"Can't we go after her the same way and trace her?"

"I don't know. I haven't had any experience with such a job."

"I've got to do something or I'll go nuts."

"Take it easy, son. Let me think about it." He smoked in

silence while Howard controlled an impulse to scream, break furniture, anything!

Frost knocked the ash off his cigar and placed it carefully in a tray. "I can think of one chance. It's a remote one."

"Anything!"

"I'm going to listen to the record that Estelle heard, and cross over. I'll do it wide awake, while concentrating on her. Perhaps I can establish some rapport, some extra-sensory connection, that will serve to guide me to her." Frost went immediately about his preparations as he spoke. "I want you to remain in the room when I go so that you will really believe that it can be done."

In silence Howard watched him don the head-phones. The Professor stood still, eyes closed. He remained so for nearly fifteen minutes, then took a short step forward. The ear-phones clattered to the floor. He was gone.

Frost felt himself drift off into the timeless limbo which precedes transition. He noticed again that it was exactly like the floating sensation that ushers in normal sleep, and wondered idly, for the hundredth time, whether or not the dreams of sleep were real experiences. He was inclined to think they were. Then he recalled his mission with a guilty start, and concentrated hard on Estelle.

He was walking along a road, white in the sunshine. Before him were the gates of a city. The gateman stared at his odd attire, but let him pass. He hurried down the broad tree-lined avenue which (he knew) led from the space port to Capitol Hill. He turned aside into the Way of the Gods and continued until he reached the Grove of the Priestesses. There he found the house which he sought, its marble walls pink in the sun, its fountains tinkling in the morning breeze. He turned in.

The ancient janitor, nodding in the sun, admitted him to the house. The slender maidservant, barely nubile, ushered him into the inner chamber, where her mistress raised herself on one elbow and regarded her visitor through languid eyes. Frost addressed her,

"It is time to return, Estelle."

Her eyesbrows showed her surprise. "You speak a strange and barbarous tongue, old man, and yet, here is a mystery, for I know it. What do you wish of me?"

Frost spoke impatiently. "Estelle, I say it is time to return!"

"Return? What idle talk is this? Return where? And my name is Star-Light, not Ess Tell. Who are you, and from where do you come?" She searched his face, then pointed a slender finger at him. "I know you now! You are out of my dreams. You were a Master and instructed me in the ancient wisdom."

"Estelle, do you remember a youth in those dreams?"

"That odd name again! Yes, there was a youth. He was

85

sweet—sweet and straight and tall like pine on the mountain. I have dreamed of him often." She swung about with a flash of long white limbs. "What of this youth?"

"He waits for you. It is time to return."

"Return!—There is no return to the place of dreams!"

"I can lead you there."

"What blasphemy is this? Are you a priest, that you should practice magic? Why should a sacred courtesan go to the place of dreams?"

"There is no magic in it. He is heartsick at your loss. I will lead you back to him."

She hesitated, doubt in her eyes, then she replied, "Suppose you could; why should I leave my honorable sacred station for the cold nothingness of that dream?"

He answered her gently, "What does your heart tell you, Estelle?"

She stared at him, eyes wide, and seemed about to burst into tears. Then she flung herself across the couch, and showed him her back. A muffled voice answered him,

"Be off with you! There is no youth, except in my dreams. I'll seek him there!"

She made no further reply to his importunities. Presently he ceased trying and left with a heavy heart.

Howard seized him by the arm as he returned. "Well, Professor? Well? Did you find her?"

Frost dropped wearily into his chair. "Yes, I found her."

"Was she all right? Why didn't she come back with you?"

"She was perfectly well, but I couldn't persuade her to return."

Howard looked as if he had been slapped across the mouth. "Didn't you tell her I wanted her to come back?"

"I did, but she didn't believe me."

"Not believe you?"

"You see she's forgotten most of this life, Howard. She thinks you are simply a dream."

"But that's not possible!"

Frost looked more weary than ever. "Don't you think it is about time you stopped using that term, son?"

Instead of replying he answered, "Doctor, you must take me to her!" Frost looked dubious.

"Can't you do it?"

"Perhaps I could, if you have gotten over your disbelief, but still—"

"Disbelief!—I've been forced to believe. Let's get busy."

Frost did not move. "I'm not sure that I agree. Howard, conditions are quite different where Estelle has gone. It suits her, but I'm not sure that it would be a kindness to take you through to her."

"Why not? Doesn't she want to see me?"

"Yes—I think she does. I'm sure she would welcome you, but conditions are very different."

"I don't give a damn what the conditions are. Let's go."

Frost got up. "Very well. It shall be as you wish."

He seated Jenkins in the easy cair and held the young man's eyes with his gaze. He spoke slowly in calm, unmodulated tones.

Frost assisted Howard to his feet and brushed him off. Howard laughed and wiped the white dust of the road from his hands.

"Quite a tumble, Master. I feel as if some lout had pulled a stool from under me."

"I shouldn't have had you sit down."

"I guess not." He pulled a large multi-flanged pistol from his belt and examined it. "Lucky the safety catch was set on my blaster or we might have been picking ourselves out of the stratosphere. Shall we be on our way?"

Frost looked his companion over; helmet, short military kilt, short sword and accoutrements slapping at his thighs. He blinked and answered, "Yes. Yes, of course."

As they swung into the city gates, Frost inquired, "Do you know where you are headed?"

"Yes, certainly. To Star-Light's villa in the Grove."

"And you know what to expect there?"

"Oh, you mean our discussion. I know the customs here, Master and am quite undismayed, I assure you. Star-Light and I understand each other. She's one of these 'Out of sight, out of mind' girls. Now that I'm back from Ultima Thule, she'll give up the priesthood and we'll settle down and raise a lot of fat babies."

"Ultima Thule? Do you remember my study?"

"Of course I do—and Robert and Helen and all the rest."

"Is that what you meant by Ultima Thule?"

"Not exactly. I can't explain it, Master. I'm a practical military man. I'll leave such things to you priests and teachers."

They paused in front of Estelle's house. "Coming in, Master?"

"No, I think not. I must be gettin? back."

"You know best." Howard clapped him on the shoulder. "You have been a true friend, Master. Our first brat shall be named for you."

"Thank you, Howard. Good-bye, and good luck to both of you."

"And to you." He entered the house with a confident stride.

Frost walked slowly back toward the gates, his mind pre-occupied with myriad thoughts. There seemed to be no end to the permutations and combinations; either of matter, or of mind. Martha, Robert, Helen—now Howard and Estelle. It should be possible to derive a theory that would cover them all.

As he mused, his heel caught on a loose paving block and he stumbled across his easy chair.

The absence of the five students was going to be hard to explain, Frost knew—so he said nothing to anyone. The weekend passed before anyone took the absences seriously. On Monday a policeman came to his house, asking questions.

His answers were not illuminating, for he had reasonably refrained from trying to tell the true story. The District Attorney smelled a serious crime, kidnapping or perhaps a mass murder. Or maybe one of these love cults—you can never tell about these professors!

He caused a warrant to be issued Tuesday morning; Sergeant Izowski was sent to pick him up.

The professor came quietly and entered the black wagon without protest. "Look, Doc," said the sergeant, encouraged by his docile manner, "why don't you tell us where you hid 'em? You know we're bound to dig them up in time."

Frost turned, looked him in the eyes, and smiled, "Time," he said softly, "ah, time . . . yes, you could dig them up, in Time." He then got into the wagon and sat down quietly, closed his eyes, and placed his mind in the necessary calm receptive condition.

The sergeant placed one foot on the tailboard, braced his bulk in the only door, and drew out his notebook. When he finished writing he looked up.

Professor Frost was gone.

Frost had intended to look up Howard and Estelle. Inadvertently he let his mind dwell on Helen and Robert at the crucial moment. When he "landed" it was not in the world of the future he had visited twice before. He did not know where he was—on earth apparently, somewhere and somewhen.

It was wooded rolling country, like the hills of southern Missouri, or New Jersey. Frost had not sufficient knowledge of botany to be able to tell whether the species of trees he saw around him were familiar or not. But he was given no time to study the matter.

He heard a shout, an answering shout. Human figures came bursting out of the trees in a ragged line. He thought that they were attacking him, looked wildly around for shelter, and found none. But they kept on past him, ignoring him, except that the one who passed closest to him glanced at him hastily, and shouted something. Then he, too, was gone.

Frost was left standing, bewildered, in the small natural clearing in which he had landed.

Before he had had time to integrate these events one of the fleeing figures reappeared and yelled to him, accompanying the words with a gesture unmistakable—he was to come along.

Frost hesitated. The figure ran toward and hit him with a clean tackle. The next few seconds were very confused, but he pulled himself together sufficiently to realize that he was seeing the world upside down; the stranger was carrying him at a strong dogtrot, thrown over one shoulder.

Bushes whipped at his face, then the way led downward for several yards, and he was dumped casually to the ground. He sat up and rubbed himself.

He found himself in a tunnel which ran upwards to daylight and downward the Lord knew where. Figures milled around him but ignored him. Two of them were setting up some apparatus between the group and the mouth of the tunnel. They worked with extreme urgency, completing what they were doing in seconds, and stepped back. Frost heard a soft gentle hum.

The mouth of the tunnel became slightly cloudy. He soon saw why—the apparatus was spinning a web from wall to wall, blocking the exit. The web became less tenuous, translucent, opaque. The hum persisted for minutes thereafter and the strange machine continued to weave and thicken the web. One of the figures glanced at its belt, spoke one word in the tone of command, and the humming ceased.

Frost could feel relief spread over the group like a warm glow. He felt it himself and relaxed, knowing intuitively that some acute danger had been averted.

The member of the group who had given the order to shut off the machine turned around, happened to see Frost, and approached him, asking some questions in a sweet but peremptory soprano. Frost was suddenly aware of three things; the leader was a woman, it was the leader who had rescued him, and the costume and general appearance of these people *matched that of the transformed Robert Monroe.*

A smile spread over his face. Everything was going to be all right!

The question was repeated with marked impatience. Frost felt that an answer was required, though he did not understand the language and was sure that she could not possibly know English. Nevertheless—

"Madame," he said in English, getting to his feet and giving her a courtly bow, "I do not know your language and do not understand your question, but I suspect that you have saved my life. I am grateful."

She seemed puzzled and somewhat annoyed, and demanded something else—at least Frost though it was a different question; he could not be sure. This was getting nowhere. The language difficulty was almost insuperable, he realized. It might take days, weeks, months to overcome it. In the meantime these people were busy with a war, and would be in no frame of mind to bother with a useless incoherent stranger.

He did not want to be turned out on the surface.

How annoying, he thought, how stupidly annoying! Probably Monroe and Helen were somewhere around, but he could die of old age and never find them. They might be anywhere on the planet. How would an American, dumped down in Tibet, make himself understood if his only possible interpreter were in South America? Or whereabouts unknown? How would he make the Tibetans understand that there even was an interpreter? Botheration!

Still, he must make a try. What was it Monroe had said his name was *here*? Egan—no, Igor. That was it—Igor.

"Igor," he said.

The leader cocked her head. "Igor?" she said.

Frost nodded vigorously. "Igor."

She turned and called out, "Igor!" giving it the marked guttural, the liquid "r" that Monroe had given it. A man came forward. The professor looked eagerly at him, but he was a stranger, like the rest. The leader pointed to the man and stated, "Igor."

This is growing complicated, though Frost, apparently Igor is a common name here—too common. Then he had a sudden idea:

If Monroe and Helen got through, their badly-needed chattels might have made them prominent. "Igor," he said, "Helen Fisher."

The leader was attentive at once, her face alive. "Elen Feesher?" she repeated.

"Yes, yes—Helen Fisher."

She stood quiet, thinking. It was plain that the words meant something to her. She clapped her hands together and spoke, commandingly. Two men stepped forward. She addressed them rapidly for several moments.

The two men stepped up to Frost, each taking an arm. They started to lead him away. Frost held back for a moment and said over his shoulder, "Helen Fisher?"

" 'Elen Feesher'!" the leader assured him. He had to be content with that.

Two hours passed, more or less. He had not been mistreated and the room in which they had placed him was comfortable but it was a cell—at least the door was fastened. Perhaps he had said the wrong thing, perhaps those syllables meant something quite different here from a simple proper name.

The room in which he found himself was bare and lighted only by a dim glow from the walls, as had all of this underground world which he had seen so far. He was growing tired of the place and was wondering whether or not it would do any good to set up a commotion when he heard someone at the door.

The door slid back; he saw the leader, a smile on her rather grim, middle-aged features. She spoke in her own tongue, then added, "Igor . . . Ellenfeesher."

He followed her.

Glowing passageways, busy squares where he was subjected to curious stares, an elevator which startled him by dropping suddenly when he was not aware that it *was* an elevator, and finally a capsule-like vehicle in which they were sealed airtight and which went somewhere very fast indeed to judge by the sudden surge of weight when it started and again when it stopped—through them all he followed his guide, not understanding and lacking means of inquiring. He tried to relax and enjoy the passing moment, as his companion seemed to bear him no ill-will, though her manner was brusque—that of a person accustomed to giving orders and not in the habit of encouraging casual intimacy.

They arrived at a door which she opened and strode in. Frost followed and was almost knocked off his feet by a figure which charged into him and grasped him with both arms. "Doctor! Doctor Frost!"

It was Helen Fisher, dressed in the costume worn by both sexes here. Behind her stood Robert—or Igor, his gnome-like face widened with a grin.

He detached Helen's arms gently. "My dear," he said inanely, "imagine finding you here."

"Imagine finding *you* here," she retorted. "Why, professor— you're crying!"

"Oh, no, not at all," he said hastily, and turned to Monroe. "It's good to see you, too, Robert."

"That goes double for me, Doc," Monroe agreed.

The leader said something to Monroe. He answered her rapidly in their tongue and turned to Frost. "Doctor, this is my elder sister, Margri, Actoon Margri—Major Margri, you might translate it roughly."

"She has been very kind to me," said Frost, and bowed to her, acknowledging the introduction. Margri clapped her hands smartly together at the waist and ducked her head, features impassive.

"She gave the salute of equals," explained Robert-Igor. "I translated the title doctor as best I could which causes her to assume that your rank is the same as hers."

"What should I do?"

"Return it."

Frost did so, but awkwardly.

Doctor Frost brought his erstwhile students up to "date" —using a term which does not apply, since they were on a different time axis. His predicament with the civil authorities brought a cry of dismay from Helen. "Why, you poor thing! How awful of them!"

"Oh, I wouldn't say so," protested Frost. "It was reasonable so far as they knew. But I'm afraid I can't go back."

"You don't need to," Igor assured him. "You're more than welcome here."

"Perhaps I can help out in your war."

"Perhaps—but you've already done more than anyone here by what you've enabled me to do. We are working on it now." He swung his arm in a gesture which took in the whole room.

Igor had been detached from combat duty and assigned to staff work, in order to make available earth techniques. Helen was helping. "Nobody believes my story but my sister," he admitted, "But I've been able to show them enough for them to realize that what I've got is important, so they've given me a free hand and are practically hanging over my shoulder, waiting to see what we can produce. I've already got them started on a jet fighter and attack rockets to arm it."

Frost expressed surprise. How could so much be done so fast? Were the time rates different? Had Helen and Igor crossed over many weeks before, figured along this axis?

No, he was told, but Igor's countrymen, though lacking many earth techniques, were far ahead of earth in manufacturing skill. They used a single general type of machine to manufacture almost anything. They fed into it a plan which Igor called for want of a better term the blueprints—it was in fact, a careful scale model of the device to be manufactured; the machine retooled itself and produced the artifact. One of them was, at that moment, moulding the bodies of fighting planes out of plastic, all in one piece and in one operation.

"We are going to arm these jobs with both the stasis ray and rockets," said Igor. "Freeze 'em and then shoot the damn things down while they are out of control."

They talked a few minutes, but Frost could see that Igor was getting fidgety. He guessed the reason, and asked to be excused. Igor seized on the suggestion. "We will see you a little later," he said with relief. "I'll have some one dig up quarters for you. We *are* pretty rushed. War work—I know you'll understand."

Frost fell asleep that night planning how he could help his two young friends, and their friends, in their struggle.

But it did not work out that way. His education had been academic rather than practical; he discovered that the reference books which Igor and Helen had brought along were so much Greek to him—worse, for he understood Greek. He was accorded all honor and a comfortable living because of

92

Igor's affirmation that he had been the indispensable agent whereby this planet had received the invaluable new weapons, but he soon realized that for the job at hand he was useless, not even fit to act as an interpreter.

He was a harmless nuisance, a pensioner—and he knew it.

And underground life got on his nerves. The everpresent light bothered him. He had an unreasoned fear of radio-activity, born of ignorance, and Igor's reassurances did not stifle the fear. The war depressed him. He was not temperamentally cut out to stand up under the nervous tension of war. His helplessness to aid in the war effort, his lack of companionship, and his idleness all worked to increase the malaise.

He wandered into Igor and Helen's workroom one day, hoping for a moment's chat, if they were not too busy. They were not. Igor was pacing up and down, Helen followed them with worried eyes.

He cleared his throat. "Uh—I say, something the matter?"

Igor nodded, answered, "Quite a lot," and dropped back into his preoccupation.

"It's like this," said Helen. "In spite of the new weapons, things are still going against us. Igor is trying to figure out what to try next."

"Oh, I see. Sorry." He started to leave.

"Don't go. Sit down." He did so, and started mulling the matter over in his mind. It was annoying, very annoying!

"I'm afraid I'm not much use to you," he said at last to Helen. "Too bad Howard Jenkins isn't here."

"I don't suppose it matters," she answered. "We have the cream of modern earth engineering in these books."

"I don't mean that. I mean Howard himself, as he is where he's gone. They had a little gadget there in the future called a blaster. I gathered that it was a very powerful weapon indeed."

Igor caught some of this and whirled around. "What was it? How did it work?"

"Why, really," said Frost, "I can't say. I'm not up on such things, you know. I gathered that it was sort of a disintegrating ray."

"Can you sketch it? Think, man, think!"

Frost tried. Presently he stopped and said, "I'm afraid this isn't any good. I don't remember clearly and anyhow I don't know anything about the inside of it."

Igor sighed, sat down, and ran his hand through his hair.

After some minutes of gloomy silence, Helen said, "Couldn't we go get it?"

"Eh? How's that? How would you find him?"

"Could you find him, Professor?"

Frost sat up. "I don't know," he said slowly, "—but I'll try!"

There was the city. Yes, and there was the same gate he had passed through once before. He hurried on.

Star Light was glad to see him, but not particularly surprised. Frost wondered if anything could surprise this dreamy girl. But Howard more than made up for her lack of enthusiasm. He pounded Frost's back hard enough to cause pleurisy. "Welcome home, Master! Welcome home! I didn't know whether or not you would ever come, but we are ready for you. I had a room built for you and you alone, in case you ever showed up. What do you think of that? You are to live with us, you know. No sense in ever going back to that grubby school."

Frost thanked him, but added, "I came on business. I need your help, urgently."

"You do? Well, tell me, man, tell me!"

Frost explained. "So you see, I've got to take the secret of your blaster back to them. They need it. They must have it."

"And they shall have it," agreed Howard.

Some time later the problem looked more complicated. Try as he would Frost was simply not able to soak up the technical knowledge necessary to be able to take the secret back. The pedagogical problem presented was as great as if an untutored savage were to be asked to comprehend radio engineering sufficiently to explain to engineers unfamiliar with radio how to build a major station. And Frost was by no means sure that he could take a blaster with him through the country of Time.

"Well," said Howard at last, "I shall simply have to go with you."

Star Light, who had listened quietly, showed her first acute interest. "Darling! You must not—"

"Stop it," said Howard, his chin set stubbornly. "This is a matter of obligation and duty. You keep out of it."

Frost felt the acute embarrassment one always feels when forced to overhear a husband and wife having a difference of opinion.

When they were ready, Frost took Howard by the wrist. "Look me in the eyes," he said. "You remember how we did it before?"

Howard was trembling. "I remember. Master, do you think you can do it—and not lose me?"

"I hope so," said Frost, "now relax."

They got back to the chamber from which Frost had started, a circumstance which Frost greeted with relief. It would have been awkward to have to cross half a planet to find his friends. He was not sure yet just how the spatial dimensions fitted into the time dimensions. Someday he would have to study the matter, work out an hypothesis and try to check it.

Igor and Howard wasted little time on social amenities. They were deep into engineering matters before Helen had finished greeting the professor.

At long last— "There," said Howard, "I guess that covers everything. I'll leave my blaster for a model. Any more questions?"

"No," said Igor, "I understand it, and I've got every word you've said recorded. I wonder if you know what this means to us, old man? It unquestionably will win the war for us."

"I can guess," said Howard. "This little gadget is the mainstay of our systemwide pax. Ready, Doctor. I'm getting kinda anxious."

"But you're not going, Doctor?" cried Helen. It was both a question and a protest.

"I've got to guide him back," said Frost.

"Yes," Howard confirmed, "but he is staying to live with us. Aren't you, Master?"

"Oh, no!" It was Helen again.

Igor put an arm around her. "Don't coax him," he told her. "You know he has not been happy here. I gather that Howard's home would suit him better. If so, he's earned it."

Helen thought about it, then came up to Frost, placed both hands on his shoulders, and kissed him, standing on tiptoe to do so. "Goodbye, Doc," she said in a choky voice, "or anyhow, *au revoir!*"

He reached up and patted one of her hands.

Frost lay in the sun, letting the rays soak into his old bones. It was certainly pleasant here. He missed Helen and Igor a little, but he suspected that they did not really miss him. And life with Howard and Star Light was more to his liking. Officially he was tutor to their children, if and when. Actually he was just as lazy and useless as he had always wanted to be, with time on his hands. Time . . . Time.

There was just one thing that he would liked to have known: What did Sergeant Izowski say when he looked up and saw that the police wagon was empty? Probably thought it was impossible.

It did not matter. He was too lazy and sleepy to care. Time enough for a little nap before lunch. Time enough . . . Time.

THE END

CHAPTER ONE

LOST LEGACY

"Ye Have Eyes to See With!"

"HI-YAH, BUTCHER!" Doctor Philip Huxley put down the dice cup he had been fiddling with as he spoke, and shoved out a chair with his foot. "Sit down."

The man addressed ostentatiously ignored the salutation while handing a yellow slicker and soggy felt hat to the Faculty Clubroom attendant, but accepted the chair. His first words were to the negro attendant.

"Did you hear that, Pete? A witch doctor, passing himself off as a psychologist, has the effrontery to refer to me—to *me*, a licensed physician and surgeon, as a butcher." His voice was filled with gentle reproach.

"Don't let him kid you, Pete. If Doctor Coburn ever got you into an operating theatre, he'd open up your head just to see what makes you tick. He'd use your skull to make an ash-tray."

The colored man grinned as he wiped the table, but said nothing.

Coburn clucked and shook his head. "That from a witch doctor. Still looking for the Little Man Who Wasn't There, Phil?"

"If you mean parapsychology, yes."

"How's the racket coming?"

"Pretty good. I've got one less lecture this semester, which is just as well—I get awfully tired of explaining to the wide-eyed innocents how little we really know about what goes on inside their think-tanks. I'd rather do research."

"Who wouldn't? Struck any pay dirt lately?"

"Some. I'm having a lot of fun with a law student just now, chap named Valdez."

Coburn lifted his brows. "So? E.S.P.?"

"Kinda. He's sort of a clairvoyant; if he can see one side of an object, he can see the other side, too."

"Nuts!"

" 'If you're so smart, why ain't you rich?' I've tried him

96

out under carefully controlled conditions, and he can do it—see around corners."

"Hmmmm—well, as my Grandfather Stonebender used to say, 'God has more aces up his sleeve than were ever dealt in the game.' He would be a menace at stud poker."

"Matter of fact, he made his stake for law school as a professional gambler."

"Found out how he does it?"

"No, damn it." Huxley drummed on the table top, a worried look on his face. "If I just had a little money for research, I might get enough data to make this sort of thing significant. Look at what Rhine accomplished at Duke."

"Well, why don't you holler? Go before the Board and bite 'em in the ear for it. Tell 'em how you're going to make Western University famous."

Huxley looked still more morose. "Fat chance. I talked with my dean and he wouldn't even let me take it up with the President. Scared that the old fathead will clamp down on the department even more than he has. You see, officially, we are supposed to be behaviorists. Any suggestion that there might be something to consciousness that can't be explained in terms of physiology and mechanics is about as welcome as a Saint Bernard in a telephone booth."

The telephone signal glowed red back of the attendant's counter. He switched off the newscast and answered the call. "Hello . . . Yes, ma'am, he is. I'll call him. Telephone for you, Doctuh Coburn."

"Switch it over here." Coburn turned the telephone panel at the table around so that it faced him; as he did so it lighted up with the face of a young woman. He picked up the handset. "What is it? . . . What's that? How long ago did it happen? . . . Who made the diagnosis? . . . Read that over again . . . Let me see the chart." He inspected its image reflected in the panel, then added, "Very well. I'll be right over. Prepare the patient for operating." He switched off the instrument and turned to Huxley. "Got to go, Phil—emergency."

"What sort?"

"It'll interest you. Trephining. Maybe some cerebral excision. Car accident. Come along and watch it, if you have time." He was putting on his slicker as he spoke. He turned and swung out the west door with a long, loose-limbed stride. Huxley grabbed his own raincoat and hurried to catch up with him.

"How come," he asked as he came abreast, "they had to search for you?"

"Left my pocketphone in my other suit," Coburn returned briefly. "On purpose—I wanted a little peace and quiet. No luck."

They worked north and west through the arcades and

passages that connected the Union with the Science group, ignoring the moving walkways as being too slow. But when they came to the conveyor subway under Third Avenue opposite the Pottenger Medical School, they found it flooded, its machinery stalled, and were forced to detour west to the Fairfax Avenue conveyor. Coburn cursed impartially the engineers and the planning commission for the fact that spring brings torrential rains to Southern California, Chamber of Commerce or no.

They got rid of their wet clothes in the Physicians' Room and moved on to the gowning room for surgery. An orderly helped Huxley into white trousers and cotton shoe covers, and they moved to the next room to scrub. Coburn invited Huxley to scrub also in order that he might watch the operation close up. For three minutes by the little sand glass they scrubbed away with strong green soap, then stepped through a door and were gowned and gloved by silent, efficient nurses. Huxley felt rather silly to be helped on with his clothes by a nurse who had to stand on tip-toe to get the sleeves high enough. They were ushered through the glass door into surgery III, rubber-covered hands held out, as if holding a skein of yarn.

The patient was already in place on the table, head raised up and skull clamped immobile. Someone snapped a switch and a merciless circle of blue-white lights beat down on the only portion of him that was exposed, the right side of his skull. Coburn glanced quickly around the room, Huxley following his glance—light green walls, two operating nurses, gowned, masked, and hooded into sexlessness, a 'dirty' nurse, busy with something in the corner, the anesthetist, the instruments that told Coburn the state of the patient's heart action and respiration.

A nurse held the chart for the surgeon to read. At a word from Coburn, the anesthetist uncovered the patient's face for a moment. Lean brown face, acquiline nose, closed sunken eyes. Huxley repressed an exclamation. Coburn raised his eyebrows at Huxley.

"What's the trouble?"

"It's Juan Valdez!"

"Who's he?"

"The one I was telling you about—the law student with the trick eyes."

"Hmm—Well, his trick eyes didn't see around enough corners this time. He's lucky to be alive. You'll see better, Phil, if you stand over there."

Coburn changed to impersonal efficiency, ignored Huxley's presence and concentrated the whole of his able intellect on the damaged flesh before him. The skull had been crushed, or punched, apparently by coming into violent contact with some hard object with moderately sharp edges. The wound lay above the right ear, and was, superficially, two inches, or more, across. It was impossible, before exploration, to tell just how much damage had been suffered by the bony structure and the grey matter behind.

Undoubtedly there was some damage to the brain itself. The wound had been cleaned up on the surface and the area around it shaved and painted. The trauma showed up as a definite hole in the cranium. It was bleeding slightly and was partly filled with a curiously nauseating conglomerate of clotted purple blood, white tissue, grey tissue, pale yellow tissue.

The surgeon's lean slender fingers, unhuman in their pale orange coverings, moved gently, deftly in the wound, as if imbued with a separate life and intelligence of their own. Destroyed tissue, too freshly dead for the component cells to realize it, was cleared away,—chipped fragments of bone, lacerated mater dura, the grey cortical tissue of the cerebrum itself.

Huxley became fascinated by the minuscule drama, lost track of time, and of the sequence of events. He remembered terse orders for assistance, "Clamp!" "Retractor!" "Sponge!" The sound of the tiny saw, a muffled whine, then the tooth-tingling grind it made in cutting through solid living bone. Gently a spatulate instrument was used to straighten out the tortured convolutions. Incredible and unreal, he watched a scalpel whittle at the door of the mind, shave the thin wall of reason.

Three times a nurse wiped sweat from the surgeon's face.

Wax performed its function. Vitallium alloy replaced bone, dressing shut out infection. Huxley had watched uncounted operations, but felt again that almost insupportable sense of relief and triumph that comes when the surgeon turns away, and begins stripping off his gloves as he heads for the gowning room.

When Huxley joined Coburn, the surgeon had doused his mask and cap, and was feeling under his gown for cigarets. He looked entirely human again. He grinned at Huxley and inquired,

"Well, how did you like it?"

"Swell. It was the first time I was able to watch that type of thing so closely. You can't see so well from behind the glass, you know. Is he going to be all right?"

Coburn's expression changed. "He is a friend of yours, isn't he? That had slipped my mind for the moment. Sorry. He'll be all right, I'm pretty sure. He's young and strong, and he came through the operation very nicely. You can come see for yourself in a couple of days."

"You excised quite a lot of the speech center, didn't you?

99

Will he be able to talk when he gets well? Isn't he likely to have aphasia, or some other speech disorder?"

"Speech center? Why, I wasn't even close to the speech centers."

"Huh?"

"Put a rock in your right hand, Phil, so you'll know it next time. You're turned around a hundred and eighty degrees. I was working in the *right* cerebral lobe, not the left lobe."

Huxley looked puzzled, spread both hands out in front of him, glanced from one to the other, then his face cleared and he laughed. "You're right. You know, I have the damndest time with that. I never can remember which way to deal in a bridge game. But wait a minute—I had it so firmly fixed in my mind that you were on the left side in the speech centers that I am confused. What do you think the result will be on his neurophysiology?"

"Nothing—if past experience is any criterion. What I took away he'll never miss. I was working in terra incognita, pal —No Man's Land. If that portion of the brain that I was in has any function, the best physiologists haven't been able to prove it."

CHAPTER TWO

Three Blind Mice

BRRRINNG!

Joan Freeman reached out blindly with one hand and shut off the alarm clock, her eyes jammed shut in the vain belief that she could remain asleep if she did. Her mind wondered. Sunday. Don't have to get up early on Sunday. Then why had she set the alarm? She remembered suddenly and rolled out of bed, warm feet on a floor cold in the morning air. Her pajamas landed on that floor as she landed in the shower, yelled, turned the shower to warm, then back to cold again.

The last item from the refrigerator had gone into a basket, and a thermos jug was filled by the time she heard the sound of a car on the hill outside, the crunch of tires on granite in the driveway. She hurriedly pulled on short boots, snapped the loops of her jodhpurs under them, and looked at herself in the mirror. Not bad, she thought. Not Miss America, but she wouldn't frighten any children.

A banging at the door was echoed by the doorbell, and a baritone voice, "Joan! Are you decent?"

"Practically. Come on in, Phil."

Huxley, in slacks and polo shirt, was followed by another figure. He turned to him. "Joan, this is Ben Coburn, Doctor Ben Coburn. Doctor Coburn, Miss Freeman."

"Awfully nice of you to let me come, Miss Freeman."

"Not at all, Doctor. Phil had told me so much about you that I have been anxious to meet you." The conventionalities flowed with the ease of all long-established tribal taboo.

"Call him Ben, Joan. It's good for his ego."

While Joan and Phil loaded the car Coburn looked over the young woman's studio house. A single large room, panelled in knotty pine and dominated by a friendly field-stone fireplace set about with untidy bookcases, gave evidence of her personality. He had stepped through open french doors into a tiny patio, paved with mossy bricks and fitted with a barbecue pit and a little fishpond, brilliant in the morning sunlight, when he heard himself called.

"Doc! Stir your stumps! Time's awastin'!"

He glanced again around the patio, and rejoined the others at the car. "I like your house, Miss Freeman. Why should we bother to leave Beachwood Drive when Griffith Park can't be any pleasanter?"

"That's easy. If you stay at home, it's not a picnic—it's just breakfast. My name's Joan."

"May I put in a request for 'just breakfast' here some morning—Joan?"

"Lay off o' that mug, Joan," advised Phil in a stage whisper. "His intentions ain't honorable."

Joan straightened up the remains of what had recently been a proper-sized meal. She chucked into the fire three well-picked bones to which thick sirloin steaks were no longer attached, added some discarded wrapping paper and one lonely roll. She shook the thermos jug. It gurgled slightly. "Anybody want some more grapefruit juice?" she called.

"Any more coffee?" asked Coburn, then continued to Huxley, "His special talents are gone completely?"

"Plenty," Joan replied. "Serve yourselves."

The Doctor filled his own cup and Huxley's. Phil answered, "Gone entirely, I'm reasonably certain. I thought it might be hysterical shock from the operation, but I tried him under hypnosis, and the results were still negative—completely. Joan, you're some cook. Will you adopt me?"

"You're over twenty-one."

"I could easily have him certified as incompetent," volunteered Coburn.

"Single women aren't favored for adoption."

"Marry me, and it will be all right—we can both adopt him and you can cook for all of us."

101

"Well, I won't say that I won't and I won't say that I will, but I will say that it's the best offer I've had today. What were you guys talking about?"

"Make him put it in writing, Joan. We were talking about Valdez."

"Oh! You were going to run those last tests yesterday, weren't you? How did you come out?"

"Absolutely negative insofar as his special clairvoyance was concerned. It's gone."

"Hmm—How about the control tests?"

"The Humm-Wadsworth Temperament Test showed exactly the same profile as before the accident, within the inherent limits of accuracy of the technique. His intelligence quotient came within the technique limit, too. Association tests didn't show anything either. By all the accepted standards of neuro-psychology he is the same individual, except in two respects; he's minus a chunk of his cortex, and he is no longer able to see around corners. Oh, yes, and he's annoyed at losing that ability."

After a pause she answered, "That's pretty conclusive, isn't it?"

Huxley turned to Coburn. "What do you think, Ben?"

"Well, I don't know. You are trying to get me to admit that that piece of grey matter I cut out of his head gave him the ability to see in a fashion not possible to normal sense organs and not accounted for by orthodox medical theory, aren't you?"

"I'm not trying to make you admit anything. I'm trying to find out something."

"Well, since you put it that way, I would say if we stipulate that all your primary data were obtained with care under properly controlled conditions—"

"They were."

"—and that you have exercised even greater care in obtaining your negative secondary data—"

"I have. Damn it, I tried for three weeks under all conceivable conditions."

"Then we have the inescapable conclusions, first—" He ticked them off on his fingers. "—that this subject could see without the intervention of physical sense organs; and second, that this unusual, to put it mildly, ability was in some way related to a portion of his cerebrum in the dexter lobe."

"Bravo!" This was Joan's contribution.

"Thanks, Ben," acknowledged Phil. "I had reached the same conclusions, of course, but it's very encouraging to have someone else agree with me."

"Well, now that you are there, where are you?"

"I don't know exactly. Let me put it this way; I got into psychology for the same reason a person joins a church—

because he feels an overpowering need to understand himself and the world around him. When I was a young student, I thought modern psychology could tell me the answers, but I soon found out that the best psychologists didn't know a damn thing about the real core of the matter. Oh, I am not disparaging the work that has been done; it was badly needed and has been very useful in its way. None of 'em know what life is, what thought is, whether free will is a reality or an illusion, or whether that last question means anything. The best of 'em admit their ignorance; the worst of them make dogmatic assertions that are obvious absurdities—for example some of the mechanistic behaviorists that think just because Pavlov could condition a dog to drool at the sound of a bell that, therefore, they knew all about how Paderewski made music!"

Joan, who had been lying quietly in the shade of the big liveoaks and listening, spoke up. "Ben, you are a brain surgeon, aren't you?"

"One of the best," certified Phil.

"You've seen a lot of brains, furthermore you've seen 'em while they were *alive*, which is more than most psychologists have. What do you believe thought is? What do you think makes us tick?"

He grinned at her. "You've got me, kid. I don't pretend to know. It's not my business; I'm just a tinker."

She sat up. "Give me a cigaret, Phil. I've arrived just where Phil is, but by a different road. My father wanted me to study law. I soon found out that I was more interested in the principles behind law and I changed over to the School of Philosophy. But philosophy wasn't the answer. There really isn't anything to philosophy. Did you ever eat that cotton candy they sell at fairs? Well, philosophy is like that—it looks as if it were really something, and it's awfully pretty, and it tastes sweet, but when you go to bite it you can't get your teeth into it, and when you try to swallow, there isn't anything there. Philosophy is word-chasing, as significant as a puppy chasing its tail.

"I was about to get my Ph.D. in the School of Philosophy, when I chucked it and came to the science division and started taking courses in psychology. I thought that if I was a good little girl and patient, all would be revealed to me. Well, Phil has told us what that leads to. I began to think about studying medicine, or biology. You just gave the show away on that. Maybe it was a mistake to teach women to read and write."

Ben laughed. "This seems to be experience meeting at the village church; I might as well make my confession. I guess most medical men start out with a desire to know all about man and what makes him tick, but it's a big field, the final answers are elusive and there is always so much work that

103

needs to be done right now, that we quit worrying about the final problems. I'm as interested as I ever was in knowing what life, and thought, and so forth, really are, but I have to have an attack of insomnia to find time to worry about them. Phil, are you seriously proposing to tackle such things?"

"In a way, yes. I've been gathering data on all sorts of phenomena that run contrary to orthodox psychological theory —all the junk that goes under the general name of metapsychics—telepathy, clairvoyance, so-called psychic manifestations, clairaudience, levitation, yoga stuff, stigmata, anything of that sort I can find."

"Don't you find that most of that stuff can be explained in an ordinary fashion?"

"Quite a lot of it, sure. Then you can strain orthodox theory all out of shape and ignore the statistical laws of probability to account for most of the rest. Then by attributing anything that is left over to charlatanism, credulity, and self-hypnosis, and refuse to investigate it, you can go peacefully back to sleep."

"Occam's razor," murmured Joan.

"Huh?"

"William of Occam's Razor. It's a name for a principle in logic; whenever two hypotheses both cover the facts, use the simpler of the two. When a conventional scientist has to strain his orthodox theories all out of shape, 'til they resemble something thought up by Rube Goldberg, to account for unorthodox phenomena, he's ignoring the principle of Occam's Razor. It's simpler to draw up a new hypothesis to cover all the facts than to strain an old one that was never intended to cover the non-conforming data. But scientists are more attached to their theories than they are to their wives and families."

"My," said Phil admiringly, "to think that that came out from under a permanent wave."

"If you'll hold him, Ben, I'll beat him with this here thermos jug."

"I apologize. You're absolutely right, darling. I decided to forget about theories, to treat these outcast phenomena like any ordinary data, and to see where it landed me."

"What sort of stuff," put in Ben, "have you dug up, Phil?"

"Quite a variety, some verified, some mere rumor, a little of it carefully checked under laboratory conditions, like Valdez. Of course, you've heard of all the stunts attributed to Yoga. Very little of it has been duplicated in the Western Hemisphere, which counts against it; nevertheless a lot of odd stuff in India has been reported by competent, cool-minded observers— telepathy, accurate soothsaying, clairvoyance, fire walking, and so forth."

"Why do you include fire walking in metapsychics?"

"On the chance that the mind can control the body and other material objects in some esoteric fashion."

"Hmm."

"Is the idea any more marvelous than the fact that you can cause your hand to scratch your head? We haven't any more idea of the actual workings of volition on matter in one case than in the other. Take the Tierra del Fuegans. They slept on the ground, naked, even in zero weather. Now the body can't make any such adjustment in its economy. It hasn't the machinery; any physiologist will tell you so. A naked human being caught outdoors in zero weather must exercise, or die. But the Tierra del Fuegans didn't know about metabolic rates and such. They just slept—nice, and warm, and cozy."

"So far you haven't mentioned anything close to home. If you are going to allow that much latitude, my Grandfather Stonebender had much more wonderful experiences."

"I'm coming to them. Don't forget Valdez."

"What's this about Ben's grandfather?" asked Joan.

"Joan, don't ever boast about anything in Ben's presence. You'll find that his Grandfather Stonebender did it faster, easier, and better."

A look of more-in-sorrow-than-in-anger shone out of Coburn's pale blue eyes. "Why, Phil, I'm surprised at you. If I weren't a Stonebender myself, and tolerant, I'd be inclined to resent that remark. But your apology is accepted."

"Well, to bring matters closer home, besides Valdez, there was a man in my home town, Springfield, Missouri, who had a clock in his head."

"What do you mean?"

"I mean he knew the exact time without looking at a clock. If your watch disagreed with him, your watch was wrong. Besides that, he was a lightning calculator—knew the answer instantly to the most complicated problems in arithmetic you cared to put to him. In other ways he was feeble-minded."

Ben nodded. "It's a common phenomenon—*idiots savants.*"

"But giving it a name doesn't explain it. Besides which, while a number of the people with erratic talents are feeble-minded, not all of them are. I believe that by far the greater per cent of them are not, but that we rarely hear of them because the intelligent ones are smart enough to know that they would be annoyed by the crowd, possibly persecuted, if they let the rest of us suspect that they were different."

Ben nodded again. "You got something there, Phil. Go ahead."

"There have been a lot of these people with impossible talents who were not subnormal in other ways and who were right close to home. Boris Sidis, for example—"

"He was that child prodigy, wasn't he? I thought he played out?"

"Maybe. Personally, I think he grew cagy and decided not to let the other monkeys know that he was different. In any case he had a lot of remarkable talents, in intensity, if not in kind. He must have been able to read a page of print just by glancing at it, and he undoubtedly had complete memory. Speaking of complete memory, how about Blind Tom, the negro pianist who could play any piece of music he had ever heard once? Nearer home, there was this boy right here in Los Angeles County not so very many years ago who could play ping-pong blind-folded, or anything else, for which normal people require eyes. I checked him myself, and he could do it. And there was the 'Instantaneous Echo.' "

"You never told me about him, Phil," commented Joan. "What could he do?"

"He could talk along with you, using your words and intonations, in any language whether he knew the language or not. And he would keep pace with you so accurately that anyone listening wouldn't be able to tell the two of you apart. He could imitate your speech and words as immediately, as accurately, and as effortlessly as your shadow follows the movements of your body."

"Pretty fancy, what? And rather difficult to explain by behaviorist theory. Ever run across any cases of levitation, Phil?"

"Not of human beings. However I have seen a local medium —a nice kid, non-professional, used to live next door to me— make articles of furniture in my own house rise up off the floor and float. I was cold sober. It either happened or I was hypnotized; have it your own way. Speaking of levitating, you know the story they tell about Nijinsky?"

"Which one?"

"About him floating. There are thousands of people here and in Europe (unless they died in the Collapse) who testify that in *Le Spectre de la Rose* he used to leap up into the air, pause for a while, then come down when he got ready. Call it mass hallucination—I didn't see it."

"Occam's Razor again," said Joan.

"So?"

"Mass hallucination is harder to explain than one man floating in the air for a few seconds. Mass hallucination not proved —mustn't infer it to get rid of a troublesome fact. It's comparable to the "There aint no sech animal' of the yokel who saw the rhinoceros for the first time."

"Maybe so. Any other sort of trick stuff you want to hear about, Ben? I got a million of 'em."

"How about forerunners, and telepathy?"

"Well, telepathy is positively proved, though still unexplained, by Dr. Rhine's experiments. Of course a lot of people had observed it before then, with such frequency as to make

106

questioning it unreasonable. Mark Twain, for example. He wrote about it fifty years before Rhine, with documentation and circumstantial detail. He wasn't a scientist, but he had hard common sense and shouldn't have been ignored. Upton Sinclair, too. Forerunners are a little harder. Every one has heard dozens of stories of hunches that came true, but they are hard to follow up in most cases. You might try J. W. Dunne's *Experiment with Time* for a scientific record under controlled conditions of forerunners in dreams."

"Where does all this get you, Phil? You aren't just collecting Believe-it-or-nots?"

"No, but I had to assemble a pile of data—you ought to look over my notebooks—before I could formulate a working hypothesis. I have one now."

"Well?"

"You gave it to me—by operating on Valdez. I had begun to suspect sometime ago that these people with odd and apparently impossible mental and physical abilities were no different from the rest of us in any sense of abnormality, but that they had stumbled on potentialities inherent in all of us. Tell me, when you had Valdez' cranium open did you notice anything abnormal in its appearance?"

"No. Aside from the wound, it presented no special features."

"Very well. Yet when you excised that damaged portion, he no longer possessed his strange clairvoyant power. You took that chunk of his brain out of an uncharted area—no known function. Now it is a primary datum of psychology and physiology that large areas of the brain have no *known* function. It doesn't seem reasonable that the most highly developed and highly specialized part of the body should have large areas with *no* function; it is more reasonable to assume that the functions are unknown. And yet men have had large pieces of their cortices cut out without any *apparent* loss in their mental powers—as long as the areas controlling the normal functions of the body were left untouched.

"Now in this one case, Valdez, we have established a direct connection between an uncharted area of the brain and an odd talent, to wit, clairvoyance. My working hypothesis comes directly from that: All normal people are potentially able to exercise all (or possibly most) of the odd talents we have referred to—telepathy, clairvoyance, special mathematical ability, special control over the body and its functions, and so forth. The potential ability to do these things is lodged in the unassigned areas of the brain."

Coburn pursed his lips. "Mmm—I don't know. If we all have these wonderful abilities, which isn't proved, how is it that we don't seem able to use them?"

"I haven't proved anything—yet. This is a working hypothe-

…s. But let me give you an analogy. These abilities aren't like sight, hearing, and touch which we can't avoid using from birth; they are more like the ability to talk, which has its own special centers in the brain from birth, *but which has to be trained into being.* Do you think a child raised exclusively by deaf-mutes would ever learn to talk? Of course not. To outward appearance he would be a deaf-mute."

"I give up," conceded Coburn. "You set up an hypothesis and made it plausible. But how are you going to check it? I don't see any place to get hold of it. It's a very pretty speculation, but without a working procedure, it's just fantasy."

Huxley rolled over and stared unhappily up through the branches. "That's the rub. I've lost my best wild talent case. I don't know where to begin."

"But, Phil," protested Joan. "You want normal subjects, and then try to develop special abilities in them. I think it's wonderful. When do we start?"

"When do we start what?"

"On *me*, of course. Take that ability to do lightning calculations, for example. If you could develop that in me, you'd be a magician. I got bogged down in first year algebra. I don't know the multiplication tables even now!"

CHAPTER THREE

"Every Man His Own Genius"

"SHALL WE GET BUSY?" asked Phil.

"Oh, let's not," Joan objected. "Let's drink our coffee in peace and let dinner settle. We haven't seen Ben for two weeks. I want to hear what he's been doing up in San Francisco."

"Thanks, darling," the doctor answered, "but I'd much rather hear about the Mad Scientist and his Trilby."

"Trilby, hell," Huxley protested, "She's as independent as a hog on ice. However, we've got something to show you this time, Doc."

"Really? That's good. What?"

"Well, as you know, we didn't make much progress for the first couple of months. It was all up hill. Joan developed a fair telepathic ability, but it was erratic and unreliable. As for mathematical ability, she had learned her multiplication tables, but as for being a lightning calculator, she was a washout."

Joan jumped up, crossed between the men and the fireplace, and entered her tiny Pullman kitchen. "I've got to scrape these dishes and put them to soak before the ants get at 'em. Talk loud, so I can hear you."

"What can Joan do now, Phil?"

"I'm not going to tell you. You wait and see. Joan! Where's the card table?"

"Back of the couch. No need to shout. I can hear plainly since I got my Foxy Grandma Stream-lined Ear Trumpet."

"Okay, wench, I found it. Cards in the usual place?"

"Yes, I'll be with you in a moment." She reappeared, whisking off a giddy kitchen apron, and sat down on the couch, hugging her knees. "The Great Gaga, the Ghoul of Hollywood is ready. Sees all, knows all, and tells a darnsight more. Fortunetelling, teethpulling, and refined entertainment for the entire family."

"Cut out the clowning. We'll start out with a little straight telepathy. Throw every thing else out of gear. Shuffle the cards, Ben."

Coburn did so. "Now what?"

"Deal 'em off, one at a time, letting you and me see 'em, but not Joan. Call 'em off, kid."

Ben dealt them out slowly. Joan commenced to recite in a sing-song voice, "Seven of diamonds; jack of hearts; ace of hearts; three of spades; ten of diamonds; six of clubs; nine of spades; eight of clubs—"

"Ben, that's the first time I've ever seen you look amazed."

"Right through the deck without a mistake. Grandfather Stonebender couldn't have done better."

"That's high praise, chum. Let's try a variation. I'll sit out this one. Don't let me see them. I don't know how it will work, as we never worked with anyone else. Try it."

A few minutes later Coburn put down the last card. "Perfect! Not a mistake."

Joan got up and came over to the table. "How come this deck has two tens of hearts in it?" She riffled through the deck, and pulled out one card. "Oh! You thought the seventh card was the ten of hearts; it was the ten of diamonds. See?"

"I guess I did," Ben admitted. "I'm sorry I threw you a curve. The light isn't any too good."

"Joan prefers artistic lighting effects to saving her eyes," explained Phil. "I'm glad it happened; it shows she was using telepathy, not clairvoyance. Now for a spot of mathematics. We'll skip the usual stunts like cube roots, instantaneous addition, logarithms of hyperbolic functions, and stuff. Take my word for it; she can do 'em. You can try her later on those simple tricks. Here's a little honey I shot in my own kitchen. It involves fast reading, complete memory, handling of unbelievable number of permutations and combinations, and mathematical investigation of alternatives. You play solitaire, Ben?"

"Sure."

"I want you to shuffle the cards thoroughly, then lay out a Canfield solitaire, dealing from left to right, then play it out, three cards at a time, going through the deck again and again, until you are stuck and can't go any farther."

"Okay. What's the gag?"

"After you have shuffled and cut, I want you to riffle the cards through once, holding them up so that Joan gets a quick glimpse of the index on each card. Then wait a moment."

Silently he did what he had been asked to do. Joan checked him. "You'll have to do it again, Ben. I saw only fifty-one cards."

"Two of them must have stuck together. I'll do it more carefully." He repeated it.

"Fifty-two that time. That's fine."

"Are you ready, Joan?"

"Yes, Phil. Take it down; hearts to the six, diamonds to the four, spades to the deuce, no clubs."

Coburn looked incredulous. "Do you mean that is the way this game is going to come out?"

"Try it and see."

He dealt the cards out from left to right, then played the game out slowly. Joan stopped him at one point. "No, play the king of hearts' stack into that space, rather than the king of spades. The king of spades play would have gotten the ace of clubs out, but three less hearts would play out if you did so." Coburn made no comment, but did as she told him to do. Twice more she stopped him and indicated a different choice of alternatives.

The game played out exactly as she had predicted.

Coburn ran his hand through his hair and stared at the cards. "Joan," he said meekly, "does your head ever ache?"

"Not from doing that stuff. It doesn't seem to be an effort at all."

"You know," put in Phil, seriously, "there isn't any real reason why it should be a strain. So far as we know, thinking requires no expenditure of energy at all. A person ought to be able to think straight and accurately with no effort. I've a notion that it is faulty thinking that makes headaches."

"But how in the devil does she do it, Phil? It makes my head ache just to try to imagine the size of that problem, if it were worked out long hand by conventional mathematics."

"I don't know how she does it. Neither does she."

"Then how did she *learn* to do it?"

"We'll take that up later. First, I want to show you our *piece de resistance*."

"I can't take much more. I'm groggy now."

"You'll like this."

"Wait a minute, Phil. I want to try one of my own. How fast can Joan read?"

"As fast as she can see."

"Hmm—". The doctor hauled a sheaf of typewritten pages out of his inside coat pocket. "I've got the second draft of a paper I've been working on. Let's try Joan on a page of it. Okay, Joan?"

He separated an inner page from the rest and handed it to her. She glanced at it and handed it back at once. He looked puzzled and said:

"What's the matter?"

"Nothing. Check me as I read back." She started in a rapid singsong, " 'page four. —now according to Cunningham, fifth edition, page 547,: "Another strand of fibres, videlicet, the fasciculus spinocerebellaris (posterior), prolonged upwards in the lateral furniculus of the medulla spinallis, gradually leaves this portion of the medulla oblongata. This tract lies on the surface, and is—"

"That's enough, Joan, hold it. God knows how you did it, but you read and memorized that page of technical junk in a split second." He grinned slyly. "But your pronunciation was a bit spotty. Grandfather Stonebender's would have been perfect."

"What can you expect? I don't know what half of the words mean."

"Joan, how did you learn to do all this stuff?"

"Truthfully, Doctor, I don't know. It's something like learning to ride a bicycle—you take one spill after another, then one day you get on and just ride away, easy as you please. And in a week you are riding without handle-bars and trying stunts. It's been like that—I knew what I wanted to do, and one day I could. Come on, Phil's getting impatient."

Ben maintained a puzzled silence and permitted Phil to lead him to a little desk in the corner. "Joan, can we use any drawer? OK. Ben, pick out a drawer in this desk, remove any articles you wish, add anything you wish. Then, without looking into the drawer, stir up the contents and remove a few articles and drop them into another drawer. I want to eliminate the possibility of telepathy."

"Phil, don't worry about my housekeeping. My large staff of secretaries will be only too happy to straighten out that desk after you get through playing with it."

"Don't stand in the way of science, little one. Besides," he added, glancing into a drawer, "this desk obviously hasn't been straightened for at least six months. A little more stirring up won't hurt it."

"Humph! What can you expect when I spend all my time learning parlor tricks for you? Besides, I know where everything is."

111

"That's just what I am afraid of, and why I want Ben to introduce a little more of the random element—if possible. Go ahead, Ben."

When the doctor had complied and closed the drawer, Phil continued, "Better use pencil and paper on this one, Joan. First list everything you see in the drawer, then draw a little sketch to show approximate locations and arrangement."

"OK." She sat down at the desk and commenced to write rapidly:

One large black leather handbag
Six-inch ruler

Ben stopped her. "Wait a minute. This is all wrong. I would have noticed anything as big as a handbag."

She wrinkled her brow. "Which drawer did you say?"

"The second on the right."

"I thought you said the top drawer."

"Well, perhaps I did."

She started again:

Brass paper knife
Six assorted pencils and a red pencil
Thirteen rubber bands
Pearl-handled penknife

"That must be your knife, Ben. It's very pretty; why haven't I seen it before?"

"I bought it in San Francisco. Good God, girl. You haven't seen it *yet*."

One paper of matches, advertising the Sir Francis Drake Hotel
Eight letters and two bills
Two ticket stubs, the Follies Burlesque Theatre—"Doctor, I'm *surprised* at you."

"Get on with your knitting."

"Provided you promise to take me the next time you go."

One fever thermometer with a pocket clip
Art gum and a typewriter eraser
Three keys, assorted
One lipstick, Max Factor #3
A scratch pad and some file cards, used on one side
One small brown paper sack containing one pair stockings, size nine, shade Creole. —"I'd forgotten that I had bought them; I searched all through the house for a decent pair this morning."

"Why didn't you just use your X-ray eyes, Mrs. Houdini?"

She looked startled. "Do you know, it just didn't occur to me. I haven't gotten around to trying to *use* this stuff yet."

"Anything else in the drawer?"

"Nothing but a box of notepaper. Just a sec: I'll make the sketch." She sketched busily for a couple of minutes, her

112

tongue between her teeth, her eyes darting from the paper toward the closed drawer and back again. Ben inquired,

"Do you have to look in the direction of the drawer to see inside it?"

"No, but it helps. It makes me dizzy to *see* a thing when I am looking away from it."

The contents and arrangement of the drawer were checked and found to be exactly as Joan had stated they were. Doctor Coburn sat quietly, making no comment, when they had finished. Phil, slightly irked at his lack of demonstrativeness, spoke to him.

"Well, Ben, what did you think of it? How did you like it?"

"You know what I thought of it. You've proved your theory up to the hilt—but I'm thinking about the implications, some of the possibilities. I *think* we've just been handed the greatest boon a surgeon ever had to work with. Joan, can you see inside a human body?"

"I don't know. I've never—"

"Look at me."

She stared at him for a silent moment. "Why—why, I can see your heart beat! I can see—"

"Phil, can you teach me to see the way she does?"

Huxley rubbed his nose. "I don't know. Maybe—"

Joan bent over the big chair in which the doctor was seated. "Won't he go under, Phil?"

"Hell, no. I've tried everything but tapping his skull with a bungstarter. I don't believe there's any brain there to hypnotize."

"Don't be pettish. Let's try again. How do you feel, Ben?"

"All right, but wide awake."

"I'm going out of the room this time. Maybe I'm a distracting factor. Now be a good boy and go sleepy-bye." She left them.

Five minutes later Huxley called out to her, "Come on back in, kid. He's under."

She came in and looked at Coburn where he lay sprawled in her big easy chair, quiet, eyes half closed. "Ready for me?" she asked, turning to Huxley.

"Yes. Get ready." She lay down on the couch. "You know what I want; get in rapport with Ben as soon as you go under. Need any persuasion to get to sleep?"

"No."

"Very well, then—Sleep!"

She became quiet, lax.

"Are you under, Joan?"

"Yes, Phil."

"Can you reach Ben's mind?"

A short pause: "Yes."

"What do you find?"

"Nothing. It's like an empty room, but friendly. Wait a moment—he greeted me."

"What did he say?"

"Just a greeting. It wasn't in words."

"Can you hear me, Ben?"

"Sure, Phil."

"You two are together?"

"Yes. Yes, indeed."

"Listen to me, both of you. I want you to wake up slowly, remaining in rapport. Then Joan is to teach Ben how to perceive that which is not seen. Can you do it?"

"Yes, Phil, we can." It was as if one voice had spoken.

CHAPTER FOUR

Holiday

"FRANKLY, MR. HUXLEY, I can't understand your noncooperative attitude." The President of Western University let the stare from his slightly bulging eyes rest on the second button of Phil's vest. "You have been given every facility for sound useful research along lines of proven worth. Your program of instructing has been kept light in order that you might make use of your undoubted ability. You have been acting chairman of your sub-department this past semester. Yet instead of profiting by your unusual opportunities, you have, by your own admission, been, shall we say, frittering away your time in the childish pursuit of old wives' tales and silly superstitions. Bless me, man, I don't understand it!"

Phil answered, with controlled exasperation, "But Doctor Brinckley, if you would permit me to show you—"

The president interposed a palm. "Please, Mr. Huxley. It is not necessary to go over that ground again. One more thing, it has come to my attention that you have been interfering in the affairs of the medical school."

"The medical school! I haven't set foot inside it in weeks."

"It has come to me from unquestioned authority that you have influenced Doctor Coburn to disregard the advice of the staff diagnosticians in performing surgical operations— the best diagnosticians, let me add, on the West Coast."

Huxley maintained his voice at toneless politeness. "Let us suppose for the moment that I have influenced Doctor Coburn —I do not concede the point—has there been any case in

114

which Coburn's refusal to follow diagnosis has failed to be justified by the subsequent history of the case?"

"That is beside the point. The point is—I can't have my staff from one school interfering in the affairs of another school. You see the justice of that, I am sure."

"I do not admit that I have interfered. In fact, I deny it."

"I am afraid I shall have to be the judge of that." Brinckley rose from his desk and came around to where Huxley stood. "Now Mr. Huxley—may I call you Philip? I like to have my juniors in our institution think of me as a friend. I want to give you the same advice that I would give to my son. The semester will be over in a day or two. I think you need a vacation. The Board has made some little difficulty over renewing your contract inasmuch as you have not yet completed your doctorate. I took the liberty of assuring them that you would submit a suitable thesis this coming academic year—and I feel sure that you can if you will only devote your efforts to sound, constructive work. You take your vacation, and when you come back you can outline your proposed thesis to me. I am quite sure the Board will make no difficulty about your contract then."

"I had intended to write up the results of my current research for my thesis."

Brinckley's brows raised in polite surprise. "Really? But that is out of the question, my boy, as you know. You do need a vacation. Good-bye then; if I do not see you again before commencement, let me wish you a pleasant holiday now."

When a stout door separated him from the president, Huxley dropped his pretense of good manners and hurried across the campus, ignoring students and professors alike. He found Ben and Joan waiting for him at their favorite bench, looking across the La Brea Tar Pits toward Wilshire Boulevard.

He flopped down on the seat beside them. Neither of the men spoke, but Joan was unable to control her impatience. "Well, Phil? What did the old fossil have to say?"

"Gimme a cigaret." Ben handed him a pack and waited. "He didn't say much—just threatened me with the loss of my job and the ruination of my academic reputation if I didn't knuckle under and be his tame dog—all in the politest of terms of course."

"But Phil, didn't you offer to bring me in and show him the progress you had already made?"

"I didn't bring your name into it; it was useless. He knew who you were well enough—he made a sidelong reference to the inadvisability of young instructors seeing female students socially except under formal, fully chaperoned conditions—

115

talked about the high moral tone of the university, and our obligation to the public!"

"Why, the dirty minded old so-and-so! I'll tear him apart for that!"

"Take it easy, Joan." Ben Coburn's voice was mild and thoughtful. "Just how did he threaten you, Phil?"

"He refused to renew my contract at this time. He intends to keep me on tenterhooks all summer, then if I come back in the fall and make a noise like a rabbit, he might renew— if he feels like it. Damn him! The thing that got me the sorest was a suggestion that I was slipping and needed a rest."

"What are you going to do?"

"Look for a job, I guess. I've got to eat."

"Teaching job?"

"I suppose so, Ben."

"Your chances aren't very good, are they, without a formal release from Western? They can blacklist you pretty effectively. You've actually got about as much freedom in the matter as a professional ballplayer."

Phil looked glum and said nothing. Joan sighed and looked out across the marshy depression surrounding the tar pits. Then she smiled and said, "We could lure old Picklepuss down here and push him in."

Both men smiled but did not answer. Joan muttered to herself something about sissies. Ben addressed Phil. "You know, Phil, the old boy's idea about a vacation wasn't too stupid; I could do with one myself."

"Anything in particular in mind?"

"Why, yes, more or less. I've been out here seven years and never really seen the state. I'd like to start out and drive, with no particular destination in mind. Then we could go on up past Sacramento and into northern California. They says it's magnificent country up there. We could take in the High Sierras and the Big Trees on the way back."

"That certainly sounds inviting."

"You could take along your research notes and we could talk about your ideas as we drove. If you decided you wanted to write up some phase, we could just lay over while you did it."

Phil stuck out his hand. "It's a deal, Ben. When do we start?"

"As soon as the term closes."

"Let's see—we ought to be able to get underway late Friday afternoon then. Which car will we use, yours or mine?"

"My coupe ought to be about right. It has lots of baggage space."

Joan, who had followed the conversation with interest, broke in on them. "Why use your car, Ben? Three people can't be comfortable in a coupe."

"Three people? Wha' d'yu mean, three people? You aren't going, bright eyes."

"So? That's what you think. You can't get rid of me at this point; I'm the laboratory case. Oh no, you can't leave me behind."

"But Joan, this is a stag affair."

"Oh, so you want to get rid of me?"

"Now Joan, we didn't say that. It just would look like the devil for you to be barging about the country with a couple of men—"

"Sissies! Tissyprissles! Pantywaists! Worried about your reputations."

"No, we're not. We're worried about yours."

"It won't wash. No girl who lives alone has any reputation. She can be as pure as Ivory soap and the cats on the campus, both sexes, will take her to pieces anyway. What are you so scared of? We aren't going to cross any state lines."

Coburn and Huxley exchanged the secret look that men employ when confronted by the persistence of an unreasonable woman.

"Look out, Joan!" A big red Santa Fe bus took the shoulder on the opposite side of the highway and slithered past. Joan switched the tail of the grey sedan around an oil tanker truck and trailer on their own side of the road before replying. When she did, she turned her head to speak directly to Phil who was riding in the back seat.

"What's the matter, Phil?"

"You darn near brought us into a head on collision with about twenty tons of the Santa Fe's best rolling stock!"

"Don't be nervous; I've been driving since I was sixteen and I've never had an accident."

"I'm not surprised; you'll never have but one. Anyhow," Phil went on, "can't you keep your eyes on the road? That's not too much to ask, is it?"

"I don't need to watch the road. Look." She turned her head far around and showed him that her eyes were jammed shut. The needle of the speedometer hovered around ninety.

"Joan! Please!"

She opened her eyes and faced front once more. "But I don't have to look in order to see. You taught me that yourself, Smarty. Don't you remember?"

"Yes, yes, but I never thought you'd apply it to driving a car!"

"Why not? I'm the safest driver you ever saw; I can see everything that's on the road, even around a blind curve. If I need to, I read the other driver's minds to see what they are going to do next."

"She's right, Phil. The few times I've paid attention to

her driving she's been doing just exactly what I would have done in the same circumstances. That's why I haven't been nervous."

"All right. All right," Phil answered, "but would you two supermen keep in mind that there is a slightly nervous ordinary mortal in the back seat who can't see around corners?"

"I'll be good," said Joan soberly. "I didn't mean to scare you, Phil."

"I'm interested," resumed Ben, "in what you said about not looking toward anything you wanted to see. I can't do it too satisfactorily. I remember once you said it made you dizzy to look away and still use direct perception."

"It used to, Ben, but I got over it, and so will you. It's just a matter of breaking old habits. To me, every direction is in 'front'—all around and up and down. I can focus my attention in any direction, or two or three directions at once. I can even pick a point of away from where I am physically, and look at the other side of things—but that is harder."

"You two make me feel like the mother of the Ugly Duckling," said Phil bitterly. "Will you still think of me kindly when you have passed beyond human communication?"

"Poor Phil!" exclaimed Joan, with sincere sympathy in her voice. "You taught us, but no one has bothered to teach you. Tell you what, Ben, let's stop tonight at an auto camp—pick a nice quiet one on the outskirts of Sacramento—and spend a couple of days doing for Phil what he has done for us."

"Okay by me. It's a good idea."

"That's mighty white of you, pardner," Phil conceded, but it was obvious that he was pleased and mollified. "After you get through with me will I be able to drive a car on two wheels, too?"

"Why not learn to levitate?" Ben suggested "It's simpler —less expensive and nothing to get out of order."

"Maybe we will some day," returned Phil, quite seriously, "there no telling where this line of investigation may lead."

"Yeah, you're right," Ben answered him with equal sobriety. "I'm getting so that I can believe seven impossible things before breakfast. What were you saying just before we passed that oil tanker?"

"I was just trying to lay before you an idea I've been mulling over in my mind the past several weeks. It's a big idea, so big that I can hardly believe it myself."

"Well, spill it."

Phil commenced checking points off on his fingers. "We've proved, or tended to prove, that the normal human mind has powers previously unsuspected, haven't we?"

"Tentatively—yes. It looks that way."

"Powers way beyond any that the race as a whole makes regular use of."

"Yes, surely. Go on."

"And we have reason to believe that these powers exist, have their being, by virtue of certain areas of the brain to which functions were not previously assigned by physiologists? That is to say, they have organic basis, just as the eye and the sight centers in the brain are the organic basis for normal sight?"

"Yes, of course."

"You can trace the evolution of any organ from a simple beginning to a complex, highly developed form. The organ develops through use. In an evolutionary sense function begets organ."

"Yes. That's elementary."

"Don't you see what that implies?"

Coburn looked puzzled, then a look of comprehension spread over his face. Phil continued, with delight in his voice, "You see it, too?" The conclusion is inescapable: there must have been a time when the entire race used these strange powers as easily as they heard, or saw, or smelled. And there must have been a long, long period—hundreds of thousands, probably millions of years—during which these powers were developed as a race. Individuals couldn't do it, any more than I could grow wings. It had to be done racially, over a long period of time. Mutation theory is no use either—mutation goes by little jumps, with use confirming the change. No indeed—these strange powers are vestigial—hangovers from a time when the whole race had 'em and used 'em."

Phil stopped talking, and Ben did not answer him, but sat in a brown study while some ten miles spun past. Joan started to speak once, then thought better of it. Finally Ben commenced to speak slowly.

"I can't see any fault in your reasoning. It's not reasonable to assume that whole areas of the brain with complex functions 'jest growed'. But, brother, you've sure raised hell with modern anthropology:"

"That worried me when I first got the notion, and that's why I kept my mouth shut. Do you know anything about anthropology?"

"Nothing except the casual glance that any medical student gets."

"Neither did I, but I had quite a lot of respect for it. Professor Whoosistwitchell would reconstruct one of our great grand-daddies from his collar bone and his store teeth and deliver a long dissertation on his most intimate habits, and I would swallow it, hook, line, and sinker, and be much impressed. But I began to read up on the subject. Do you know what I found?"

"Go ahead."

"In the first place there isn't a distinguished anthropologist in the world but what you'll find one equally distinguished who will call him a diamond-studded liar. They can't agree on the simplest elements of their alleged science. In the second place, there isn't a corporal's guard of really decent exhibits to back up their assertions about the ancestry of mankind. I never saw so much stew from one oyster. They write book after book and what have they got to go on?—The Dawson Man, the Pekin Man, the Heidelberg Man and a couple of others. And those aren't complete skeletons, a damaged skull, a couple of teeth, maybe another bone or two."

"Oh now, Phil, there were lots of specimens found of Cro-Magnon men."

"Yes, but they were true men. I'm talking about submen, our evolutionary predecessors. You see, I was trying to prove myself wrong. If man's ascent had been a long steady climb, submen into savages, savages to barbarians, barbarians perfecting their cultures into civilization . . . all this with only minor setbacks of a few centuries, or a few thousands years at the most . . . and with our present culture the highest the race had ever reached . . . If all that was true, then my idea was wrong.

"You follow me, don't you? The internal evidence of the brain proves that mankind, sometime in its lost history, climbed to heights undreamed of today. In some fashion the race slipped back. And this happened so long ago that we have found no record of it anywhere. These brutish submen, that the anthropologists set such store by, *can't* be our ancestors; they are too new, too primitive, too young. They are too recent; they allow for no time for the race to develop these abilities whose existence we have proved. Either anthropology is all wet, or Joan can't do the things we have seen her do."

The center of the controversy said nothing. She sat at the wheel, as the big car sped along, her eyes closed against the slanting rays of the setting sun, seeing the road with an inner impossible sight.

Five days were spent in coaching Huxley and a sixth on the open road. Sacramento lay far behind them. For the past hour Mount Shasta had been visible from time to time through openings in the trees. Phil brought the car to a stop on a view point built out from the pavement of U.S. Highway 99. He turned to his passengers. "All out, troops," he said. "Catch a slice of scenery."

The three stood and stared over the canyon of the Sacramento River at Mount Shasta, thirty miles away. It was sweater weather and the air was as clear as a child's gaze. The peak was framed by two of the great fir trees which marched down the side of the canyon. Snow still lay on the slopes of the cone and straggled down as far as the timberline.

Joan muttered something. Ben turned his head. "What did you say, Joan?"

"Me? Nothing—I was saying over a bit of poetry to myself."

"What was it?"

"Tietjens' *Most Sacred Mountain:*

" 'Space and the twelve clean winds are here;
And with them broods eternity—a swift white peace, a
    presence manifest.
The rhythm ceases here. Time has no place. This is the
    end that has no end'."

Phil cleared his throat and self-consciously broke the silence. "I think I see what you mean."

Joan faced them. "Boys," she stated, "I am going to climb Mount Shasta."

Ben studied her dispassionately. "Joan," he pronounced, "You are full of hop."

"I mean it. I didn't say you were going to—I said I was."

"But we are responsible for your safety and welfare—and I for one don't relish the thought of a fourteen-thousand foot climb."

"You are *not* responsible for my safety; I'm a free citizen. Anyhow a climb wouldn't hurt you any; it would help to get rid of some of that fat you've been storing up against winter."

"Why," inquired Phil, "are you so determined so suddenly to make this climb?"

"It's really not a sudden decision, Phil. Ever since we left Los Angeles I've had a recurring dream that I was climbing, climbing, up to some high place . . . and that I was very happy because of it. Today I know that it was Shasta I was climbing."

"How do you know it?"

"I know it."

"Ben, what do you think?"

The doctor picked up a granite pebble and shied it out in the general direction of the river. He waited for it to come to rest several hundred feet down the slope. "I guess," he said, "we'd better buy some hobnailed boots."

Phil paused and the two behind him on the narrow path were forced to stop, too. "Joan," he asked, with a worried tone, "is this the way we came?"

They huddled together, icy wind cutting at their faces like rusty razor blades and gusts of snow eddying about them and stinging their eyes, while Joan considered her answer. "I think so," she ventured at last, "but even with my eyes closed this snow makes everything look different."

"That's my trouble, too. I guess we pulled a boner when we

decided against a guide . . . but who would have thought that a beautiful summer day could end up in a snow storm?"

Ben stamped his feet and clapped his hands together. "Let's get going," he urged. "Even if this is the right road, we've got the worst of it ahead of us before we reach the rest cabin. Don't forget that stretch of glacier we crossed."

"I wish I could forget it," Phil answered him soberly. "I don't fancy the prospect of crossing it in this nasty weather."

"Neither do I, but if we stay here we freeze."

With Ben now in the lead they resumed their cautious progress, heads averted to the wind, eyes half closed. Ben checked them again after a couple of hundred yards. "Careful, gang," he warned, "the path is almost gone here, and it's slippery." He went forward a few steps. "It's rather—" They heard him make a violent effort to recover his balance, then fall heavily.

"Ben! Ben!" Phil called out, "are you all right?"

"I guess so," he gasped. "I gave my left leg an awful bang. Be careful."

They saw that he was on the ground, hanging part way over the edge of the path. Cautiously they approached until they were alongside him. "Lend me a hand, Phil. Easy, now."

Phil helped him wiggle back onto the path. "Can you stand up?"

"I'm afraid not. My left leg gave me the devil when I had to move just now. Take a look at it, Phil. No, don't bother to take the boot off; look right through it."

"Of course. I forgot." Phil studied the limb for a moment. "It's pretty bad, fella—a fracture of the shin bone about four inches below the knee."

Coburn whistled a couple of bars of *Suwannee River,* then said, "Isn't that just too, too lovely? Simple or compound fracture, Phil?"

"Seems like a clean break, Ben."

"Not that it matters much one way or the other just now. What do we do next?"

Joan answered him. "We must build a litter and get you down the mountain!"

"Spoken like a true girl scout, kid. Have you figured how you and Phil can maneuver a litter, with me in it, over that stretch of ice?"

"We'll *have* to—somehow." But her voice lacked confidence.

"It won't work, kid. You two will have to straighten me out and bed me down, then go on down the mountain and stir out a rescue party with proper equipment. I'll get some sleep while you're gone. I'd appreciate it if you'd leave me some cigarets."

"No!" Joan protested. "We won't leave you here alone."

Phil added his objections. "Your plan is as bad as Joan's,

122

Ben. It's all very well to talk about sleeping until we get back, but you know as well as I do that you would die of exposure if you spent a night like this on the ground with no protection."

"I'll just have to chance it. What better plan can you suggest?"

"Wait a minute. Let me think." He sat down on the ledge beside his friend and pulled at his left ear. "This is the best I can figure out: We'll have to get you to some place that is a little more sheltered, and build a fire to keep you warm. Joan can stay with you and keep the fire going while I go down after help."

"That's all right," put in Joan, "except that I will be the one to go after help. You couldn't find your way in the dark and the snow, Phil. You know yourself that your direct perception isn't reliable as yet—you'd get lost."

Both men protested. "Joan, you're not going to start off alone."—"We can't permit that, Joan."

"That's a lot of gallant nonsense. Of course I'm going."

"No." It was a duet.

"Then we all stay here tonight, and huddle around a fire. I'll go down in the morning."

"That might do," Ben conceded, "if—"

"Good evening, friends." A tall, elderly man stood on the ledge behind them. Steady blue eyes regarded them from under shaggy white eyebrows. He was smooth shaven but a mane of white hair matched the eyebrows. Joan thought he looked like Mark Twain.

Coburn recovered first. "Good evening," he answered, "if it is a good evening—which I doubt."

The stranger smiled with his eyes. "My name is Ambrose, ma'am. But your friend is in need of some assistance. If you will permit me, sir—" He knelt down and examined Ben's leg, without removing the boot. Presently he raised his head. "This will be somewhat painful. I suggest, son, that you go to sleep." Ben smiled at him, closed his eyes, and gave evidence by his slow, regular breathing that he was asleep.

The man who called himself Ambrose slipped away into the shadows. Joan tried to follow him with perception, but this she found curiously hard to do. He returned in a few minutes with several straight sticks which he broke to a uniform length of about twenty inches. These he proceeded to bind firmly to Ben's left shin with a roll of cloth which he had removed from his trouser pocket.

When he was satisfied that the primitive splint was firm, he picked Coburn up in his arms, handling the not inconsiderable mass as if it were a child. "Come," he said.

They followed him without a word, back the way they had come, single file through the hurrying snowflakes. Five hundred yards, six hundred yards, then he took a turn that had not been on the path followed by Joan and the two men, and strode confidently away in the gloom. Joan noticed that he was wearing a light cotton shirt with neither coat nor sweater, and wondered that he had come so far with so little protection against the weather. He spoke to her over his shoulder,

"I like cold weather, ma'am."

He walked between two large boulders, apparently disappeared into the side of the mountain. They followed him and found themselves in a passageway which led diagonally into the living rock. They turned a corner and were in an octagonal living room, high ceilinged and panelled in some mellow, light-colored wood. It was softly illuminated by indirect lighting, but possessed no windows. One side of the octagon was a fireplace with a generous hearth in which a wood fire burned hospitably. There was no covering on the flagged floor, but it was warm to the feet.

The old man paused with his burden and indicated the comfortable fittings of the room—three couches, old-fashioned heavy chairs, a chaise longue—with a nod. "Be seated, friends, and make yourselves comfortable. I must see that your companion is taken care of, then we will find refreshment for you." He went out through a door opposite the one by which they had entered, still carrying Coburn in his arms.

Phil looked at Joan and Joan looked at Phil. "Well," he said, "what do you make of it?"

"I think we've found a 'home from home'. This is pretty swell."

"What do we do next?"

"I'm going to pull that chaise longue up to the fire, take off my boots, and get my feet warm and my clothes dry."

When Ambrose returned ten minutes later he found them blissfully toasting their tired feet before the fire. He was bearing a tray from which he served them big steaming bowls of onion soup, hard rolls, apple pie, and strong black tea. While doing so he stated, "Your friend is resting. There is no need to see him until tomorrow. When you have eaten, you will find sleeping rooms in the passageway, with what you need for your immediate comfort." He indicated the door from which he had just come. "No chance to mistake them; they are the lighted rooms immediately at hand. I bid you goodnight now." He picked up the tray and turned to leave.

"Oh, I say," began Phil hesitantly, "This is awfully good of you, Mister, uh—"

"You are very welcome, sir. Bierce is my name. Ambrose Bierce. Goodnight." And he was gone.

CHAPTER FIVE

"—Through a Glass, Darkly"

WHEN PHIL ENTERED the living room the next morning he found a small table set with a very sound breakfast for three. While he was lifting plate covers and wondering whether good manners required him to wait until joined by others, Joan entered the room. He looked up.

"Oh! It's you. Good morning, and stuff. They set a proper table here. Look." He lifted a plate cover. "Did you sleep well?"

"Like a corpse." She joined his investigations. "They do understand food, don't they? When do we start?"

"When number three gets here, I guess. Those aren't the clothes you had on last night."

"Like it?" She turned around slowly with a swaying mannequin walk. She had on a pearl grey gown that dropped to her toes. It was high waisted; two silver cords crossed between her breasts and encircled her waist, making a girdle. She was shod in silver sandals. There was an air of ancient days about the whole costume.

"It's swell. Why is it a girl always looks prettier in simple clothes?"

"Simple—hmmf! If you can buy this for three hundred dollars on Wilshire Boulevard, I'd like to have the address of the shop."

"Hello, troops." Ben stood in the doorway. They both stared at him. "What's the trouble?"

Phil ran his eye down Ben's frame. "How's your leg, Ben?"

"I wanted to ask you about that. How long have I been out? The leg's all well. Wasn't it broken after all?"

"How about it, Phil?" Joan seconded. "You examined it— I didn't."

Phil pulled his ear. "It was broken—or I've gone completely screwy. Let's have a look at it."

Ben was dressed in pajamas and bathrobe. He slid up the pajama leg, and exposed a shin that was pink and healthy. He pounded it with his fist. "See that? Not even a bruise."

"Hmm—You haven't been out long, Ben. Just since last night. Maybe ten or eleven hours."

"Huh?"

"That's right."

"Impossible."

"Maybe so. Let's eat breakfast."

They ate in thoughtful silence, each under pressing necessity of taking stock and reaching some reasonable reorientation. Toward the end of the meal they all happened to look up at once. Phil broke the silence,

"Well . . . How about it?"

"I've just doped it out," volunteered Joan. "We all died in the snow storm and went to Heaven. Pass the marmalade, will you, please?"

"That can't be right," objected Phil, as he complied, "else Ben wouldn't be here. He led a sinful life. But seriously, things have happened which require explanation. Let's tick 'em off: One; Ben breaks a leg last night, it's all healed this morning."

"Wait a minute—are we sure he broke his leg?"

"I'm sure. Furthermore, our host acted as if he thought so too—else why did he bother to carry him? Two; our host has direct perception, or an uncanny knowledge of the mountainside."

"Speaking of direct perception," said Joan, "have either of you tried to look around you and size up the place?"

"No, why?"—"Neither have I."

"Don't bother to. I tried, and it can't be done. I can't perceive past the walls of the room."

"Hmm—we'll put that down as point three. Four; our host says that his name is Ambrose Bierce. Does he mean that he is *the* Ambrose Bierce? You know who Ambrose Bierce was, Joan?"

"Of course I do—I got eddication. He disappeared sometime before I was born."

"That's right—at the time of the outbreak of the first World War. If this is the same man, he must be over a hundred years old."

"He didn't look that old by forty years."

"Well, we'll put it down for what it's worth. Point five; —We'll make this one an omnibus point—why does our host live up here? How come this strange mixture of luxury hotel and cliff dwellers cave anyhow? How can one old man run such a joint? Say, have either of you seen anyone else around the place?"

"I haven't," said Ben. "Someone woke me, but I think it was Ambrose."

"I have," offered Joan. "It was a woman who woke me. She offered me this dress."

"Mrs. Bierce, maybe?"

"I don't think so—she wasn't more than thirty-five. I didn't really get acquainted—she was gone before I was wide awake."

126

Phil looked from Joan to Ben. "Well, what have we got? Add it up and give us an answer."

"Good morning, young friends!" It was Bierce, standing in the doorway, his rich, virile voice resounding around the many-sided room. The three started as if caught doing something improper.

Coburn recovered first. He stood up and bowed. "Good morning, sir. I believe that you saved my life. I hope to be able to show my gratitude."

Bierce bowed formally. "What service I did I enjoyed doing, sir. I hope that you are all rested?"

"Yes, thank you, and pleasantly filled from your table."

"That is good. Now, if I may join you, we can discuss what you wish to do next. Is it your pleasure to leave, or may we hope to have your company for a while longer?"

"I suppose," said Joan, rather nervously, "that we should get started down as soon as possible. How is the weather?"

"The weather is fair, but you are welcome to remain here as long as you like. Perhaps you would like to see the rest of our home and meet the other members of our household?"

"Oh, I think that would be lovely!"

"It will be my pleasure, ma'am."

"As a matter of fact, Mr. Bierce—" Phil leaned forward a little, his face and manner serious. "—we are quite anxious to see more of your place here and to know more about you. We were speaking of it when you came in."

"Curiosity is natural and healthy. Please ask any question you wish."

"Well—" Phil plunged in. "Ben had a broken leg last night. Or didn't he? It's well this morning."

"He did indeed have a broken leg. It was healed in the night."

Coburn cleared his throat. "Mr. Bierce, my name is Coburn. I am a physician and surgeon, but my knowledge does not extend to such healing as that. Will you tell me more about it?"

"Certainly. You are familiar with regeneration as practiced by the lower life forms. The principle used is the same, but it is consciously controlled by the will and the rate of healing is accelerated. I placed you in hypnosis last night, then surrendered control to one of our surgeons who directed your mind in exerting its own powers to heal its body."

Coburn looked baffled. Bierce continued, "There is really nothing startling about it. The mind and will have always the possibility of complete domination over the body. Our operator simply directs your will to master its body. The technique is simple; you may learn it, if you wish. I assure you that to learn it is easier than to explain it in our cumbersome and imperfect language. I spoke of mind and will as if they were separate. Language forced me to that ridiculous misstatement. There is neither mind, nor will, as entities; there is only—" His voice stopped. Ben felt a blow within his mind like the shock of a sixteen inch rifle, yet it was painless and gentle. What ever it was, it was as alive as a hummingbird, or a struggling kitten, yet it was calm and untroubled.

He saw Joan nodding her head in agreement, her eyes on Bierce.

Bierce went on in his gentle, resonant voice. "Was there any other matter troubling any one of you?"

"Why, yes, Mr. Bierce," replied Joan, "several things. What is this place where we are?"

"It is my home, and the home of several of my friends. You will understand more about us as you become better acquainted with us."

"Thank you. It is difficult for me to understand how such a community could exist on this mountaintop without a being a matter of common knowledge."

"We have taken certain precautions, ma'am, to avoid notoriety. Our reasons, and the precautions they inspired will become evident to you."

"One more question; this is rather personal; you may ignore it if you like. Are you the Ambrose Bierce who disappeared a good many years ago?"

"I am. I first came up here in 1880 in search of a cure for asthma. I retired here in 1914 because I wished to avoid direct contact with the tragic world events which I saw coming and was powerless to stop." He spoke with some reluctance, as if the subject were distasteful, and turned the conversation. "Perhaps you would like to meet some of my friends now?"

The apartments extended for a hundred yards along the face of the mountain and for unmeasured distances into the mountain. The thirty-odd persons in residence were far from crowded; there were many rooms not in use. In the course of the morning Bierce introduced them to most of the inhabitants.

They seemed to be of all sorts and ages and of several nationalities. Most of them were occupied in one way, or another, usually with some form of research, or with creative art. At least Bierce assured them in several cases that research was in progress—cases in which no apparatus, no recording device, nothing was evident to indicate scientific research.

Once they were introduced to a group of three, two women and a man, who were surrounded by the physical evidence of their work—biological research. But the circumstances were still confusing; two of the trio sat quietly by, doing nothing, while the third labored at a bench. Bierce explained that they were doing some delicate experiments in the possibility of activating artificial colloids. Ben inquired,

"Are the other two observing the work?"

Bierce shook his head. "Oh, no. They are all three engaged actively in the work, but at this particular stage they find it expedient to let three brains in rapport direct one set of hands."

Rapport, it developed, was the usual method of collaboration. Bierce had led them into a room occupied by six persons. One or two of them looked up and nodded, but did not speak. Bierce motioned for the three to come away. "They were engaged in a particularly difficult piece of reconstruction; it would not be polite to disturb them."

"But Mr. Bierce," Phil commented, "two of them were playing chess."

"Yes. They did not need that part of their brains, so they left it out of rapport. Nevertheless they were very busy."

It was easier to see what the creative artists were doing. In two instances, however, their methods were startling. Bierce had taken them to the studio of a little gnome of a man, a painter in oil, who was introduced simply as Charles. He seemed glad to see them and chatted vivaciously, without ceasing his work. He was doing, with meticulous realism but with a highly romantic effect, a study of a young girl dancing, a wood nymph, against a pine forest background.

The young people each made appropriate appreciative comments, Coburn commented that it was remarkable that he should be able to be so accurate in his anatomical detail without the aid of a model.

"But I have a model," he answered. "She was here last week. See?" He glanced toward the empty model's throne. Coburn and his companions followed the glance, and saw, poised on the throne, a young girl, obviously the model for the picture, frozen in the action of the painting. She was as real as bread and butter.

Charles glanced away. The model's throne was again vacant.

The second instance was not so dramatic, but still less comprehensible. They had met, and chatted with, a Mrs. Draper, a comfortable, matronly soul, who knitted and rocked as they talked. After they had left her Phil inquired about her.

"She is possibly our most able and talented artist," Bierce told him.

"In what field?"

Bierce's shaggy eyebrows came together as he chose his words. "I don't believe I can tell you adequately at this time. She composes moods—arranges emotional patterns in harmonic sequences. It's our most advanced and our most completely human form of art, and yet, until you have experienced it, it is very difficult for me to tell you about it."

"How is it possible to *arrange* emotions?"

"Your great grandfather no doubt thought it impossible to record music. We have a technique for it. You will understand later."

"Is Mrs. Draper the only one who does this?"

"Oh, no. Most of us try our hand at it. It's our favorite art form. I work at it myself but my efforts aren't popular—too gloomy."

The three talked it over that night in the living room they had first entered. This suite had been set aside for their use, and Bierce had left them with the simple statement that he would call on them on the morrow.

They felt a pressing necessity to exchange views, and yet each was reluctant to express opinion. Phil broke the silence.

"What kind of people are these? They make me feel as if I were a child who had wandered in where adults were working, but that they were too polite to put me out."

"Speaking of working—there's something odd about the way they work. I don't mean what it is they do—that's odd, too, but it's something else, something about their attitude, or the tempo at which they work."

"I know what you mean, Ben," Joan agreed, "they are busy all the time, and yet they act as if they had all eternity to finish it. Bierce was like that when he was strapping up your leg. They never hurry." She turned to Phil. "What are you frowning about?"

"I don't know. There is something else we haven't mentioned yet. They have a lot of special talents, sure, but we three know something about special talents—that ought not to confuse us. But there is something else about them that is *different*."

The other two agreed with him but could offer no help. Sometime later Joan said that she was going to bed and left the room. The two men stayed for a last cigaret.

Joan stuck her head back in the room. "I know what it is that is so different about these people," she anounced,—"They are so *alive*."

CHAPTER SIX

Ichabod!

PHILIP HUXLEY WENT TO BED and to sleep as usual. From there on nothing was usual.

He became aware that he was inhabiting another's body, thinking with another's mind. The Other was aware of Huxley, but did not share Huxley's thoughts.

The Other was at home, a home never experienced by Huxley, yet familiar. It was on Earth, incredibly beautiful, each tree and shrub fitting into the landscape as if placed there in the harmonic scheme of an artist. The house grew out of the ground.

The Other left the house with his wife and prepared to leave for the capital of the planet. Huxley thought of the destination as a "capital" yet he knew that the idea of government imposed by force was foreign to the nature of these people. The "capital" was merely the accustomed meeting place of the group whose advice was followed in matters affecting the entire race.

The Other and his wife, accompanied by Huxley's awareness, stepped into the garden, shot straight up into the air, and sped over the countryside, flying hand in hand. The country was green, fertile, parklike, dotted with occasional buildings, but nowhere did Huxley see the jammed masses of a city.

They passed rapidly over a large body of water, perhaps as large as the modern Mediterranean, and landed in a clearing in a grove of olive trees.

The Young Men—so Huxley thought of them—demanded a sweeping change in custom, first, that the ancient knowledge should henceforth be the reward of ability rather than common birthright, and second, that the greater should rule the lesser. Loki urged their case, his arrogant face upthrust and crowned with bright red hair. He spoke in words, a method which disturbed Huxley's host, telepathic rapport being the natural method of mature discussion. But Loki had closed his mind to it.

Jove answered him, speaking for all:

"My son, your words seem vain and without serious meaning. We can not tell your true meaning, for you and your brothers have decided to shut your minds to us. You ask that the ancient knowledge be made the reward of ability. Has it not always been so? Does our cousin, the ape, fly through the air? Is not the infant soul bound by hunger, and sleep, and the ills of the flesh? Can the oriole level the mountain with his glance? The powers of our kind that set us apart from the younger spirits on this planet are now exercised by those who possess the ability, and none other. How can we make that so which is already so?

"You demand that the greater shall rule the lesser. Is it not so now? Has it not always been so? Are you ordered about by the babe at the breast? Does the waving of the grass cause the wind? What dominion do you desire other than over yourself? Do you wish to tell your brother when to sleep and when to eat? If so, to what purpose?"

Vulcan broke in while the old man was still speaking. Huxley felt a stir of shocked repugnance go through the council at this open disregard of good manners.

"Enough of this playing with words. We know what we want; you know what we want. We are determined to take it, council or no. We are sick of this sheeplike existence. We are tired of this sham equality. We intend to put on end to it. We are the strong and the able, the natural leaders of mankind. The rest shall follow us and serve us, as is the natural order of things."

Jove's eyes rested thoughtfully on Vulcan's crooked leg. "You should let me heal that twisted limb, my son."

"No one can heal my limb!"

"No. No one but yourself. And until you heal the twist in your mind, you can not heal the twist in your limb."

"There is no twist in my mind!"

"Then heal your limb."

The young man stirred uneasily. They could see that Vulcan was making a fool of himself. Mercury separated himself from the group and came forward.

"Hear me, Father. We do not purpose warring with you. Rather it is our intention to add to your glory. Declare yourself king under the sun. Let us be your legates to extend your rule to every creature that walks, or crawls, or swims. Let us create for you the pageantry of dominion, the glory of conquest. Let us conserve the ancient knowledge for those who understand it, and provide instead for lesser beings the drama they need. There is no reason why every way should be open to everyone. Rather, if the many serve the few, then will our combined efforts speed us faster on our way, to the profit of master and servant alike. Lead us, Father! Be our King!"

Slowly the elder man shook his head. "Not so. There is no knowledge, other than knowledge of oneself, and that should be free to every man who has the wit to learn. There is no power, other than the power to rule oneself, and that can be neither given, nor taken away. As for the poetry of empire, that has all been done before. There is no need to do it again. If such romance amuses you, enjoy it in the records—there is no need to bloody the planet again."

"That is the final word of the council, Father?"

"That is our final word." He stood up and gathered his robe about him, signifying that the session had ended. Mercury shrugged his shoulders and joined his fellows.

There was one more session of the council—the last—called to decide what to do about the ultimatum of the Young Men. Not every member of the council thought alike; they were as diverse as many group of human beings. They *were* human beings—not supermen. Some held out for opposing the Young Men with all the forces at their command—translate them to another dimension, wipe their minds clean, even crush them by major force.

But to use force on the Young Men was contrary to their whole philosophy. "Free will is the primary good of the Cosmos. Shall we degrade, destroy, all that we have worked for by subverting the will of even one man?"

Huxley became aware that these Elders had no need to remain on Earth. They were anxious to move on to another place, the nature of which escaped Huxley, save that it was not of the time and space he knew.

The issue was this: Had they done what they could to help the incompletely developed balance of the race? Were they justified in abdicating?

The decision was yes, but a female member of the council, whose name, it seemed to Huxley, was Demeter, argued that records should be left to help those who survived the inevitable collapse. "It is true that each member of the race must make himself strong, must make himself wise. We cannot make them wise. Yet, after famine and war and hatred have stalked the earth, should there not be a message, telling them of their heritage?"

The council agreed, and Huxley's host, recorder for the council, was ordered to prepare records and to leave them for those who would come after. Jove added an injunction:

"Bind the force patterns so that they shall not dissipate while this planet endures. Place them where they will outlast any local convulsions of the crust, so that some at least will carry down through time."

So ended that dream. But Huxley did not wake—he started at once to dream another dream, not through the eyes of another, but rather as if he watched a stereo-movie, every scene of which was familiar to him.

The first dream, for all its tragic content, had not affected

133

him tragically; but throughout the second dream he was oppressed by a feeling of heartbreak and overpowering weariness.

After the abdication of the Elders, the Young Men carried out their purpose, they established their rule. By fire and sword, searing rays and esoteric forces, chicanery and deception. Convinced of their destiny to rule, they convinced themselves that the end justified the means.

The end was empire—Mu, mightiest of empires and mother of empires.

Huxley saw her in her prime and felt almost that the Young Men had been right—for she was glorious! The heart-choking magnificence filled his eyes with tears; he mourned for the glory, the beautiful breathtaking glory that was hers, and is no more.

Gargantuan silent liners in her skies, broadbeamed vessels at her wharves, loaded with grain and hides and spices, procession of priest and acolyte and humble believer, pomp and pageantry of power—he saw her intricate patterns of beauty and mourned her passing.

But in her swelling power there was decay. Inevitably Atlantis, her richest colony, grew to political maturity and was irked by subordinate status. Schism and apostasy, disaffection and treason, brought harsh retaliation—and new rebellion.

Rebellions rose, were crushed. At last one rose that was not crushed. In less than a month two-thirds of the people of the globe were dead; the remainder were racked by disease and hunger, and left with germ plasm damaged by the forces they had loosed.

But priests still held the ancient knowledge.

Not priests secure in mind and proud of their trust, but priests hunted and fearful, who had seen their hierarchy totter. There were such priests on both sides—and they unchained forces compared with which the previous fighting had been gentle.

The forces disturbed the isostatic balance of the earth's crust.

Mu shuddered and sank some two thousand feet. Tidal waves met at her middle, broke back, surged twice around the globe, climbed the Chinese plains, lapped the feet of Alta Himalaya.

Atlantis shook and rumbled and split for three days before the water covered it. A few escaped by air, to land on ground still wet with the ooze of exposed seabottom, or on peaks high enough to fend off the tidal waves. There they had still to wring a living from the bare soil, with minds unused to primitive art—but some survived.

Of Mu there was not a trace. As for Atlantis, a few islands, mountaintops short days before, marked the spot. Waters rolled over the twin Towers of the Sun and fish swam through the gardens of the viceroy.

The woebegone feeling which had pursued Huxley now overwhelmed him. He seemed to hear a voice in his head:

"Woe! Cursed be Loki! Cursed be Venus! Cursed be Vulcan! Thrice cursed am I, their apostate servant, Orab, Archpriest of the Isles of the Blessed. Woe is me! Even as I curse I long for Mu, mighty and sinful. Twenty-one years ago, seeking a place to die, on this mountaintop I stumbled on this record of the mighty ones who were before us. Twenty-one years I have labored to make the record complete, searching the dim recesses of my mind for knowledge long unused, roaming the other planes for knowledge I never had. Now in the eight hundred and ninety-second year of my life, and of the destruction of Mu the three hundred and fifth, I, Orab, return to my fathers."

Huxley was very happy to wake up.

CHAPTER SEVEN

"The Fathers Have Eaten Sour Grapes, and the Children's Teeth are Set on Edge."

BEN WAS IN THE LIVING ROOM when Phil came in to breakfast. Joan arrived almost on Phil's heels. There were shadows under her eyes and she looked unhappy. Ben spoke in a tone that was almost surly,

"What's troubling you, Joan? You look like the wrath to come."

"Please, Ben," she answered, in a tired voice, "don't heckle me. I've had bad dreams all night."

"That so? Sorry—but if you think you had bad dreams all night, you should have seen the cute little nightmares I've been riding."

Phil looked at the two of them. "Listen—have you both had odd dreams all night?"

"Wasn't that what we were just saying?" Ben sounded exasperated.

"What did you dream about?"

Neither one answered him.

"Wait a minute. I had some very strange dreams myself." He pulled his notebook out of a pocket and tore out three sheets. "I want to find out something. Will you each write

135

down what your dreams were about, before anyone says anything more? Here's a pencil, Joan."

They balked a little, but complied.

"Read them aloud, Joan."

She picked up Ben's slip and read, " 'I dreamed that your theory about the degeneracy of the human race was perfectly correct.' "

She put it down and picked up Phil's slip. " 'dreamt that I was present at the Twilight of the Gods, and that I saw the destruction of Mu and Atlantis.' "

There was dead silence as she took the last slip, her own.

"My dream was about how the people destroyed themselves by rebelling against Odin."

Ben was first to commit himself. "Anyone of those slips could have applied to my dreams." Joan nodded. Phil got up again, went out, and returned at once with his diary. He opened it and handed it to Joan.

"Kid, will you read that aloud—starting with 'June sixteenth'?"

She read it through slowly, without looking up from the pages. Phil waited until she had finished and closed the book before speaking. "Well," he said, "well?"

Ben crushed out a cigaret which had burned down to his fingers. "It's a remarkably accurate description of my dream, except that the elder you call Jove, I thought of as Ahuramazda."

"And I thought Loki was Lucifer."

"You're both right," agreed Phil. "I don't remember any spoken names for any of them. It just seemed that I knew what their names were."

"Me, too."

"Say," interjected Ben, "we are talking as if these dreams were real—as if we had all been to the same movie."

Phil turned on him. "Well, what do *you* think?"

"Oh, the same as you do, I guess. I'm stumped. Does anybody mind if I eat breakfast—or drink some coffee, at least?"

Bierce came in before they had a chance to talk it over after breakfast—by tacit consent they had held their tongues during a sketchy meal.

"Good morning, ma'am. Good morning, gentlemen."

"Good morning, Mr. Bierce."

"I see," he said, searching their faces, "that none of you look very happy this morning. That is not surprising; no one does immediately after experiencing the records."

Ben pushed back his chair and leaned across the table at Bierce. "Those dreams were deliberately arranged for us?"

"Yes, indeed—but we were sure that you were ready to profit by them. But I have come to ask you to interview the

136

Senior. If you can hold your questions for him, it will be simpler."

"The Senior?"

"You haven't met him as yet. It is the way we refer to the one we judge best fitted to co-ordinate our activities."

Ephraim Howe had the hills of New England in his face, lean gnarled cabinet-maker's hands. He was not young. There was courtly grace in his lanky figure. Everything about him —the twinkle in his pale blue eyes, the clasp of his hand, his drawl—bespoke integrity.

"Sit yourselves down," he said, "I'll come straight to the point"—he called it 'pint.' "You've been exposed to a lot of curious things and you've a right to know why. You've seen the Ancient Records now—part of 'em. I'll tell you how this institution came about, what it's for, and why you are going to be asked to join us.

"Wait a minute, Waaaait a minute," he added, holding up a hand. "Don't say anything just yet . . ."

When Fra Junipero Serra first laid eyes on Mount Shasta in 1781, the Indians told him it was a holy place, only for medicine men. He assured them that he was a medicine man, serving a greater Master, and to keep face, dragged his sick, frail old body up to the snow line, where he slept before returning.

The dream he had there—of the Garden of Eden, the Sin, the Fall, and the Deluge—convinced him that it was indeed a holy place. He returned to San Francisco, planning to found a mission at Shasta. But there was too much for one old man to do—so many souls to save, so many mouths to feed. He surrendered his soul to rest two years later, but laid an injunction on a fellow monk to carry out his intention.

It is recorded that this friar left the northernmost mission in 1785 and did not return.

The Indians fed the holy man who lived on the mountain until 1843, by which time he had gathered about him a group of neophytes, three Indians, a Russian, a Yankee mountainman. The Russian carried on after the death of the friar until joined by a Chinese, fled from his indenture. The Chinese made more progress in a few weeks than the Russian had in half of a lifetime; the Russian gladly surrendered first place to him.

The Chinese was still there over a hundred years later, though long since retired from administration. He tutored in esthetics and humor.

"And this establishment has just one purpose," continued Ephraim Howe. "We aim to see to it that Mu and Atlantis

137

don't happen again. Everything that the Young Men stood for, we are against.

"We see the history of the world as a series of crises in a conflict between two opposing philosophies. Ours is based on the notion that life, consciousness, intelligence, ego is the important thing in the world." For an instant only he touched them telepathically; they felt again the vibrantly alive thing that Ambrose Bierce had showed them and been unable to define in words. "That puts us in conflict with every force that tends to destroy, deaden, degrade the human spirit, or to make it act contrary to its nature. We see another crisis approaching; we need recruits. You've been selected.

"This crisis has been growing on us since Napoleon. Europe has gone, and Asia—surrendered to authoritarianism, nonsense like the 'leader principle,' totalitarianism, all the bonds placed on liberty which treat men as so many economic and political units with no importance as individuals. No dignity—do what you're told, believe what you are told, and shut your mouth! Workers, soldiers, breeding units . . .

"If *that* were the object of life, there would have been no point in including consciousness in the scheme at all!

"This continent," Howe went on, "has been a refuge of freedom, a place where the soul could grow. But the forces that killed enlightenment in the rest of the world are spreading here. Little by little they have whittled away at human liberty and human dignity. A repressive law, a bullying school board, a blind dogma to be accepted under pain of persecution —doctrines that will shackle men and put blinders on their eyes so that they will never regain their lost heritage.

"We need help to fight it."

Huxley stood up. "You can count on us."

Before Joan and Coburn could speak the Senior interposed. "Don't answer yet. Go back to your chambers and think about it. Sleep on it. We'll talk again."

CHAPTER EIGHT

"Precept Upon Precept . . ."

HAD THE PLACE ON MOUNT SHASTA been a university and possessed a catalog (which it did not), the courses offered therein might have included the following:

TELEPATHY. Basic course required of all students not qualified by examination. Practical instruction up to and including rapport. Prerequisite in all departments. Laboratory.

RATIOCINATION, I, II, III, IV. R.I. Memory. R.II. Perception; clairvoyance, clairaudience, discretion of mass, -time, -and-space, non-mathematical relation, order, and structure, harmonic form and interval.
R.III. Dual and parallel thought processes. Detachment.
R.IV. Meditation (seminar)

AUTOKINETICS. Discrete kinesthesia. Endocrine control with esp. application to the affective senses and to suppression of fatigue, regeneration, transformation (clinical aspects of lycanthropy), sex determination, inversion, autoanaesthesia, rejuvenation.

TELEKINETICS. Life-mass-space-time continua. Prerequisite; autokinetics. Teleportation and general action at a distance. Projection. Dynamics. Statics. Orientation.

HISTORY. Courses by arrangement. Special discussions of psychometry with reference to telepathic records, and of metempsychosis. Evaluation is a prerequisite for all courses in this department.

HUMAN ESTHETICS. Seminar. Autokinetics and technique of telepathic recording (psychometry) a prerequisite.

HUMAN ETHICS. Seminar. Given concurrently with all other courses. Consult with instructor.

Perhaps some of the value of the instruction would have been lost had it been broken up into disjointed courses as outlined above. In any case the adepts on Mount Shasta could and did instruct in all these subjects. Huxley, Coburn, and Joan Freeman learned from tutors who led them to teach themselves, and they took it as an eel seeks the sea, with a sense of returning home after a long absence.

All three made rapid progress; being possessed of rudimentary perception and some knowledge of telepathy, their in-

139

structors could teach them directly. First they learned to control their bodies. They regained the control over each function, each muscle, each tissue, each gland, that a man should possess, but has largely forgotten—save a few obscure students in the far east. There was a deep, welling delight in willing the body to obey and having it comply. They became intimately aware of their bodies, but their bodies no longer tyrannized them. Fatigue, hunger, cold, pain—these things no longer drove them, but rather were simply useful signals that a good engine needed attention.

Nor did the engine need as much attention as before; the body was driven by a mind that knew precisely both the capacity and its limitations. Furthermore, through understanding their bodies, they were enabled to increase those capacities to their full potential. A week of sustained activity, without rest, or food, or water, was as easy as a morning's work had been. As for mental labor, it did not cease at all, save when they willed it—despite sleep, digestive languor, ennui, external stimuli, or muscular activity.

The greatest delight was levitation.

To fly through the air, to hang suspended in the quiet heart of a cloud, to sleep, like Mohamet, floating between ceiling and floor—these were sensuous delights unexpected, and never before experienced, except in dreams, dimly. Joan in particular drank this new joy with lusty abandon. Once she remained away two days, never setting foot to ground, sharing the sky and wind and swallow, the icy air of the heights smoothing her bright body. She dove and soared, looped and spiralled, and dropped, a dead weight, knees drawn up to forehead, from stratosphere to treetop.

During the night she paced a transcontinental plane, flying unseen above it for a thousand miles. When she grew bored with this, she pressed her face for a moment against the one lighted port of the plane, and looked inside. The startled wholesale merchant who stared back into her eyes thought that he had been vouchsafed a glimpse of an angel. He went promptly from the airport of his destination to the office of his lawyer, who drew up for him a will establishing scholarships for divinity students.

Huxley found it difficult to learn to levitate. His inquiring mind demanded a reason why the will should apparently be able to set at naught the inexorable "law" of gravitation, and his doubt dissipated his volition. His tutor reasoned with him patiently.

"You know that intangible will can affect the course of mass in the continuum; you experience it whenever you move your hand. Are you powerless to move your hand because you can not give a full rational explanation of the mystery? Life has power to affect matter; you know that—you have

140

experienced it directly. It is a fact. Now there is no 'why' about any fact in the unlimited sense in which you ask the question. There it stands, serene, demonstrating itself. One may observe relations between facts, the relations being other facts, but to pursue those relations back to final meanings is not possible to a mind which is itself relative. First you tell me *why* you *are* . . . then I will tell you why levitation is possible.

"Now come," he continued, place yourself in rapport with me, and try to feel how I do, as I levitate."

Phil tried again. "I don't get it," he concluded miserably. "Look down."

Phil did so, gasped, and fell three feet to the floor. That night he joined Ben and Joan in a flight over the High Sierras.

Their tutor enjoyed with quiet amusement the zest with which they entered into the sport made possible by the newly acquired mastery of their bodies. He knew that their pleasure was natural and healthy, suited to their stage of development, and he knew that they would soon learn, of themselves, its relative worth, and then be ready to turn their minds to more serious work.

"Oh, no, Brother Junipero wasn't the only man to stumble on the records," Charles assured them, talking as he painted. "You must have noticed how high places have significance in the religions of every race. Some of them must be repositories of the ancient records."

"Don't you know for certain?" asked Phil.

"Indeed yes, in many cases—Alta Himalaya, for example. I was speaking of what an intelligent man might infer from matters of common knowledge. Consider how many mountains are of prime importance in as many different religions. Mount Olympus, Popocatepetl, Mauna Loa, Everest, Sinai, Tai Shan, Ararat, Fujiyama, several places in the Andes. And in every religion there are accounts of a teacher bringing back inspired messages from high places—Gautama, Jesus, Joseph Smith, Confucius, Moses. They all come down from high places and tell stories of creation, and downfall, and redemption.

"Of all the old accounts the best is found in Genesis. Making allowance for the fact that it was first written in the language of uncivilized nomads, it is an exact, careful account."

Huxley poked Coburn in the ribs. "How do you like that, my skeptical friend?" Then to Charles, "Ben has been a devout atheist since he first found out that Santa Claus wore false whiskers; it hurts him to have his fondest doubts overturned."

Coburn grinned, unperturbed. "Take it easy, son. I can express my own doubts, unassisted. You've brought to mind

141

another matter, Charles. Some of these mountains don't seem old enough to have been used for the ancient records—Shasta, for example. It's volcanic and seems a little new for the purpose."

Charles went rapidly ahead with his painting as he replied. "You are right. It seems likely that Orab made copies of the original record which he found, and placed the copies with his supplement on several high places around the globe. And it is possible that others after Orab, but long before our time, read the records and moved them for safekeeping. The copy that Junipero Serra found may have been here a mere twenty thousand years, or so."

CHAPTER NINE

Fledglings Fly

"WE COULD HANG AROUND HERE for fifty years, learning new things, but in the mean time we wouldn't be getting anywhere. I, for one, am ready to go back." Phil crushed out a cigaret and looked around at his two friends.

Coburn pursed his lips and slowly nodded his head. "I feel the same way, Phil. There is no limit to what we could learn here, of course, but there comes a time when you just have to use some of the things you learn, or it just boils up inside. I think we had better tell the Senior, and get about doing it."

Joan nodded vigorously. "Uh huh. I think so, too. There's work to be done, and the place to do it is Western U.—not up here in Never-Never land. Boy, I can hardly wait to see old Brinckley's face when we get through with him!"

Huxley sought out the mind of Ephraim Howe. The other two waited for him to confer, courteously refraining from attempting to enter the telepathic conversation. "He says he had been expecting to hear from us, and that he intends to make it a full conference. He'll meet us here."

"Full conference? Everybody on the mountain?"

"Everybody—on the mountain, or not. I gather it's customary when new members decide what their work will be."

"Whew!" exclaimed Joan, "that gives me stage fright just to think about it. Who's going to speak for us? It won't be little Joan."

"How about you, Ben?"

"Well . . . if you wish."

"Take over."

They meshed into rapport. As long as they remained so, Ben's voice would express the combined thought of the trio. Ephraim Howe entered alone, but they were aware that he was in rapport with, and spokesman for, not only the adepts on the mountainside, but also the two-hundred-odd full-geniuses scattered about the country.

The conference commenced with direct mind-to-mind exchange:

—*"We feel that it is time we were at work. We have not learned all that there is to learn, it is true; nevertheless, we need to use our present knowledge."*

—*"That is well and entirely as it should be, Benjamin. You have learned all that we can teach you at this time. Now you must take what you have learned out into the world, and use it, in order that knowledge may mature into wisdom."*

—*"Not only for that reason do we wish to leave, but for another more urgent. As you yourself have taught us, the crisis approaches. We want to fight it."*

—*"How do you propose to fight the forces bringing on the crisis?"*

—*"Well . . ."* Ben did not use the word, but the delay in his thought produced the impression. *"As we see it, in order to make men free, free so that they may develop as men and not as animals; it is necessary that we undo what the Young Men did. The Young Men refused to permit any but their own select few to share in the racial heritage of ancient knowledge. For men again to become free and strong and independent it is necessary to return to each man his ancient knowledge and his ancient powers."*

—*"That is true; what do you intend to do about it?"*

—*"We will go out and tell about it. We all three are in the educational system; we can make ourselves heard—I, in the medical school at Western; Phil and Joan in the department of psychology. With the training you have given us we can overturn the traditional ideas in short order. We can start a renaissance in education that will prepare the way for everyone to receive the wisdom that you, our elders, can offer them."*

—*"Do you think that it will be as simple as that?"*

—*"Why not? Oh, we don't expect it to be simple. We know that we will run head on into some of the most cherished misconceptions of everyone, but we can use that very fact to help. It will be spectacular; we can get publicity through it that will call attention to our work. You have taught us enough that we can prove that we are right. For example— suppose we put on a public demonstration of levitation, and proved before thousands of people that human mind could do the things we know it can? Suppose we said that anyone could learn such things who first learned the techniques of*

143

telepathy? Why, in a year, or two, the whole nation could be taught telepathy, and be ready for the reading of the records, and all that that implies!"

Howe's mind was silent for several long minutes—no message reached them. The three stirred uneasily under his thoughtful, sober gaze. Finally,

—*"If it were as simple as that, would we not have done it before?"*

It was the turn of the three to be silent. Howe continued kindly,—*"Speak up, my children. Do not be afraid. Tell us your thoughts freely. You will not offend us."*

The thought that Coburn sent in answer was hesitant—*"It is difficult . . . Many of you are very old, and we know that all of you are wise. Nevertheless, it seems to us, in our youth, that you have waited overly long in acting. We feel— we feel that you have allowed the pursuit of understanding to sap your will to action. From our standpoint, you have waited from year to year, perfecting an organization that will never be perfected, while the storm that overturns the world is gathering its force."*

The elders pondered before Ephraim Howe answered.— *"It may be that you are right, dearly beloved children, yet it does not seem so to us. We have not attempted to place the ancient knowledge in the hands of all men because few are ready for it. It is no more safe in childish minds than matches in childish hands.*

—*"And yet . . . you may be right. Mark Twain thought so, and was given permission to tell all that he had learned. He did so, writing so that anyone ready for the knowledge could understand. No one did. In desperation he set forth specifically how to become telepathic. Still no one took him seriously. The more seriously he spoke, the more his readers laughed. He died embittered.*

—*"We would not have you believe that we have done nothing. This republic, with its uncommon emphasis on personal freedom and human dignity, would not have endured as long as it has had we not helped. We chose Lincoln. Oliver Wendell Holmes was one of us. Walt Whitman was our beloved brother. In a thousand ways we have supplied help, when needed, to avert a setback toward slavery and darkness."*

The thought paused, then continued. —*"Yet each must act as he sees it. It is still your decision to do this?"*

Ben spoke aloud, in a steady voice, "It is!"

—*"So let it be! Do you remember the history of Salem?"*

—*"Salem? Where the witchcraft trials were held? . . . Do you mean to warn us that we may be persecuted as witches?"*

—*"No. There are no laws against witchcraft today, of course. It would be better if there were. We hold no monopoly on the power of knowledge; do not expect an easy victory. Be-*

*ware of those who hold some portion of the ancient knowledge
and use it to a base purpose—witches . . . black magicians!"*

The conference concluded and rapport loosed, Ephraim
Howe shook hands solemnly all around and bade them goodby.

"I envy you kids," he said, "going off like Jack the Giant
Killer to tackle the whole educational system. You've got
your work cut out for you. Do you remember what Mark
Twain said? 'God made an idiot for practice, then he made a
school board.' Still, I'd like to come along."

"Why don't you, sir?"

"Eh? No, 'twouldn't do. I don't really believe in your plan.
F'r instance—it was frequently a temptation during the years
I spent peddlin' hardware in the State of Maine to show
people better ways of doing things. But I didn't do it; people
are used to paring knives and ice cream freezers, and they
won't thank you to show them how to get along without them,
just by the power of the mind. Not all at once, anyhow. They'd
read you out of meetin'—and lynch you, too, most probably.

"Still, I'll be keeping an eye on you."

Joan reached up and kissed him good-bye. They left.

CHAPTER TEN

Lion's Mouth

PHIL PICKED HIS LARGEST CLASS to make the demonstration
which was to get the newspapers interested in them.

They had played safe to the extent of getting back to Los
Angeles and started with the fall semester before giving anyone cause to suspect that they possessed powers out of
ordinary. Joan had been bound over not to levitate, not to
indulge in practical jokes involving control over inanimate
objects, not to startle strangers with weird abilities of any
sort. She had accepted the injunctions meekly, so meekly that
Coburn claimed to be worried.

"It's not normal," he objected. "She can't grow up as fast
as all that. Let me see your tongue, my dear."

"Pooh," she answered, displaying that member in a most
undiagnostic manner, "Master Ling said I was further advanced along the Way than either one of you."

" 'The heathen Chinee is peculiar.' He was probably just
encouraging you to grow up. Seriously, Phil, hadn't we better
put her into a deep hypnosis and scoot her back up the
mountain for diagnosis and readjustment?"

"Ben Coburn, you cast an eye in my direction and I'll bung it out!"

Phil built up to his key demonstration with care. His lectures were sufficiently innocuous that he could afford to have his head of department drop in without fear of reprimand or interference. But the combined effect was to prepare the students emotionally for what was to come. Carefully selected assignments for collateral reading heightened his chances.

"Hypnosis is a subject but vaguely understood," he began his lecture on the selected day, "and formerly classed with witchcraft, magic, and so forth, as a silly superstition. But it is a commonplace thing today and easily demonstrated. Consequently the most conservative psychologists must recognize its existence and try to observe its characteristics." He went on cheerfully uttering bromides and commonplaces, while he sized up the emotional attitude of the class.

When he felt that they were ready to accept the ordinary phenomena of hypnosis without surprise, he called Joan, who had attended for the purpose, up to the front of the room. She went easily into a state of light hypnosis. They ran quickly through the small change of hypnotic phenomena—catalepsy, compulsion, post-hypnotic suggestion—while he kept up a running chatter about the relation between the minds of the operator and the subject, the possibility of direct telepathic control, the Rhine experiments, and similar matters, orthodox in themselves, but close to the borderline of heterodox thought.

Then he offered to attempt to reach the mind of the subject telepathically.

Each student was invited to write something on a slip of paper. A volunteer floor committee collected the slips, and handed them to Huxley one at a time. He solemnly went through the hocus-pocus of glancing at each one, while Joan read them off as his eyes rested on them. She stumbled convincingly once or twice. —"Nice work, kid." —"Thanks, pal. "Can't I pep it up a little?" —"None of your bright ideas. Just keep on as you are. They're eating out of our hands now."

By such easy stages he led them around to the idea that mind and will could exercise control over the body much more complete than that ordinarily encountered. He passed lightly over the tales of Hindu holy men who could lift themselves up into the air and even travel from place to place.

"We have an exceptional opportunity to put such tales to practical test," he told them. "The subject believes fully any statement made by the operator. I shall tell Miss Freeman that she is to exert her will power, and rise up off the floor. It is certain that she will believe that she can do it. Her will will be in an optimum condition to carry out the order, if it can be done. Miss Freeman!"

146

"Yes, Mr. Huxley."

"Exert your will. Rise up in the air!"

Joan rose straight up into the air, some six feet—until her head nearly touched the high ceiling. —*"How'm doin,' pal?" —Swell, kid, you're wowin' 'em. Look at 'em stare!"*

At that moment Brinckley burst into the room, rage in his eyes.

"Mr. Huxley, you have broken your word to me, and disgraced this university!" It was some ten minutes after the fiasco ending the demonstration. Huxley faced the president in Brinckley's private office.

"I made you no promise. I have not disgraced the school," Phil answered with equal pugnacity.

"You have indulged in cheap tricks of fake magic to bring your department into disrepute."

"So I'm a faker, am I? You stiff-necked old fossil—explain this one!" Huxley levitated himself until he floated three feet above the rug.

"Explain what?" To Huxley's amazement Brinckley seemed unaware that anything unusual was going on. He continued to stare at the point where Phil's head had been. His manner showed nothing but a slight puzzlement and annoyance at Huxley's apparently irrelevant remark.

Was it possible that the doddering old fool was so completely self-deluded that he could not observe anything that ran counter to his own preconceptions even when it happened directly under his eyes? Phil reached out with his mind and attempted to see what went on inside Brinckley's head. He got one of the major surprises of his life. He expected to find the floundering mental processes of near senility; he found . . . cold calculation, keen ability, set in a matrix of pure evil that sickened him.

It was just a glimpse, then he was cast out with a wrench that numbed his brain. Brinckley had discovered his spying and thrown up his defences—the hard defences of a disciplined mind.

Phil dropped back to the floor, and left the room, without a word, nor a backward glance.

From THE WESTERN STUDENT, October 3rd:

PSYCH PROF FIRED FOR FRAUD

. . . students' accounts varied, but all agreed that it had been a fine show. Fullback 'Buzz' Arnold told your reporter, "I hated to see it happen; Prof Huxley is a nice guy and he certainly put on a clever skit with some good deadpan acting. I could see how it was done, of course—it was the same the Great Arturo used in his turn at the Orpheum last spring. But I can see Doctor Brinckley's viewpoint; you can't permit monkey shines at a serious center of learning."

President Brinckley gave the STUDENT the following official statement: "It is with real regret that I announce the termination of Mr. Huxley's association with the institution—for the good of the University. Mr. Huxley had been repeatedly warned as to where his steps were leading him. He is a young man of considerable ability. Let us devoutly hope that this experience will serve as a lesson to him in whatever line of endeavor . . ."

Coburn handed the paper back to Huxley. "You know what happened to me?" he inquired.

"Something new?"

"Invited to resign . . . No publicity—just a gentle hint. My patients got well too fast; I'd quit using surgery, you know."

"How perfectly stinking!" This from Joan.

"Well," Ben considered, "I don't blame the medical director; Brinckley forced his hand. I guess we underrated the old cuss."

"Rather! Ben, he's every bit as capable as any one of us, and as for his motives—I gag when I think about it."

"And I thought he was just a were-mouse," grieved Joan. "We should have pushed him into the tar pits last spring. I told you to. What do we do now?"

"Go right ahead." Phil's reply was grim. "We'll turn the situation to our own advantage; we've gotten some publicity —we'll use it."

"What's the gag?"

"Levitation again. It's the most spectacular thing we've got for a crowd. Call in the papers, and tell 'em that we will publicly demonstrate levitation at noon tomorrow in Pershing Square."

"Won't the papers fight shy of sticking their necks out on anything that sounds as fishy as that?"

"Probably they would, but here's how we'll handle that: Make the whole thing just a touch screwball and give 'em plenty of funny angles to write up. Then they can treat it as a feature rather than as straight news. The lid's off, Joan— you can do anything you like; the screwier the better. Let's get going, troops—I'll call the News Service. Ben, you and Joan split up the dailies between you."

The reporters were interested, certainly. They were interested in Joan's obvious good looks, cynically amused by Phil's flowing tie and bombastic claims, and seriously impressed by his taste in whiskey. They began to take notice when Coburn courteously poured drinks for them without bothering to touch the bottle.

But when Joan floated around the room while Phil rode a non-existent bicycle across the ceiling, they balked. "Honest, doc," as one of them put it, "we've got to eat—you don't expect us to go back and tell a city editor anything like this. Come clean; is it the whiskey, or just plain hypnotism?"

"Put it any way you like, gentlemen. Just be sure that you say that we will do it all over again in Pershing Square at noon tomorrow."

Phil's diatribe against Brinckley came as an anticlimax to the demonstration, but the reporters obligingly noted it.

Joan got ready for bed that night with a feeling of vague depression. The exhilaration of entertaining the newspaper boys had worn off. Ben had proposed supper and dancing to mark their last night of private life, but it had not been a success. To start with, they had blown a tire while coming down a steep curve on Beachwood Drive, and Phil's gray sedan had rolled over and over. They would have all been seriously injured had it not been for the automatic body control which they possessed.

When Phil examined the wreck, he expressed puzzlement as to its cause. "Those tires were perfectly all right," he maintained. "I had examined them all the way through this morning." But he insisted on continuing with their evening of relaxation.

The floor show seemed dull, the jokes crude and callous, after the light, sensitive humor they had learned to enjoy through association with Master Ling. The ponies in the chorus were young and beautiful—Joan had enjoyed watching them, but she made the mistake of reaching out to touch their minds. The incongruity of the vapid, insensitive spirits she found—in almost every instance—added to her malaise.

She was relieved when the floor show ended and Ben asked her to dance. Both of the men were good dancers, especially Coburn, and she fitted herself into his arms contentedly. Her pleasure didn't last; a drunken couple bumped into them repeatedly. The man was quarrelsome, the woman shrilly vitriolic. Joan asked her escorts to take her home.

These things bothered her as she prepared for bed. Joan, who had never known acute physical fear in her life, feared just one thing—the corrosive, dirty emotions of the poor in spirit. Malice, envy, spite, the snide insults of twisted, petty minds; these things could hurt her, just by being in her presence, even if she were not the direct object of the attack. She was not yet sufficiently mature to have acquired a smooth armor of indifference to the opinions of the unworthy.

After a summer in the company of men of good will, the

149

incident with the drunken couple dismayed her. She felt dirtied by the contact. Worse still, she felt an outlander, a stranger in a strange land.

She awakened sometime in the night with the sense of loneliness increased to overwhelming proportions. She was acutely aware of the three-million-odd living beings around her, but the whole city seemed alive only with malignant entities, jealous of her, anxious to drag her down to their own ignoble status. This attack on her spirit, this attempt to despoil the sanctity of her inner being, assumed an almost corporate nature. It seemed to her that it was nibbling at the edges of her mind, snuffling at her defences.

Terrified, she called out to Ben and Phil. There was no answer; her mind could not find them.

The filthy thing that threatened her was aware of her failure; she could feel it leer. In open panic she called to the Senior.

No answer. This time the thing spoke—"That way, too, is closed."

As hysteria claimed her, as her last defences crumbled, she was caught in the arms of a stronger spirit, whose calm, untroubled goodness encysted her against the evil thing that stalked her.

"Ling!" she cried, "Master Ling!" before racking sobs claimed her.

She felt the quiet, reassuring humor of his smile while the fingers of his mind reached out and smoothed away the tensions of her fear. Presently she slept.

His mind stayed with her all through the night, and talked with her, until she awakened.

Ben and Phil listened to her account of the previous night with worried faces. "That settles it," Phil decided. "We've been too careless. From now on until this thing is finished, we stay in rapport day and night, awake and asleep. As a matter of fact, I had a bad time of it myself last night, though nothing equal to what happened to Joan."

"So did I, Phil. What happened to you?"

"Nothing very much—just a long series of nightmares in which I kept losing confidence in my ability to do any of the things we learned on Shasta. What about you?"

"Same sort of thing, with variations. I operated all night long, and all of my patients died on the table. Not very pleasant—but something else happened that wasn't a dream. You know I still use an old-fashioned straight-razor; I was shaving away, paying no attention to it, when it jumped in my hand and cut a big gash in my throat. See? It's not entirely healed yet." He indicated a thin red line which ran diagonally down the right side of his neck.

"Why, Ben!" squealed Joan, "you might have been killed."

"That's what I thought," he agreed dryly.

"You know, kids," Phil said slowly, "these things aren't accidental—"

"Open up in there!" The order was bawled from the other side of the door. As one mind, their senses of direct perception jumped through solid oak and examined the speaker. Plainclothes did not conceal the profession of the over-size individual waiting there, even had they not been able to see the gold shield on his vest. A somewhat smaller, but equally officious, man waited with him.

Ben opened the door and inquired gently, "What do you want?"

The larger man attempted to come in. Coburn did not move.

"I asked you your business."

"Smart guy, eh? I'm from police headquarters. You Huxley?"

"No."

"Coburn?" Ben nodded.

"You'll do. That Huxley behind you? Don't either of you ever stay home? Been here all night?"

"No," said Coburn frostily, "not that it is any of your business."

"I'll decide about that. I want to talk to you two. I'm from the bunco squad. What's this game you were giving the boys yesterday?"

"No game, as you call it. Come down to Pershing Square at noon today, and see for yourself."

"You won't be doing anything in Pershing Square today, Bud."

"Why not?"

"Park Commission's orders."

"What authority?"

"Huh?"

"By what act, or ordinance, do they deny the right of private citizens to make peaceful use of a public place? Who is that with you?"

The smaller man identified himself. "Name's Ferguson, D.A.'s office. I want your pal Huxley on a criminal libel complaint. I want you two's witnesses."

Ben's stare became colder, if possible. "Do either of you," he inquired, in gently snubbing tones, "have a warrant?"

They looked at each other and failed to reply. Ben continued, "Then it is hardly profitable to continue this conversation, is it?" and closed the door in their faces.

He turned around to his companions and grinned. "Well, they are closing in. Let's see what the papers gave us."

They found just one story. It said nothing about their proposed demonstration, but related that Doctor Brinckley had

151

sworn a complaint charging Phil with criminal libel. "That's the first time I ever heard of four metropolitan papers refusing a juicy news story," was Ben's comment, "what are you going to do about Brinckley's charge?"

"Nothing," Phil told him, "except possibly libel him again. If he goes through with it, it will be a beautiful opportunity to prove our claims in court. Which reminds me—we don't want our plans interfered with today; those bird dogs may be back with warrants most any time. Where'll we hide out?"

On Ben's suggestion they spent the morning buried in the downtown public library. At five minutes to twelve, they flagged a taxi, and rode to Pershing Square.

They stepped out of the cab into the arms of six sturdy policemen.

—"Ben, Phil, how much longer do I have to put up with this?"
—"Steady, kid. Don't get upset."
—"I'm not, but why should we stay pinched when we can duck out anytime?"
—"That's the point; we can escape anytime. We've never been arrested before; let's see what it's like."

They were gathered that night late around the fireplace in Joan's house. Escape had presented no difficulties, but they had waited until an hour when the jail was quiet to prove that stone walls do not a prison make for a person adept in the powers of the mind.

Ben was speaking, "I'd say we had enough data to draw a curve now."

"Which is?"

"You state it."

"All right. We came down from Shasta thinking that all we had to overcome was stupidity, ignorance, and a normal amount of human contrariness and cussedness. Now we know better. Any attempt to place the essentials of the ancient knowledge in the hands of the common people is met by a determined, organized effort to prevent it, and to destroy, or disable the one who tries it."

"It's worse than that," amended Ben, "I spent our rest in the clink looking over the city. I wondered why the district attorney should take such an interest in us, so I took a look into his mind. I found out who his boss was, and took a look at *his* mind. What I found there interested me so much that I had to run up to the state capital and see what made things tick there. That took me back to Spring Street and the financial district. Believe it or not, from there I had to look up some of the most sacred cows in the community—clergymen, clubwomen, business leaders, and stuff." He paused.

"Well, what about it? Don't tell me everybody is out of step but Willie—I'll break down and cry."

"No—that was the odd part about it. Nearly all of these heavyweights were good Joes, people you'd like to know. But usually—not always, but usually—the good Joes were dominated by someone they trusted, someone who had helped them to get where they were, and these dominants were not good Joes, to state it gently. I couldn't get into all of their minds, but where I was able to get in, I found the same sort of thing that Phil found in Brinckley—cold calculated awareness that their power lay in keeping the people in ignorance."

Joan shivered. "That's a sweet picture you paint, Ben— just the right thing for a bed-time story. What's our next move?"

"What do you suggest?"

"Me? I haven't reached any conclusion. Maybe we should take on these tough babies one at a time, and smear 'em."

"How about you, Phil?"

"I haven't anything better to offer. We'll have to plan a shrewd campaign, however."

"Well, I do have something to suggest myself."

"Let's have it."

"Admit that we blindly took on more than we could handle. Go back to Shasta and ask for help."

"Why, Ben!" Joan's dismay was matched by Phil's unhappy face. Ben went on stubbornly, "Sure, I know it's gravelling, but pride is too expensive and the job is too—"

He broke off when he noticed Joan's expression. "What is it kid?"

"We'll have to make some decision quickly—that is a police car that just stopped out in front."

Ben turned back to Phil. "What'll it be; stay and fight, or go back for re-inforcements?"

"Oh, you're right. I've known it ever since I got a look at Brinckley's mind—but I hated to admit it."

The three stepped out into the patio, joined hands, and shot straight up into the air.

CHAPTER ELEVEN

"A Little Child Shall Lead Them."

"WELCOME HOME!" Ephraim Howe met them when they landed. "Glad to have you back." He led them into his own private apartment. "Rest yourselves while I stir up the fire a mite." He chucked a wedge of pinewood into the wide grate, pulled his homely old rocking chair around so that it faced both the fire and his guests, and settled down. "Now suppose you tell me all about it. No, I'm not hooked in with the others —you can make a full report to the council when you're ready."

"As a matter of fact, don't you already know everything that happened to us, Mr. Howe?" Phil looked directly at the Senior as he spoke.

"No, I truly don't. We let you go at it your own way, with Ling keeping an eye out to see that you didn't get hurt. He has made no report to me."

"Very well, sir." They took turns telling him all that had happened to them, occasionally letting him see directly through their minds the events they had taken part in.

When they were through Howe gave them his quizzical smile and inquired, "So you've come around to the viewpoint of the council?"

"No, sir!" It was Phil who answered him. "We are more convinced of the need for positive, immediate action than we were when we left—but we are convinced, too, that we aren't strong enough nor wise enough to handle it alone. We've come back to ask for help, and to urge the council to abandon its policy of teaching only those who show that they are ready, and, instead, to reach out and teach as many minds as can accept your teachings.

"You see, sir, our antagonists don't wait. They are active all the time. They've won in Asia, they are in the ascendancy in Europe, they may win here in America, while we wait for an opportunity."

"Have you any method to suggest for tackling the problem?"

"No, that's why we came back. When we tried to teach others what we knew, we were stopped."

"That's the rub," Howe agreed. "I've been pretty much of your opinion for a good many years, but it is hard to do.

154

What we have to give can't be printed in a book, nor broadcast over the air. It must be passed directly from mind to mind, wherever we find a mind ready to receive it."

They finished the discussion without finding a solution. Howe told them not to worry. "Go along," he said, "and spend a few weeks in meditation and rapport. When you get an idea that looks as if it might work, bring it in and we'll call the council together to consider it."

"But, Senior," Joan protested for the trio, "you see— Well, we had hoped to have the advice of the council in working out a plan. We don't know where to start, else we wouldn't have come back."

He shook his head. "You are the newest of the brethren, the youngest, the least experienced. Those are your virtues, not your disabilities. The very fact that you have not spent years of this life in thinking in terms of eons and races gives you an advantage. Too broad a viewpoint, too philosophical an outlook paralyzes the will. I want you three to consider it alone."

They did as he asked. For weeks they discussed it in rapport as a single mind, hammered at it in spoken conversation, meditated its ramifications. They roamed the nation with their minds, examining the human spirits that lay behind political and social action. With the aid of the archives they learned the techniques by which the brotherhood of adepts had interceded in the past when freedom of thought and action in America had been threatened. They proposed and rejected dozens of schemes.

"We should go into politics," Phil told the other two, "as our brothers did in the past. If we had a Secretary of Education, appointed from among the elders, he could found a national academy in which freedom of thought would really prevail, and it could be the source from which the ancient knowledge could spread."

Joan put in an objection.

"Suppose you lose the election?"

"Huh?"

"Even with all the special powers that the adepts have, it 'ud be quite a chore to line up delegates for a national convention to get our candidate nominated, then get him elected in the face of all the political machines, pressure groups, newspapers, favorite sons, et cetera, et cetera, et cetera.

"And remember this, the opposition can fight as dirty as it pleases, but we have to fight fair, or we defeat our own aims."

Ben nodded. "I am afraid she is right, Phil. But you are absolutely right in one thing; this is a problem of education." He stopped to meditate, his mind turned inward.

Presently he resumed. "I wonder if we have been tackling this job from the right end? We've been thinking of reeducating adults, already set in their ways. How about the children? They haven't crystallized; wouldn't they be easier to teach?"

Joan sat up, her eyes bright. "Ben, you've got it!"

Phil shook his head doggedly. "No. I hate to throw cold water, but there is no way to go about it. Children are constantly in the care of adults; we couldn't get to them. Don't think for a moment that you could get past local school boards; they are the tightest little oligarchies in the whole political system."

They were sitting in a group of pine trees on the lower slopes of Mount Shasta. A little group of human figures came into view below them and climbed steadily toward the spot where the three rested. The discussion was suspended until the group moved beyond earshot. The trio watched them with casual, friendly interest.

They were all boys, ten to fifteen years old, except the leader, who bore his sixteen years with the serious dignity befitting one who is responsible for the safety and wellbeing of younger charges. They were dressed in khaki shorts and shirts, campaign hats, neckerchiefs embroidered with a conifer and the insignia ALPINE PATROL, TROOP I, Each carried a staff and a knapsack.

As the procession came abreast of the adults, the patrol leader gave them a wave in greeting, the merit badges on his sleeve flashing in the sun. The three waved back and watched them trudge out of sight up the slope.

Phil watched them with a faraway look. "Those were the good old days," he said; "I almost envy them."

"Were you one?" Ben said, his eyes still on the boys. "I remember how proud I was the day I got my merit badge in first aid."

"Born to be a doctor, eh, Ben?" commented Joan, her eyes maternal, approving. "I didn't—say!"

"What's up?"

"Phil! That's your answer! That's how to reach the children in spite of parents and school boards."

She snapped into telepathic contact, her ideas spilling excitedly into their minds. They went into rapport and ironed out the details. After a time Ben nodded and spoke aloud. "It might work," he said, "let's go back and talk it over with Ephraim."

"Senator Moulton, these are the young people I was telling you about." Almost in awe, Joan looked at the face of the little white-haired, old man whose name had become a synonym for integrity. She felt the same impulse to fold her hands

156

across her middle and bow which Master Ling inspired. She noted that Ben and Phil were having trouble not to seem gawky and coltish.

Ephraim Howe continued, "I have gone into their scheme and I think it is practical. If you do too, the council will go ahead with it. But it largely depends on you."

The Senator took them to himself with a smile, the smile that had softened the hearts of two generations of hard politicians. "Tell me about it," he invited.

They did so—how they had tried and failed at Western University, how they had cudgeled their brains for a way, how a party of boys on a hike up the mountain had given them an inspiration. "You see, Senator, if we could just get enough boys up here all at once, boys too young to have been corrupted by their environment, and already trained, as these boys are, in the ideals of the ancients,—human dignity, helpfulness, self-reliance, kindness, all those things set forth in their code—if we could get even five thousand such boys up here all at once, we could train them in telepathy, and how to impart telepathy to others.

"Once they were taught, and sent back to their homes, each one would be a center for spreading the knowledge. The antagonists could never stop it; it would be too wide spread, epidemic. In a few years every child in the country would be telepathic, and they would even teach their elders—those that haven't grown too calloused to learn.

"And once a human being is telepathic, we can lead him along the path of the ancient wisdom!"

Moulton was nodding, and talking to himself. "Yes. Yes indeed. It could be done. Fortunately Shasta is a national park. Let me see, who is on that committee? It would take a joint resolution and a small appropriation. Ephraim, old friend, I am afraid I shall have to practice a little logrolling to accomplish this, will you forgive me?"

Howe grinned broadly.

"Oh, I mean it," Moulton continued, "people are so cynical, so harsh, about political expediency—even some of our brothers. Let me see, this will take about two years, I think, before the first camp can be held—"

"As long as that?" Joan was disappointed.

"Oh, yes, my dear. There are two bills to get before Congress, and much arranging to do to get them passed in the face of a full legislative calendar. There are arrangements to be made with the railroads and bus companies to give the boys special rates so that they can afford to come. We must start a publicity campaign to make the idea popular. Then there must be time for as many of our brothers as possible to get into the administration of the movement in order that the camp executives may be liberally interspersed with adepts. Fortunately

I am a national trustee of the organization. Yes, I can manage it in two years' time, I believe."

"Good heavens!" protested Phil; "why wouldn't it be more to the point to teleport them here, teach them, and teleport them back?"

"You do not know what you are saying, my son. Can we abolish force by using it? Every step must be voluntary, accomplished by reason and persuasion. Each human being must free himself; freedom cannot be thrust on him. Besides, is two years long to wait to accomplish a job that has been waiting since the Deluge?"

"I'm sorry, sir."

"Do not be. Your youthful impatience has made it possible to do the job at all."

CHAPTER TWELVE

"Ye Shall Know the Truth—"

ON THE LOWER SLOPES of Mount Shasta, down near McCloud, the camp grew up. When the last of the spring snow was still hiding in the deeper gullies and on the north sides of ridges, U.S. Army Quartermaster trucks came lumbering over a road built the previous fall by the army engineers. Pyramid tents were broken out and were staked down in rows on the bosom of a gently rolling alp. Cook shacks, an infirmary, a headquarters building took shape. Camp Mark Twain was changing from blueprint to actuality.

Senator Moulton, his toga laid aside for breeches, leggings, khaki shirt, and a hat marked CAMP DIRECTOR, puttered around the field, encouraging, making decisions for the straw bosses, and searching, ever searching the minds of all who came into or near the camp for any purpose. Did anyone suspect? Had anyone slipped in who might be associated with partial adepts who opposed the real purpose of the camp? Too late to let anything slip now—too late, and too much at stake.

In the middle west, in the deep south, in New York City and New England, in the mountains and on the coast, boys were packing suitcases, buying special Shasta Camp round-trip tickets, talking about it with their envious contemporaries.

And all over the country the antagonists of human liberty, of human dignity—the racketeers, the crooked political figures, the shysters, the dealers in phony religions, the sweat-shoppers, the petty authoritarians, all of the key figures among the traffickers in human misery and human oppression, themselves somewhat adept in the arts of the mind and acutely aware of the danger of free knowledge—all of this unholy breed stirred uneasily and wondered what was taking place. Moulton had never been associated with anything but ill for them; Mount Shasta was one place they had never been able to touch—they hated the very name of the place. They recalled old stories, and shivered.

They shivered, but they acted.

Special transcontinental buses loaded with the chosen boys —could the driver be corrupted? Could his mind be taken over? Could tires, or engine, be tampered with? Trains were taken over by the youngsters. Could a switch be thrown? Could the drinking water be polluted?

Other eyes watched. A trainload of boys moved westward; in it, or flying over it, his direct perception blanketing the surrounding territory, and checking the motives of every mind within miles of his charges, was stationed at least one adept whose single duty it was to see that those boys reached Shasta safely.

Probably some of the boys would never have reached there had not the opponents of human freedom been caught off balance, doubtful, unorganized. For vice has this defect; it cannot be truly intelligent. Its very motives are its weakness. The attempts made to prevent the boys reaching Shasta were scattered and abortive. The adepts had taken the offensive for once, and their moves were faster and more rationally conceived than their antagonists'.

Once in camp a tight screen surrounded the whole of Mount Shasta National Park. The Senior detailed adepts to point patrol night and day to watch with every sense at their command for mean or malignant spirits. The camp itself was purged. Two of the councilors, and some twenty of the boys, were sent home when examination showed them to be damaged souls. The boys were not informed of their deformity, but plausible excuses were found for the necessary action.

The camp resembled superficially a thousand other such camps. The courses in woodcraft were the same. The courts of honor met as usual to examine candidates. There were the usual sings around the campfire in the evening, the same setting-up exercises before breakfast. The slightly greater emphasis on the oath and the law of the organization was not noticeable.

Each one of the boys made at least one overnight hike in the course of the camp. In groups of fifteen or twenty they would set out in the morning in company of a councilor. That each councilor supervising such hikes was an adept was not evident, but it so happened. Each boy carried his blanket roll,

159

and knapsack of rations, his canteen, knife, compass, and hand axe.

They camped that night on the bank of a mountain stream, fed by the glaciers, whose rush sounded in their ears as they ate supper.

Phil started out with such a group one morning during the first week of the camp. He worked around the mountain to the east in order to keep well away from the usual tourist haunts.

After supper they sat around the campfire. Phil told them stories of the holy men of the east and their reputed powers, and of Saint Francis and the birds. He was in the middle of one of his yarns when a figure appeared within the circle of firelight.

Or rather figures. They saw an old man, in clothes that Davy Crockett might have worn, flanked by two beasts, on his left side a mountain lion, who purred when he saw the fire, on his right a buck of three points, whose soft brown eyes stared calmly into theirs.

Some of the boys were alarmed at first, but Phil told them quietly to widen their circle and make room for the strangers. They sat in decent silence for a while, the boys getting used to the presence of the animals. In time one of the boys timidly stroked the big cat, who responded by rolling over and presenting his soft belly. The boy looked up at the old man and asked,

"What is his name, Mister—"

"Ephraim. His name is Freedom."

"My, but he's tame! How do you get him to be so tame?"

"He reads my thoughts and trusts me. Most things are friendly when they know you—and most people."

The boy puzzled for a moment. "How can he read your thoughts?"

"It's simple. You can read his, too. Would you like to learn how?"

"Jiminy!"

"Just look into my eyes for a moment. There! Now look into his."

"Why—Why—I really believe I can!"

—"*Of course you can. And mine, too. I'm not talking out loud. Had you noticed?*"

—"*Why, so you're not. I'm reading your thoughts!*"

—"*And I'm reading yours. Easy, isn't it?*"

With Phil's help Howe had them all conversing by thought transference inside an hour. Then to calm them down he told them stories for another hour, stories that constituted an important part of their curriculum. He helped Phil get them to sleep, then left, the animals following after him.

The next morning Phil was confronted at once by a young

sceptic. "Say, did I dream all that about an old man and a puma and a deer?"

—"Did you?"

—"You're doing it now!"

—"Certainly I am. And so are you. Now go tell the other boys the same thing."

Before they got back to camp, he advised them not to speak about it to any other of the boys who had not as yet had their overnight hike, but that they test their new powers by trying it on any boy who had had his first all-night hike.

All was well until one of the boys had to return home in answer to a message that his father was ill. The elders would not wipe his mind clean of his new knowledge; instead they kept careful track of him. In time he talked, and the word reached the antagonists almost at once. Howe ordered the precautions of the telepathic patrol redoubled.

The patrol was able to keep out malicious persons, but it was not numerous enough to keep everything out. Forest fire broke out on the windward side of the camp late one night. No human being had been close to the spot; telekinetics was the evident method.

But what control over matter from a distance can do, it can also undo. Moulton squeezed the flame out with his will, refused it permisson to burn, bade its vibrations to stop.

For the time being the enemy appeared to cease attempts to do the boys physical harm. But the enemy had not given up. Phil received a frantic call from one of the younger boys to come at once to the tent the boy lived in; his patrol leader was very sick. Phil found the lad in a state of hysteria, and being restrained from doing himself an injury by the other boys in the tent. He had tried to cut his throat with his jack knife and had gone berserk when one of the other boys had grabbed his hand.

Phil took in the situation quickly and put in a call to Ben.

—"Ben! Come at once. I need you."

Ben did so, zipping through the air and flying in through the door of the tent almost before Phil had time to lay the boy on his cot and start forcing him into a trance. The lad's startled tent mates did not have time to decide that Dr. Ben had been flying before he was standing in a normal fashion alongside their councilor.

Ben greeted him with tight communication, shutting the boys out of the circuit. —"What's up?"

—"They've gotten to him . . . and damn near wrecked him."

—"How?"

—"Preyed on his mind. Tried to make him suicide. But I

161

tranced back the hookup. *Who do you think tried to do him in?—Brinckley!*"

—"*No!*"

—"*Definitely. You take over here; I'm going after Brinckley. Tell the Senior to have a watch put on all the boys who have been trained to be sensitive to telepathy. I'm afraid that any of them may be gotten at before we can teach them how to defend themselves.*" With that he was gone, leaving the boys half convinced of levitation.

He had not gone very far, was still gathering speed, when he heard a welcome voice in his head,

—"*Phil! Phil! Wait for me.*"

He slowed down for a few seconds. A smaller figure flashed alongside his and grasped his hand. "It's a good thing I stay hooked in with you two. You'd have gone off to tackle that dirty old so-and-so without me."

He tried to maintain his dignity. "If I had thought that you should be along on this job, I'd have called you, Joan."

"Nonsense! And also fiddlesticks! You might get hurt, tackling him all alone. Besides, I'm going to push him into the tar pits."

He sighed and gave up. "Joan, my dear, you are a blood-thirsty wench with ten thousand incarnations to go before you reach beatitude."

"I don't want to reach beatitude; I want to do old Brinckley in."

"Come along, then. Let's make some speed."

They were south of the Tehachapi by now and rapidly approaching Los Angeles. They flitted over the Sierra Madre range, shot across San Fernando Valley, clipped the top of Mount Hollywood, and landed on the lawn of the President's Residence at Western University. Brinckley saw, or felt, them coming and tried to run for it, but Phil grappled with him.

He shot one thought to Joan. —"*You stay out of this, kid, unless I yell for help.*"

Brinckley did not give up easily. His mind reached out and tried to engulf Phil's. Huxley felt himself slipping, giving way before the evil onslaught. It seemed as though he were being dragged down, drowned, in filthy quicksand.

But he steadied himself and fought back.

When Phil had finished that which was immediately necessary with Brinckley, he stood up and wiped his hands, as if to cleanse himself of the spiritual slime he had embraced. "Let's get going," he said to Joan, "we're pushed for time."

"What did you do to him, Phil?" She stared with fascinated disgust at the thing on the ground.

"Little enough. I placed him in stasis. I've got to save him

162

for use—for a time. Up you go, girl. Out of here—before we're noticed."

Up they shot, with Brinckley's body swept along behind by tight telekinetic bond. They stopped above the clouds. Brinckley floated beside them, starfished, eyes popping, mouth loose, his smooth pink face expressionless. —*"Ben!"* Huxley was sending, *"Ephraim Howe! Ambrose! To me! To me! Hurry!"*

—*"Coming, Phil!"* came Coburn's answer.

—*"I hear."* The strong calm thought held the quality of the Senior. *"What is it, son? Tell me."*

—*"Not time!"* snapped Phil. *"Yourself, Senior, and all others that can. Rendezvous! Hurry!"*

—*"We come."* The thought was still calm, unhurried. But there were two ragged holes in the roof of Moulton's tent. Moulton and Howe were already out of sight of Camp Mark Twain.

Slashing, slicing through the air they came, the handful of adepts who guarded the fire. From five hundred miles to the north they came, racing pigeons hurrying home. Camp councilors, two-thirds of the small group of camp matrons, some few from scattered points on the continent, they came in response to Huxley's call for help and the Senior's unprecedented tocsin. A housewife turned out the fire in the oven and disappeared into the sky. A taxi driver stopped his car and left his fares without a word. Research groups on Shasta broke their tight rapport, abandoned their beloved work, and came—fast!

"And now, Philip?" Howe spoke orally as he arrested his trajectory and hung beside Huxley.

Huxley flung a hand toward Brinckley. "He has what we need to know to strike now! Where's Master Ling?"

"He and Mrs. Draper guard the Camp."

"I need him. Can she do it alone?"

Clear and mellow, her voice rang in his head from half a state away. —*"I can!"*

—*"The tortoise flies."* The second thought held the quality of deathless merriment which was the unmistakable characteristic of the ancient Chinese.

Joan felt a soft touch at her mind, then Master Ling was among them, seated carefully tailor-fashion on nothingness. "I attend; my body follows," he announced. "Can we not proceed?"

Whereupon Joan realized that he had borrowed the faculties of her mind to project himself into their presence more quickly than he could levitate the distance. She felt unreasonably flattered by the attention.

Huxley commenced at once. "Through *his* mind—" He indicated Brinckley, "I have learned of many others with whom there can be no truce. We must search them out, deal

163

with them at once, before they can rally from what has happened to him. But I need help. Master, will you extend the present and examine him?"

Ling had tutored them in discrimination of time and perception of the present, taught them to stand off and perceive duration from eternity. But he was incredibly more able than his pupils. He could split the beat of a fly's wing into a thousand discrete instants, or grasp a millenium as a single flash of experience. His discrimination of time and space was bound neither by his metabolic rate nor by his molar dimensions.

Now he poked gingerly at Brinckley's brain like one who seeks a lost jewel in garbage. He felt out the man's memory patterns and viewed his life as one picture. Joan, with amazement, saw his everpresent smile give way to a frown of distaste. His mind had been left open to any who cared to watch. She peered through his mind, then cut off. If there were that many truely vicious spirits in the world, she preferred to encounter them one at a time, as necessary, not experience them all at once.

Master Ling's body joined the group, melted into his projection.

Huxley, Howe, Moulton, and Bierce followed the Chinese's delicate work with close attention. Howe's face was bleakly impassive; Moulton's face, aged to androgynous sensitivity, moved from side to side while he clucked disapproval of such wickedness. Bierce looked more like Mark Twain than ever, Twain in an implacable, lowering rage.

Master Ling looked up. "Yes, yes," said Moulton, "I suppose we must act, Ephraim."

"We have no choice," Huxley stated, with a completely unconscious disregard of precedent. "Will you assign the tasks, Senior?"

Howe glanced sharply at him. "No, Philip. No. Go ahead. Carry on."

Huxley checked himself in surprise for the briefest instant, then took his cue. "You'll help me, Master Ling. Ben!"

"Waiting!"

He meshed mind to mind, had Ling show him his opponent and the data he needed. —"*Got it? Need any help?*"

—"*Grandfather Stonebender is enough.*"

—"*Okay. Nip off and attend to it.*"

—"*Chalk it up.*" He was gone, a rush of air in his wake.

—"*This one is yours, Senator Moulton.*"

—"*I know.*" And Moulton was gone.

By ones and twos he gave them their assignments, and off they went to do that which must be done. There was no argument. Many of them had been aware long before Huxley was that a day of action must inevitably come to pass, but

164

they had waited with quiet serenity, busy with the work at hand, till time should incubate the seed.

In a windowless study of a mansion on Long Island, soundproofed, cleverly locked and guarded, ornately furnished, a group of five was met—three men, one woman, and a thing in a wheel chair. It glared at the other four in black fury, glared without eyes, for its forehead dropped unbroken to its cheekbones, a smooth sallow expanse.

A lap robe, tucked loosely across the chair masked, but did not hide, the fact that the creature had no legs.

It gripped the arms of the chair. "Must I do *all* the thinking for you fools?" it asked in a sweet gentle voice. "You, Arthurson—you let Moulton slip that Shasta Bill past the Senate. Moron." The epithet was uttered caressingly.

Arthurson shifted in his chair. "I examined his mind. The bill was harmless. It was a swap on the Missouri Valley deal. I told you."

"You examined his mind, eh? Hmm—he led you on a personally conducted tour, you fool. A *Shasta* bill! When will you mindless idiots learn that no good ever came out of Shasta?" It smiled approvingly.

"Well, how was I to know? I thought a camp near the mountain might confuse . . . *them*."

"Mindless idiot. The time will come when I will find you dispensable." The thing did not wait for the threat to sink in, but continued, "Enough of that now. We must move to repair the damage. *They* are on the offensive now. Agnes—"

"Yes." The woman answered.

"Your preaching has got to pick up—"

"I've done my best."

"Not good enough. I've got to have a wave of religious hysteria that will wash out the Bill of Rights—*before* the Shasta camp breaks up for the summer. We will have to act fast before that time and we can't be hampered by a lot of legalisms."

"It can't be done."

"Shut up. It can be done. Your temple will receive endowments this week which you are to use for countrywide television hookups. At the proper time you will discover a new messiah."

"Who?"

"Brother Artemis."

"*That* cornbelt pipsqueak? Where do I come in on this?"

"You'll get yours. But you can't head this movement; the country won't take a woman in the top spot. The two of you will lead a march on Washington and take over. The Sons of '76 will fill out your ranks and do the street fighting. Weems, that's your job."

The man addressed demurred. "It will take three, maybe four months to indoctrinate them."

"You have three weeks. It would be well not to fail."

The last of the three men broke his silence. "What's the hurry, Chief? Seems to me that you are getting yourself in a panic over a few kids."

"I'll be the judge. Now you are to time an epidemic of strikes to tie the country up tight at the time of the march on Washington."

"I'll need some incidents."

"You'll get them. You worry about the unions; I'll take care of the Merchants' and Commerce League myself. You give me one small strike tomorrow. Get your pickets out and I will have four or five of them shot. The publicity will be ready. Agnes, you preach a sermon about it."

"Slanted which way?"

It rolled its non-existent eyes up to the ceiling. "Must I think of everything? It's elementary. Use your minds."

The last man to speak laid down his cigar carefuly and said, "What's the real rush, Chief?'

"I've told you."

"No, you haven't. You've kept your mind closed and haven't let us read your thoughts once. You've known about the Shasta camp for months. Why this sudden excitement? You aren't slipping, are you? Come on, spill it. You can't expect us to follow if you are slipping."

The eyeless one looked him over carefully. "Hanson," he said, in still sweeter tones, "you have been feeling your size for months. Would you care to match your strength with mine?"

The other looked at his cigar. "I don't mind if I do."

"You will. But not tonight. I haven't time to select and train new lieutenants. Therefore I will tell you what the urgency is. I can't raise Brinckley. He's fallen out of communication. There is not *time*—"

"You are correct," said a new voice. "There is not time."

The five jerked puppetlike to face its source. Standing side by side in the study were Ephraim Howe and Joan Freeman.

Howe looked at the thing. "I've waited for this meeting," he said cheerfully, "and I've saved you for myself."

The creature got out of its wheelchair and moved through the air at Howe. Its height and position gave an unpleasant sensation that it walked on invisible legs. Howe signalled to Joan—"*It starts. Can you hold the others, my dear?*"

—"*I think so.*"

—"*Now!*" Howe brought to bear everything he had learned in one hundred and thirty busy years, concentrated on the single problem of telekinetic control. He avoided, refused

166

contact with the mind of the evil thing before him and turned his attention to destroying its physical envelope.

The thing stopped.

Slowly, slowly, like a deepsea diver caught in an implosion, like an orange in a squeezer, the spatial limits in which it existed were reduced. A spherical locus in space enclosed it, diminished.

The thing was drawn in and in. The ungrown stumps of its legs folded against its thick torso. The head ducked down against the chest to escape the unrelenting pressure. For a single instant it gathered its enormous perverted power and fought back. Joan was disconcerted, momentarily nauseated, by the backwash of evil.

But Howe withstood it without change of expression; the sphere shrank again.

The eyeless skull split. At once, the sphere shrank to the least possible dimension. A twenty-inch ball hung in the air, a ball whose repulsive superficial details did not invite examination.

Howe held the harmless, disgusting mess in place with a fraction of his mind, and inquired—*"Are you all right, my dear?"*

—*"Yes, Senior. Master Ling helped me once when I needed it."*

—*"That I anticipated. Now for the others."* Speaking aloud he said, "Which do you prefer: To join your leader, or to forget what you know?" He grasped air with his fingers and made a squeezing gesture.

The man with the cigar screamed.

"I take that to be an answer," said Howe. "Very well, Joan, pass them to me, one at a time."

He operated subtly on their minds, smoothing out the patterns of colloidal gradients established by their corporal experience.

A few minutes later the room contained four sane but infant adults—and a gory mess on the rug.

* * *

Coburn stepped into a room to which he had not been invited. "School's out, boys," he announced cheerfully. He pointed a finger at one occupant. "That goes for you." Flame crackled from his finger tip, lapped over his adversary. "Yes, and for you." The flames spouted forth a second time. "And for you." A third received his final cleansing.

Brother Artemis, "God's Angry Man," faced the television pick-up. "And if these things be not true," he thundered, "then may the Lord strike me down dead!"

The coroner's verdict of heart failure did not fully account for the charred condition of his remains.

A political rally adjourned early because the principal speaker failed to show up. An anonymous beggar was found collapsed over his pencils and chewing gum. A director of nineteen major corporations caused his secretary to have hysterics by breaking off in the midst of dictating to converse with the empty air before lapsing into cheerful idiocy. A celebrated stereo and television star disappeared. Obituary stories were hastily dug out and completed for seven members of Congress, several judges, and two governors.

The usual evening sing at Camp Mark Twain took place that night without the presence of Camp Director Moulton. He was attending a full conference of the adepts, assembled all in the flesh for the first time in many years.

Joan looked around as she entered the hall. "Where is Master Ling?" she inquired of Howe.

He studied her face for a moment. For the first time since she had first met him nearly two years before she thought he seemed momentarily at a loss. "My dear," he said gently, "you must have realized that Master Ling remained with us, not for his own benefit, but for ours. The crisis for which he waited has been met; the rest of the work we must do alone."

A hand went to her throat. "You . . . you mean . . .?"

"He was very old and very weary. He had kept his heart beating, his body functioning, by continuous control for these past forty-odd years."

"But why did he not renew and regenerate?"

"He did not wish it. We could not expect him to remain here indefinitely after he had grown up."

"No." She bit her trembling lip. "No. That it true. We are children and he has other things to do . . . but—Oh, Ling! Ling! Master Ling!" She buried her head on Howe's shoulder.

—*"Why are you weeping, Little Flower?"*

Her head jerked up.—*"Master Ling!"*

—*"Can that not be which has been? Is there past or future? Have you learned my lessons so poorly? Am I not now with you, as always?"* She felt in the thought the vibrant timeless merriment, the gusto for living which was the hallmark of the gentle Chinese.

With a part of her mind she squeezed Howe's hand. "Sorry," she said. "I was wrong." She relaxed as Ling had taught her, let her consciousness flow in the revery which encompasses time in a single deathless now.

Howe, seeing that she was at peace, turned his attention to the meeting.

He reached out with his mind and gathered them together into the telepathic network of full conference.—"*I think that you all know why we meet*," he thought.—"*I have served my time; we enter another and more active period when other qualities than mine are needed. I have called you to consider and pass on my selection of a successor.*"

Huxley was finding the thought messages curiously difficult to follow. I must be exhausted from the effort, he thought to himself.

But Howe was thinking aloud again.—"*So be it; we are agreed.*" He looked at Huxley. "*Philip, will you accept the trust?*"

"What?!!"

"You are Senior now—by common consent."

"But . . . but . . . I am not ready."

"We think so," answered Howe evenly. "Your talents are needed now. You will grow under responsibility."

—"*Chin up, pal!*" It was Coburn, in private message.

—"*It's all right, Phil.*" Joan, that time.

For an instant he seemed to hear Ling's dry chuckle, his calm acceptance.

"I will try!" he answered.

On the last day of camp Joan sat with Mrs. Draper on a terrace of the Home on Shasta, overlooking the valley. She sighed. Mrs. Draper looked up from her knitting and smiled. "Are you sad that the camp is over?"

"Oh, no! I'm glad it is."

"What is it, then?"

"I was just thinking . . . we go to all this effort and trouble to put on this camp. Then we have to fight to keep it safe. Tomorrow those boys go home—then they must be watched, each one of them, while they grow strong enough to protect themselves against all the evil things there are still in the world. Next year there will be another crop of boys, and then another, and then another. Isn't there any end to it?"

"Certainly there is an end to it. Don't you remember, in the ancient records, what became of the elders? When we have done what there is for us to do here, we move on to where there is more to do. The human race was not meant to stay here forever."

"It still seems endless."

"It does, when you think of it that way, my dear. The way to make it seem short and interesting is to think about what you are going to do next. For example, what are you going to do next?"

"Me?" Joan looked perplexed. Her face cleared. "Why . . . why I'm going to get married!"

"I thought so." Mrs. Draper's needles clicked away.

"—and the Truth Shall Make You Free!'

THE GLOBE STILL SWUNG AROUND THE SUN. The seasons came and the seasons went. The sun still shone on the mountainsides the hills were green, and the valleys lush. The river sought the bosom of the sea, then rode the cloud, and found the hills as rain. The cattle cropped in the brown plains, the fox stalked the hare through the brush. The tides answered the sway of the moon, and the gulls picked at the wet sand in the wake of the tide. The earth was fair and the earth was full; it teemed with life, swarmed with life, overflowed with life—a stream in spate.

Nowhere was man.

Seek the high hills; search him in the plains. Hunt for his spoor in the green jungles; call for him; shout for him. Follow where he has been in the bowels of earth; plumb the dim deeps of the sea.

Man is gone; his house stands empty; the door open.

A great ape, with a brain too big for his need and a spirit that troubled him, left his tribe and sought the quiet of the high place that lay above the jungle. He climbed it, hour after hour, urged on by a need that he half understood. He reached a resting place, high above the green trees of his home, higher than any of his tribe had ever climbed. There he found a broad flat stone, warm in the sun. He lay down upon it and slept.

But his sleep was troubled. He dreamed strange dreams, unlike anything he knew. They woke him and left him with an aching head.

It would be many generations before one of his line could understand what was left there by those who had departed.

THE END

JERRY WAS A MAN

DON'T BLAME THE MARTIANS. The human race would have developed plasto-biology in any case.

Look at the older registered Kennel Club breeds—glandular giants like the St. Bernard and the Great Dane, silly little atrocities like the Chihuahua and the Pekingese. Consider fancy goldfish.

The damage was done when Dr. Morgan produced new breeds of fruit flies by kicking around their chromosomes with X-ray. After that, the third generation of the Hiroshima survivors did not teach us anything new; those luckless monstrosities merely publicized standard genetic knowledge.

Mr. and Mrs. Bronson van Vogel did not have social reform in mind when they went to the Phoenix Breeding Ranch; Mr. van Vogel simply wanted to buy a Pegasus. He had mentioned it at breakfast. "Are you tied up this morning, my dear?"

"Not especially. Why?"

"I'd like to run out to Arizona and order a Pegasus designed."

"A Pegasus? A flying horse? Why, my sweet?"

He grinned. "Just for fun. Pudgy Dodge was around the Club yesterday with a six-legged dachshund—must have been over a yard long. It was clever, but he swanked so much I want to give him something to stare at. Imagine, Martha—me landing on the Club 'copter platform on a winged horse. That'll snap his eyes back!"

She turned her eyes from the Jersey shore to look indulgently at her husband. She was not fooled; this would be expensive. But Brownie was such a dear! "When do we start?"

They landed two hours earlier than they started. The airsign read, in letters fifty feet high:

PHOENIX BREEDING RANCH
Controlled Genetics—licensed Labor Contractors

" 'Labor Contractors'?" she read. "I thought this place was used just to burbank new animals?"

"They both design and produce," he explained importantly. "They distribute through the mother corporation 'Workers'.

You ought to know; you own a big chunk of Workers common."

"You mean I own a bunch of apes? Really?"

"Perhaps I didn't tell you. Haskell and I—" He leaned forward and informed the field that he would land manually; he was a bit proud of his piloting.

He switched off the robot and added, briefly as his attention was taken up by heading the ship down, "Haskell and I have been plowing your General Atomics dividends back into Workers, Inc. Good diversification—still plenty of dirty work for the anthropoids to do." He slapped the keys; the scream of the nose jets stopped conversation.

Bronson had called the manager in flight; they were met—not with red carpet, canopy, and footmen, though the manager strove to give that impression. "Mr. van Vogel? And *Mrs.* van Vogel! We are honored indeed!" He ushered them into a tiny, luxurious unicar; they jeeped off the field, up a ramp, and into the lobby of the administration building. The manager, Mr. Blakesly, did not relax until he had seated them around a fountain in the lounge of his offices, struck cigarettes for them, and provided tall, cool drinks.

Bronson van Vogel was bored by the attention, as it was obviously inspired by his wife's Dun & Bradstreet rating (ten stars, a sunburst, and heavenly music). He preferred people who could convince him that he had invented the Briggs fortune, instead of marrying it.

"This is business Blakesly. I've an order for you."

"So? Well, our facilities are at your disposal. What would you like, sir?"

"I want you to make me a Pegasus."

"A Pegasus? A flying horse?"

"Exactly."

Blakesly pursed his lips. "You seriously want a horse that will fly? An animal like the mythical Pegasus?"

"Yes, yes—that's what I said."

"You embarrass me, Mr. van Vogel. I assume you want a unique gift for your lady. How about a midget elephant, twenty inches high, perfectly housebroken, and able to read and write? He holds the stylus in his trunk—very cunning."

"Does he talk?" demanded Mrs. van Vogel.

"Well, now, my dear lady, his voice box, you know—and his tongue—he was not designed for speech. If you insist on it, I will see what our plasticians can do."

"Now, Martha—"

"You can have your Pegasus, Brownie, but I think I may want this toy elephant. May I see him?"

"Most surely. Hartstone!"

The air answered Blakesly. "Yes, boss?"

"Bring Napoleon to my lounge."

172

"Right away, sir."

"Now about your Pegasus, Mr. van Vogel . . . I see difficulties but I need expert advice. Dr. Cargrew is the real heart
of this organization, the most eminent bio-designer—of ter-
restrial origin, of course—on the world today." He raised
his voice to actuate relays. "Dr. Cargrew!"

"What is it, Mr. Blakesly?'

"Doctor, will you favor me by coming to my office?"

"I'm busy. Later."

Mr. Blakesly excused himself, went into his inner office,
then returned to say that Dr. Cargrew would be in shortly.
In the mean time Napoleon showed up. The proportions of
his noble ancestors had been preserved in miniature; he
looked like a statuette of an elephant, come amazingly to life.

He took three measured steps into the lounge, then saluted
them each with his trunk. In saluting Mrs. van Vogel he
dropped on his knees as well.

"Oh, how cute!" she gurgled. "Come here, Napoleon."

The elephant looked at Blakesly, who nodded. Napoleon
ambled over and laid his trunk across her lap. She scratched
his ears; he moaned contentedly.

"Show the lady how you can write," ordered Blakesly.
"Fetch your things from my room."

Napoleon waited while she finished treating a particularly
satisfying itch, then oozed away to return shortly with several
sheets of heavy white paper and an oversize pencil. He spread
a sheet in front of Mrs. van Vogel, held it down daintily with
a fore foot, grasped the pencil with his trunk finger, and
printed in large, shaky letters, "I LIKE YOU."

"The darling!" She dropped to her knees and put her arms
around his neck. "I simply must have him. How much is he?"

"Napoleon is part of a limited edition of six," Blakesly
said carefully. "Do you want an exclusive model, or may the
others be sold?"

"Oh, I don't care. I just want Nappie. Can I write him a
note?"

"Certainly, Mrs. van Vogel. Print large letters and use
Basic English. Napoleon knows most of it. His price, non-
exclusive is $350,000. That includes five years salary for his
attending veterinary."

"Give the gentleman a check, Brownie," she said over her
shoulder.

"But Martha—"

"Don't be tiresome, Brownie." She turned back to her pet
and began printing. She hardly looked up when Dr. Cargrew
came in.

Cargrew was a chilly figure in white overalls and skull cap.
He shook hands brusquely, struck a cigarette and sat down.
Blakesly explained.

Cargrew shook his head. "It's a physical impossibility."

Van Vogel stood up. "I can see," he said distantly, "That I should have taken my custom to NuLife Laboratories. I came here because we have a financial interest in this firm and because I was naive enough to believe the claims of your advertisements."

"Siddown, young man!" Cargrew ordered. "Take your trade to those thumb-fingered idiots if you wish—but I warn you they couldn't grow wings on a grasshopper. First you listen to me.

"We can grow anything and make it live. I can make you a living thing—I won't call it an animal—the size and shape of that table over there. It wouldn't be good for anything, but it would be alive. It would ingest food, use chemical energy, give off excretions, and display irritability. But it would be a silly piece of manipulation. Mechanically a table and an animal are two different things. Their functions are different, so their shapes are different. Now I can make you a winged horse—"

"You just said you couldn't."

"Don't interrupt. I can make a winged horse that will look just like the pictures in the fairy stories. If you want to pay for it; we'll make it—we're in business. But it won't be able to fly."

"Why not?"

"Because it's not built for flying. The ancient who dreamed up that myth knew nothing about aerodynamics and still less about biology. He stuck wings on a horse, just stuck them on, thumb tacks and glue. But that doesn't make a flying machine. Remember, son, that an animal is a machine, primarily a heat engine with a control system to operate levers and hydraulic systems, according to definite engineering laws. You savvy aerodynamics?"

"Well, I'm a pilot."

"Hummph! Well, try to understand this. A horse hasn't got the heat engine for flight. He's a hayburner and that's not efficient. We might mess around with a horse's insides so that he could live on a diet of nothing but sugar and then he might have enough energy to fly short distances. But he still would not look like the mythical Pegasus. To anchor his flying muscles he would need a breast bone maybe ten feet long. He might have to have as much as eighty feet wing spread. Folded, his wings would cover him like a tent. You're up against the cube-square disadvantage."

"Huh?"

Cargrew gestured impatiently. "Lift goes by the square of a given dimension; dead load by the cube of the same dimension, other things being equal. I might be able to make you a

Pegasus the size of a cat without distorting the proportions too much."

"No, I want one I can ride. I don't mind the wing spread and I'll put up with the big breast bone. When can I have him?"

Cargrew looked disgusted, shrugged, and replied, "I'll have to consult with B'na Kreeth." He whistled and chirped; a portion of the wall facing them dissolved and they found themselves looking into a laboratory. A Martian, life-size, showed in the forepart of the three-dimensional picture.

When the creature chirlupped back at Cargrew, Mrs. van Vogel looked up, then quickly looked away. She knew it was silly but she simply could not stand the sight of Martians—and the ones who had modified themselves to a semi-manlike form disgusted her the most.

After they had twittered and gestured at each other for a minute or two Cargrew turned back to van Vogel. "B'na says that you should forget it; it would take too long. He wants to know how you'd like a fine unicorn, or a pair, guaranteed to breed true?"

"Unicorns are old hat. How long would the Pegasus take?"

After another squeaky-door conversation Cargrew answered, "Ten years probably, sixteen years on the guarantee."

"Ten years? That's ridiculous!"

Cargrew looked shirty. "*I* thought it would take fifty, but if B'na says that he can do it three to five generations, then he can do it. B'na is the finest bio-micrurgist in two planets. His chromosome surgery in unequalled. After all, young man, natural processes would take upwards of a million years to achieve the same result, if it were achieved at all. Do you expect to be able to buy miracles?"

Van Vogel had the grace to look sheepish. "Excuse me, Doctor. Let's forget it. Ten years really is too long. How about the other possibility? You said you could make a picture-book Pegasus, as long as I did not insist on flight. Could I ride him? On the ground?"

"Oh, certainly. No good for polo, but you could ride him."

"I'll settle for that. Ask Benny creeth, or what ever his name is, how long it would take."

The Martian had faded out of the screens. "I don't need to ask him," Cargrew asserted. "This is my job—purely manipulation. B'na's collaboration is required only for rearrangement and transplanting of genes—true genetic work. I can let you have the beast in eighteen months."

"Can't you do better than that?"

"What do you expect, man? It takes eleven months to grow a new-born colt. I want one month of design and planning. The embryo will be removed on the fourth day and will be developed in an extra-uterine capsule. I'll operate ten or twelve

175

times during gestation, grafting and budding and other things you've heard of. One year from now we'll have a baby colt, with wings. Thereafter I'll deliver to you a six-months-old Pegasus."

"I'll take it."

Cargrew made some notes, then read, "One alate horse, not capable of flight and not to breed true. Basic breed your choice—I suggest a Palomino, or an Arabian. Wings designed after a condor, in white. Simulated pin feathers with a grafted fringe of quill feathers, or reasonable facsimile." He passed the sheet over. "Initial that and we'll start in advance of formal contract."

"It's a deal," agreed van Vogel. "What is the fee?" He placed his monogram under Cargrew's.

Cargrew made further notes and handed them to Blakesly —estimates of professional man-hours, technician man-hours, purchases, and overhead. He had padded the figures to subsidize his collateral research but even he raised his eyebrows at the dollars-and-cents interpretation Blakesly put on the data. "That will be an even two million dollars."

Van Vogel hesitated; his wife had looked up at the mention of money. But she turned her attention back to the scholarly elephant.

Blakesly added hastily, "That is for an exclusive creation, of course."

"Naturally," van Vogel agreed briskly, and added the figure to the memorandum.

Van Vogel was ready to return, but his wife insisted on seeing the "apes", as she termed the anthropoid workers. The discovery that she owned a considerable share in these sub-human creatures had intrigued her. Blakesly eagerly suggested a trip through the laboratories in which the workers were developed from true apes.

They were arranged in seven buildings, the seven "Days of Creation". "First Day" was a large building occupied by Cargrew, his staff, his operating rooms, incubators, and laboratories. Martha van Vogel stared in horrified fascination at living organs and even complete embryos, living artificial lives sustained by clever glass and metal recirculating systems and exquisite automatic machinery.

She could not appreciate the techniques; it seemed depressing. She had about decided against plasto-biology when Napoleon, by tugging at her skirts, reminded her that it produced good things as well as horrors.

The building "Second Day" they did not enter; it was occupied by B'na Kreeth and his racial colleagues. "We could not stay alive in it, you understand," Blakesly explained. Van Vogel nodded; his wife hurried on—she wanted no Martians, even behind plastiglass.

176

From there on the buildings were for development and production of commercial workers. "Third Day" was used for the development of variations in the anthropoids to meet constantly changing labor requirements. "Fourth Day" was a very large building devoted entirely to production-line incubators for commercial types of anthropoids. Blakesly explained that they had dispensed with normal birth. "The policy permits exact control of forced variations, such as for size, and saves hundreds of thousands of worker-hours on the part of the female anthropoids.'

Martha van Vogel was delighted with "Fifth Day", the anthropoid kindergarten where the little tykes learned to talk and were conditioned to the social patterns necessary to their station in life. They worked at simple tasks such as sorting buttons and digging holes in sand piles, with pieces of candy given as incentives for fast and accurate work.

"Six Day" completed the anthropoids' educations. Each learned the particular sub-trade it would practice, cleaning, digging, and especially agricultural semi-skills such as weeding, thinning, and picking. "One Nisei farmer working three neo-chimpanzees can grow as many vegetables as a dozen old-style farm hands," Blakesly asserted. "They really *like* to work —when we get through with them."

They admired the almost incredibly heavy tasks done by modified gorillas and stopped to gaze at the little neo-Capuchins doing high picking on prop trees, then moved on toward "Seventh Day."

This building was used for the radioactive mutation of genes and therefore located some distance away from the others. They had to walk, as the sidewalk was being repaired; the detour took them past workers' pens and barracks. Some of the anthropoids crowded up to the wire and began calling to them: "Sigret! Sigret! Preese, Missy! Preese, Boss! Sigret!"

"What are they saying?" Martha van Vogel inquired.

"They are asking for cigarettes," Blakesly answered in annoyed tones. "They know better, but they are like children. Here—I'll put a stop to it." He stepped up to the wire and shouted to an elderly male, "Hey! Strawboss!"

The worker addressed wore, in addition to the usual short canvas kilt, a bedraggled arm band. He turned and shuffled toward the fence. "Strawboss," ordered Blakesly, "get those Joes away from here."

"Okay, Boss," the old fellow acknowledged and started cuffing those nearest him. "Scram, you Joes! Scram!"

"But I have some cigarettes," protested Mrs. van Vogel, "and I would gladly have given them some."

"It doesn't do to pamper them," the Manager told her. "They have been taught that luxuries come only from work.

177

I must apologize for my poor children; those in these pens are getting old and forgetting their manners."

She did not answer but moved further along the fence to where one old neo-chimp was pressed up against the wire, staring at them with soft, tragic eyes, like a child at a bakery window. He had taken no part in the jostling demand for tobacco and had been let alone by the strawboss. "Would you like a cigarette?" she asked him.

"Preese, Missy."

She struck one which he accepted with fumbling grace, took a long, lung-filling drag, let the smoke trickle out his nostrils, and said shyly, "Sankoo, Missy. Me Jerry."

"How do you do, Jerry?"

"Howdy, Missy." He bobbed down, bending his knees, ducking his head, and clasping his hands to his chest, all in one movement.

"Come along, Martha." Her husband and Blakesly had moved in behind her.

"In a moment," she answered. "Brownie, meet my friend Jerry. Doesn't he look just like Uncle Albert? Except that he looks so sad. Why are you unhappy, Jerry?"

"They don't understand abstract ideas," put in Blakesly.

But Jerry surprised him. "Jerry sad," he announced in tones so doleful that Martha van Vogel did not know whether to laugh or to cry.

"Why, Jerry?" she asked gently. "Why are you so sad?"

"No work," he stated. "No sigret. No candy. No work."

"These are all old workers who have passed their usefulness," Blakesly repeated. "Idleness upsets them, but we have nothing for them to do."

"Well!" she said. "Then why don't you have them sort buttons, or something like that, such as the baby ones do?"

"They wouldn't even do that properly," Blakesly answered her. "These workers are senile."

"Jerry isn't senile! You heard him talk."

"Well, perhaps not. Just a moment." He turned to the ape-man, who was squatting down in order to scratch Napoleon's head with a long forefinger thrust through the fence. "You, Joe! Come here."

Blakesly felt around the worker's hairy neck and located a thin steel chain to which was attached a small metal tag. He studied it. "You're right," he admitted. "He's not really over age, but his eyes are bad. I remember the lot—cataracts as a result of an unfortunate linked mutation." He shrugged. "But that's no reason to let him grieve his heart out in idleness."

"Really, Mrs. van Vogel, you should not upset yourself about it. They don't stay in these pens long—only a few days at the most."

"Oh," she answered, somewhat mollified, "you have some other place to retire them to, then. Do you give them something to do there? You should—Jerry wants to work. Don't you, Jerry?"

The neo-chimp had been struggling to follow the conversation. He caught the last idea and grinned. "Jerry work! Sure mike! Good worker." He flexed his fingers, then made fists, displaying fully opposed thumbs.

Mr. Blakesly seemed somewhat nonplused. "Really, Mrs. van Vogel, there is no need. You see—" He stopped.

Van Vogel had been listening irritably. His wife's enthusiasms annoyed him, unless they were also his own. Furthermore he was beginning to blame Blakesly for his own recent extravagance and had a premonition that his wife would find some way to make him pay, very sweetly, for his indulgence.

Being annoyed with both of them, he chucked in the perfect wrong remark. "Don't be silly, Martha. They don't retire them; they liquidate them."

It took a little time for the idea to soak in, but when it did she was furious. "Why . . . why—I never heard of such a thing! You ought to be ashamed. You . . . you would shoot your own grandmother."

"Mrs. van Vogel—please!"

"Don't 'Mrs. van Vogel' me! It's got to stop—you hear me?" She looked around at the death pens, at the milling hundreds of old workers therein. "It's horrible. You work them until they can't work anymore, then you take away their little comforts, and you *dispose* of them. I wonder you don't eat them!"

"They do," her husband said brutally. "Dog food."

"What! Well, we'll put a stop to that!"

"Mrs. van Vogel," Blakesly pleaded. "Let me explain."

"Hummph! Go ahead. It had better be good."

"Well, it's like this—" His eye fell on Jerry, standing with worried expression at the fence. "Scram, Joe!" Jerry shuffled away.

"Wait, Jerry!" Mrs. van Vogel called out. Jerry paused uncertainly. "Tell him to come back," she ordered Blakesly.

The Manager bit his lip, then called out, "Come back here."

He was beginning definitely to dislike Mrs. van Vogel, despite his automatic tendency to genuflect in the presence of a high credit rating. To be told how to run his own business—well, now, indeed! "Mrs. van Vogel, I admire your humanitarian spirit but you don't understand the situation. We understand our workers and do what is best for them. They die painlessly before their disabilities can trouble them. They live happy lives, happier than yours or mine. We trim off the bad part of their lives, nothing more. And don't forget, these poor beasts would never have been born had we not arranged it."

179

She shook her head. "Fiddlesticks! You'll be quoting the Bible at me next. There will be no more of it, Mr. Blakesly. I shall hold you personally responsible."

Blakesly looked bleak. "My responsibilities are to the directors."

"You think so?" She opened her purse and snatched out her telephone. So great was her agitation that she did not bother to call through, but signalled the local relay operator instead. "Phoenix? Get me Great New York Murray Hill 9Q-4004, Mr. Haskell. Priority—star subscriber 777. Make it quick." She stood there, tapping her foot and glaring, until her business manager answered. "Haskell? This is Martha van Vogel. How much Workers, Incorporated, common do I own? No, no, never mind that—what percent? . . . so? Well, it's not enough. I want 51% by tomorrow morning . . . all right, get proxies for the rest but get it . . . I didn't ask you what it would cost; I said to get it. Get busy." She disconnected abruptly and turned to her husband. "We're leaving, Brownie, and we are taking Jerry with us. Mr. Blakesly, will you kindly have him taken out of that pen? Give him a check for the amount, Brownie."

"Now, Martha—"

"My mind is made up, Brownie."

Mr. Blakesly cleared his throat. It was going to be pleasant to thwart this woman. "The workers are never sold. I'm sorry. It's a matter of policy."

"Very well then, I'll take a permanent lease."

"This worker has been removed from the labor market. He is not for lease."

"Am I going to have more trouble with you?"

"If you please, Madame! This worker is not available under any terms—but, as a courtesy to you, I am willing to transfer to you indentures for him, gratis. I want you to know that the policies of this firm are formed from a very real concern for the welfare of our charges as well as from the standpoint of good business practice. We therefore reserve the right to inspect at any time to assure ourselves that you are taking proper care of this worker." There, he told himself savagely, that will stop her clock!

"Of course. Thank you, Mr. Blakesly. You are most gracious."

The trip back to Great New York was not jolly. Napoleon hated it and let it be known. Jerry was patient but airsick. By the time they grounded the van Vogels were not on speaking terms.

"I'm sorry, Mrs. van Vogel. The shares were simply not available. We should have had proxy on the O'Toole block

180

but someone tied them up an hour before I reached them."

"Blakesly."

"Undoubtedly. You should not have tipped him off; you gave him time to warn his employers."

"Don't waste time telling me what mistakes I made yesterday. What are you going to do today?"

"Mr. dear Mrs. van Vogel, what can I do? I'll carry out any instructions you care to give."

"Don't talk nonsense. You are supposed to be smarter than I am; that's why I pay you to do my thinking for me."

Mr. Haskell looked helpless.

His principal struck a cigarette so hard she broke it. "Why isn't Weinberg here?"

"Really, Mrs. van Vogel, there are no special legal aspects. You want the stock; we can't buy it nor bind it. Therefore—"

"I pay Weinberg to know the legal angles. Get him."

Weinberg was leaving his office; Haskell caught him on a chase-me circuit. "Sidney," Haskell called out. "Come to my office, will you? Oscar Haskell."

"Sorry. How about four o'clock?"

"Sidney, I want you—now!" cut in the client's voice. "This is Martha van Vogel."

The little man shrugged helplessly. "Right away," he agreed. That woman—why hadn't he retired on his one hundred and twenty-fifth birthday, as his wife had urged him to?

Ten minutes later he was listening to Haskell's explanations and his client's interruptions. When they had finished he spread his hands. "What do you expect, Mrs. van Vogel? These workers are chattels. You have not been able to buy the property rights involved; you are stopped. But I don't see what you are worked up about. They gave you the worker whose life you wanted preserved.

She spoke forcefully under her breath, then answered him. "That's not important. What is one worker among millions? I want to stop this killing, all of it."

Weinberg shook his head. "If you were able to prove that their methods of disposing of these beasts were inhumane, or that they were negligent of their physical welfare before destroying them, or that the destruction was wanton—"

"Wanton? It certain is!"

"Probably not in a legal sense, my dear lady. There was a case, Julius Hartman et al. vs. Hartman Estate, 1972, I believe, in which a permanent injunction was granted against carrying out a term of the will which called for the destruction of a valuable collection of Persian cats. But in order to use that theory you would have to show that these creatures, when superannuated, are notwithstanding more valuable alive than dead. You cannot compel a person to maintain chattels at a loss."

181

"See here, Sidney, I didn't get you over here to tell me how this can't be done. If what I want isn't legal, then get a law passed."

Weinberg looked at Haskell, who looked embarrassed and answered, "Well, the fact of the matter is, Mrs. van Vogel, that we have agreed with the other members of the Commonwealth Association not to subsidize any legislation during the incumbency of the present administration."

"How ridiculous! Why?"

"The Legislative Guild has brought out a new fair-practices code which we consider quite unfair, a sliding scale which penalizes the well-to-do—all very nice sounding, with special provisions for nominal fees for veterans' private bills and such things—but in fact the code is confiscatory. Even the Briggs Foundation can hardly afford to take a proper interest in public affairs under this so-called code."

"Hmmph! A fine day when legislators join unions—they are professional men. Bribes should be competitive. Get an injunction."

"Mrs. van Vogel," protested Weinberg, "how can you expect me to get an injunction against an organization which has no legal existence? In a legal sense, there is no Legislative Guild, just as the practice of assisting legislation by subsidy has itself no legal existence."

"And babies come under cabbage leaves. Quit stalling me, gentlemen. What are you going to do?"

Weinberg spoke when he saw that Haskell did not intend to. "Mrs. van Vogel, I think we should retain a special shyster."

"I don't employ shysters, even—I don't undertsand the way they think. I am a simple housewife, Sidney."

Mr. Weinberg flinched at her self-designation while noting that he must not let her find out that the salary of his own staff shyster was charged to her payroll. As convention required, he maintained the front of a simple, barefoot solicitor, but he had found out long ago that Martha van Vogel's problems required an occasional dose of the more exotic branch of the law. "The man I have in mind is a creative artist," he insisted. "It is no more necessary to understand him than it is to understand the composer in order to appreciate a symphony. I do recommand that you talk with him, at least."

"Oh, very well! Get him up here."

"Here? My dear lady!" Haskell was shocked at the suggestion; Weinberg looked amazed. "It would not only cause any action you bring to be thrown out of court if it were known that you had consulted this man, but it would prejudice any Briggs enterprise for years."

Mrs. van Vogel shrugged. "You men. I never will understand the way you think. Why shouldn't one consult a shyster as openly as one consults an astrologer?"

182

James Roderick McCoy was not a large man, but he seemed large. He managed to dominate even so large a room as Mrs. van Vogel's salon. His business card read:

J. R. McCOY
"THE REAL McCOY"

Licensed Shyster—Fixing, Special Contacts,
Angles. All Work Guaranteed.

TELEPHONE SKYLINE 9-8M4554
Ask for MAC

The number given was the pool room of the notorious Three Planets Club. He wasted no time on offices and kept his files in his head—the only safe place for them.

He was sitting on the floor, attempting to teach Jerry to shoot craps, while Mrs. van Vogel explained her problem. "What do you think, Mr. McCoy? Could we approach it through the SPCA? My public relations staff could give it a build up."

McCoy got to his feet. "Jerry's eyes aren't so bad; he caught me trying to palm box cars off on him as a natural. No," he continued, "the SPCA angle is no good. It's what 'workers' will expect. They'll be ready to prove that the anthropoids actually enjoy being killed off."

Jerry rattled the dice hopefully. "That's all, Jerry. Scram."

"Okay, Boss." The ape man got to his feet and went to the big stereo which filled a corner of the room. Napoleon ambled after him and switched it on. Jerry punched a selector button and got a blues singer. Napoleon immediately punched another, then another and another until he got a loud but popular band. He stood there, beating out the rhythm with his trunk.

Jerry looked pained and switched it back to his blues singer. Napoleon stubbornly reached out with his prehensile nose and switched it off.

Jerry used a swear word.

"Boys!" called out Mrs. van Vogel. "Quit squabbling. Jerry, let Nappie play what he wants to. You can play the stereo when Nappie has to take his nap."

"Okay, Missy Boss."

McCoy was interested. "Jerry likes music?"

"Like it? He loves it. He's been learning to sing."

"Huh? This I gotta hear."

"Certainly. Nappie—turn off the stereo." The elephant complied but managed to look put upon. "Now Jerry—'Jingle Bells.'" She led him in it:

183

"Jingle bells, jingle bells, jingle all the day—", and he followed,

"Jinger bez, jinger bez, jinger awrah day;
Oh, wot fun tiz to ride in one-hoss open sray."

He was flat, he was terrible. He looked ridiculous, patting out the time with one splay foot. But it was singing.

"Say, that's fast!" McCoy commented. "Too bad Nappie can't talk—we'd have a duet."

Jerry looked puzzled. "Nappie talk good," he stated. He bent over the elephant and spoke to him. Napoleon grunted and moaned back at him. "See, Boss?" Jerry said triumphantly.

"What did he say?"

"He say, 'Can Nappie pray stereo now?'"

"Very well, Jerry," Mrs. van Vogel interceded. The ape man spoke to his chum in whispers. Napoleon squealed and did not turn on the stereo.

"Jerry!" said his mistress. "I said nothing of the sort; he does *not* have to play your blues singer. Come away, Jerry. Nappie—play what you want to."

"You mean he tried to cheat?" McCoy inquired with interest.

"He certainly did."

"Hmm—Jerry's got the makings of a real citizen. Shave him and put shoes on him and he'd get by all right in the precinct I grew up in." He stared at the anthropoid. Jerry stared back, puzzled but patient. Mrs. van Vogel had thrown away the dirty canvas kilt which was both his badge of servitude and a concession to propriety and had replaced it with a kilt in the bright Cameron war plaid, complete to sporan, and topped off with a Glengarry.

"Do you suppose he could learn to play the bagpipes?" McCoy asked. "I'm beginning to get an angle."

"Why, I don't know. What's your idea?"

McCoy squatted down cross-legged and began practicing rolls with his dice. "Never mind," he answered when it suited him, "that angle's no good. But we're getting there." He rolled four naturals, one after the other. "You say Jerry still belongs to the Corporation?"

"In a titular sense, yes. I doubt if they will ever try to repossess him."

"I wish they would try." He scooped up the dice and stood up. "It's in the bag, Sis. Forget it. I'll want to talk to your publicity man but you can quit worrying about it."

Of course Mrs. van Vogel should have knocked before entering her husband's room—but then she would not have overheard what he was saying, nor to whom.

"That's right," she heard him say, "we haven't any further need for him. Take him away, the sooner the better. Just be

184

sure the men you send have a signed order directing us to turn him over."

She was not apprehensive, as she did not understand the conversation, but merely curious. She looked over her husband's shoulder at the video screen.

There she saw Blakesly's face. His voice was saying, "Very well, Mr. van Vogel, the anthropoid will be picked up tomorrow."

She strode up to the screen. "Just a minute, Mr. Blakesly—" then, to her husband, "Brownie, what in the world do you think you are doing?"

The expression she surprised on his face was not one he had ever let her see before. "Why don't you knock?"

"Maybe it's a good thing I didn't. Brownie, did I hear you right. Were you telling Mr. Blakesly to pick up Jerry?" She turned to the screen. "Was that it, Mr. Blakesly?"

"That is correct, Mrs. van Vogel. And I must say I find this confusion most—"

"Stow it." She turned back. "Brownie, what have you to say for yourself?"

"Martha, you are being preposterous. Between that elephant and that ape this place is a zoo. I actually caught your precious Jerry smoking my special, personal cigars today . . . not to mention the fact that both of them play the stereo all day long until a man can't get a moment's peace. I certainly don't have to stand for such things in my own house."

"Whose house, Brownie?"

"That's beside the point. I will not stand for—"

"Never mind." She turned to the screen. "My husband seems to have lost his taste for exotic animals, Mr. Blakesly. Cancel the order for a Pegasus."

"Martha!"

"Sauce for the goose, Brownie. I'll pay for your whims; I'm damned if I'll pay for your tantrums. The contract is cancelled, Mr. Blakesly. Mr. Haskell will arrange the details."

Blakesly shrugged. "Your capricious behavior will cost you, of course. The penalties—"

"I said Mr. Haskell would arrange the details. One more thing, Mister Manager Blakesly—have you done as I told you to?"

"What do you mean?"

"You know what I mean—are those poor creatures still alive and well?"

"That is not your business." He had, in fact, suspended the killings; the directors had not wanted to take any chances until they saw what the Briggs trust could manage, but Blakesly would not give her the satisfaction of knowing.

She looked at him as if he were a skipped dividend. "It's not,
185

eh? Well, bear this in mind, you cold-blooded little pipsqueak: I'm holding you personally responsible. If just one of them dies from *anything*, I'll have your skin for a rug." She flipped off the connection and turned to her husband. "Brownie—"

"It's useless to say anything," he cut in, in the cold voice he normally used to bring her to heel. "I shall be at the Club. Good-bye!"

"That's just what I was going to suggest."

"What?"

"I'll have your clothes sent over. Do you have anything else in this house?"

He stared at her. "Don't talk like a fool, Martha."

"I'm not talking like a fool." She looked him up and down. "My, but you are handsome, Brownie. I guess I was a fool to think I could buy a big hunk of man with a checkbook. I guess a girl gets them free, or she doesn't get them at all. Thanks for the lesson." She turned and slammed out of the room and into her own suite.

Five minutes later, makeup repaired and nerves steadied by a few whiffs of Fly-Right, she called the pool room of the Three Planets Club. McCoy came to the screen carrying a cue. "Oh, it's you, sugar puss. Well, snap it up—I've got four bits on this game."

"This is business."

"Okay, okay—spill it."

She told him the essentials. "I'm sorry about cancelling the flying horse contract, Mr. McCoy. I hope it won't make your job any harder. I'm afraid I lost my temper."

"Fine. Go lose it again."

"Huh?"

"You're barrelling down the groove, kid. Call Blakesly up again. Bawl him out. Tell him to keep his bailiffs away from you, or you'll stuff 'em and use them for hat racks. Dare him to take Jerry away from you."

"I don't understand you."

"You don't have to, girlie. Remember this: You can't have a bull fight until you get the bull mad enough to fight. Have Weinberg get a temporary injunction restraining Workers, Incorporated, from reclaiming Jerry. Have your boss press agent give me a buzz. Then you call in the newsboys and tell them what you think of Blakesly. Make it nasty. Tell them you intend to put a stop to this wholesale murder if it takes every cent you've got."

"Well . . . all right. Will you come to see me before I talk to them?"

"Nope—gotta get back to my game. Tomorrow, maybe. Don't fret about having cancelled that silly winged-horse deal. I always did think your old man was weak in the head, and

186

it's saved you a nice piece of change. You'll need it when I send in my bill. Boy, am I going to clip you! Bye now."

The bright letters trailed around the sides of the Times Building: "WORLD'S RICHEST WOMAN PUTS UP FIGHT FOR APE MAN." On the giant video screen above showed a transcribe of Jerry, in his ridiculous Highland chief outfit. A small army of police surrounded the Briggs town house, while Mrs. van Vogel informed anyone who would listen, including several news services, that she would defend Jerry personally and to the death.

The public relations office of Workers, Incorporated, denied any intention of seizing Jerry; the denial got nowhere.

In the meantime technicians installed extra audio and video circuits in the largest court room in town, for one Jerry (no surname), described as a legal, permanent resident of these United States, had asked for a permanent injunction against the corporate person "Workers," its officers, employees, successors, or assignees, forbidding it to do him any physical harm and in particular forbidding it to kill him.

Through his attorney, the honorable and distinguished and stuffily respectable Augustus Pomfrey, Jerry brought the action *in his own name*.

Martha van Vogel sat in the court room as a spectator only, but she was surrounded by secretaries, guards, maid, publicity men, and yes men, and had one television camera trained on her alone. She was nervous. McCoy had insisted on briefing Pomfrey through Weinberg, to keep Pomfrey from knowing that he was being helped by a shyster. She had her own opinion of Pomfrey—

The McCoy had insisted that Jerry not wear his beautiful new kilt but had dressed him in faded dungaree trousers and jacket. It seemed poor theater to her.

Jerry himself worried her. He seemed confused by the lights and the noise and the crowd, about to go to pieces.

And McCoy had refused to go to the trial with her. He had told her that it was quite impossible, that his mere presence would alienate the court, and Weinberg had backed him up. Men! Their minds were devious—they seemed to *like* twisted ways of doing things. It confirmed her opinion that men should not be allowed to vote.

But she felt lost without the immediate presence of McCoy's easy self-confidence. Away from him, she wondered why she had ever trusted such an important matter to an irresponsible, jumping jack, bird-brained clown as McCoy. She chewed her nails and wished he were present.

The panel of attorneys appearing for Worker's Incorporated, began by moving that the action be dismissed without trial,

187

on the theory that Jerry was a chattel of the corporation, an integral part of it, and no more able to sue than the thumb can sue the brain.

The honorable Augustus Pomfrey looked every inch the statesman as he bowed to the court and to his opponents. "It is indeed strange," he began, "to hear the second-hand voice of a legal fiction, a soulless, imaginary quantity called a corporate 'person,' argue that a flesh-and-blood creature, a being of hopes and longings and passions, has not legal existence. I see here beside me my poor cousin Jerry." He patted Jerry on the shoulder; the ape man, needing reassurance, slid a hand into his. It went over well.

"But when I look for this abstract fancy 'Workers,' what do I find? Nothing—some words on paper, some signed bits of foolscap—"

"If the Court please, a question," put in the opposition chief attorney, "does the learned counsel contend that a limited liability stock company cannot own property?"

"Will the counsel reply?" directed the judge.

"Thank you. My esteemed colleague has set up a straw man; I contended only that the question as to whether Jerry is a chattel of Workers, Incorporated, is immaterial, nonessential, irrelevant. I am part of the corporate city of Great New York. Does that deny me my civil rights as a person of flesh and blood? In fact it does not even rob me of my right to sue that civic corporation of which I am a part, if, in my opinion, I am wronged by it. We are met today in the mellow light of equity, rather than in the cold and narrow confines of law. It seemed a fit time to dwell on the strange absurdities we live by, whereunder a nonentity of paper and legal fiction could deny the existence of this our poor cousin. I ask that the learned attorneys for the corporation stipulate that Jerry does, in fact, exist, and let us get on with the action."

They huddled; the answer was "No."

"Very well. My client asked to be examined in order that the court may determine his status and being."

"Objection! This anthropoid cannot be examined; he is a mere part and chattel of the respondent."

"That is what we are about to determine," the judge answered dryly. "Objection overruled."

"Go sit in that chair, Jerry."

"Objection! This beast cannot take an oath—it is beyond his comprehension."

"What have you to say to that, Counsel?"

"If it pleases the Court," answered Pomfrey, "the simplest thing to do is to put him in the chair and find out."

"Let him take the stand. The clerk will administer the oath." Martha van Vogel gripped the arms of her chair; McCoy had spent a full week training him for this. Would the poor thing blow up without McCoy to guide him?

The clerk droned through the oath; Jerry looked puzzled but patient.

"Your honor," said Pomfrey, "when young children must give testimony, it is customary to permit a little leeway in the wording, to fit their mental attainments. May I be permitted?" He walked up to Jerry.

"Jerry, my boy, are you a good worker?"

"Sure mike! Jerry good worker!"

"Maybe bad worker, huh? Lazy. Hide from strawboss."

"No, no, no! Jerry good worker. Dig. Weed. Not dig up vegetaber. Dig up weed. Work hard."

"You will see," Pomfrey addressed the court, "that my client has very definite ideas of what is true and what is false. Now let us attempt to find out whether or not he has moral values which require him to tell the truth. Jerry—"

"Yes, Boss."

Pomfrey spread his hand in front of the anthropoid's face. "How many fingers do you see?"

Jerry reached out and ticked them off. "One—two—sree —four, uh—five."

"Six fingers, Jerry."

"Five, Boss."

"Six fingers, Jerry. I give you cigarette. Six."

"Five, Boss. Jerry not cheat."

Pomfrey spread his hands. "Will the court accept him?"

The court did. Martha van Vogel sighed. Jerry could not count very well and she had been afraid that he would forget his lines and accept the bribe. But he had been promised all the cigarettes he wanted and chocolate as well if he would remember to insist that five was five.

"I suggest," Pomfrey went on, "that the matter has been established. Jerry is an entity; if he can be accepted as a witness, then surely he may have his day in court. Even a dog may have his day in court. Will my esteemed colleagues stipulate?"

Workers, Incorporated, through its battery of lawyers, agreed—just in time, for the judge was beginning to cloud up. He had been much impressed by the little performance.

The tide was with him; Pomfrey used it. "If it please the court and if the counsels for the respondent will permit, we can shorten these proceedings. I will state the theory under which relief is sought and then, by a few questions, it may be settled one way or another. I ask that it be stipulated that it was the intention of Workers, Incorporated, through its servants, to take the life of my client."

Stipulation was refused.

"So? Then I ask that the court take judicial notice of the

well known fact that these anthropoid workers are destroyed when they no longer show a profit; thereafter I will call witnesses, starting with Horace Blakesly, to show that Jerry was and presumably is under such sentence of death."

Another hurried huddle resulted in the stipulation that Jerry had, indeed, been scheduled for euthanasia.

"Then," said Pomfrey, "I will state my theory. Jerry is not an animal, but a man. It is not legal to kill him—it is murder."

First there was silence, then the crowd gasped. People had grown used to animals that talked and worked, but they were no more prepared to think of them as persons, humans, *men*, than were the haughty Roman citizens prepared to concede human feelings to their barbarian slaves.

Pomfrey let them have it while they were still groggy. "What is a man? A collection of living cells and tissues? A legal fiction, like this corporate 'person' that would take poor Jerry's life? No, a man is none of these things. A man is a collection of hopes and fears, of human longings, of aspirations greater than himself—more than the clay from which he came; less than the Creator which lifted him up from the clay. Jerry has been taken from his jungle and made something more than the poor creatures who were his ancestors, even as you and I. We ask that this Court recognize his manhood."

The opposing attorneys saw that the Court was moved; they drove in fast. An anthropoid, they contended, could not be a man because he lacked human shape and human intelligence. Pomfrey called his first witness—Master B'na Kreeth.

The Martian's normal bad temper had not been improved by being forced to wait around for three days in a travel tank, to say nothing of the indignity of having to interrupt his researches to take part in the childish pow-wows of terrestrials.

There was further delay to irritate him while Pomfrey forced the corporation attorneys to accept B'na as an expert witness. They wanted to refuse but could not—he was their own Director of Research. He also held voting control of all Martian-held Workers' stock, a fact unmentioned but hampering.

More delay while an interpreter was brought in to help adminster the oath—B'na Kreeth, self-centered as all Martians, had never bothered to learn English.

He twittered and chirped in answer to the demand that he tell the truth, the whole truth, and so forth; the interpreter looked pained. "He says he can't do it," he informed the judge.

Pomfrey asked for exact translation.

The interpreter looked uneasily at the judge. "He says that if he told the whole truth you fools—not 'fools' exactly; it's a

190

Martian word meaning a sort of headless worm—would not understand it."

The court discussed the idea of contempt briefly. When the Martian understood that he was about to be forced to remain in a travel tank for thirty days he came down off his high horse and agreed to tell the truth as adequately as was possible; he was accepted as a witness.

"Are you a man?" demanded Pomfrey.

"Under your laws and by your standards I am a man."

"By what theory? Your body is unlike ours; you cannot even live in our air. You do not speak our language; your ideas are alien to us. How can you be a man?"

The Martian answered carefully: *"I quote from the Terra-Martian Treaty, which you must accept as supreme law. 'All members of the Great Race, while sojourning on the Third Planet, shall have all the rights and prerogatives of the native dominant race of the Third Planet.' This clause has been interpreted by the Bi-Planet Tribunal to mean that members of the Great Race are 'men' whatever that may be."*

"Why do you refer to your sort as the 'Great Race'?"

"Because of our superior intelligence."

"Superior to men?"

"We are men."

"Superior to the intelligence of earth men?"

"That is self-evident."

"Just as we are superior in intelligence to this poor creature Jerry?"

"That is not self-evident."

"Finished with the witness," announced Pomfrey. The opposition counsels should have left bad enough alone; instead they tried to get B'na Kreeth to define the difference in intelligence between humans and worker-anthropoids. Master B'na explained meticulously that cultural differences masked the intrinsic differences, if any, and that, in any case, both anthropoids and men made so little use of their respective potential intelligences that it was really too early to tell which race would turn out to be the superior race in the Third Planet.

He had just begun to discuss how a truly superior race could be bred by combining the best features of anthropoids and men when he was hastily asked to "stand down."

"May it please the Court," said Pomfrey, "we have not advanced the theory; we have merely disposed of respondent's contention that a particular shape and a particular degree of intelligence are necessary to manhood. I now ask that the petitioner be recalled to the stand that the court may determine whether he is, in truth, human."

"If the learned court please—" The battery of lawyers had been in a huddle ever since B'na Kreeth's travel tank had been removed from the room; the chief counsel now spoke.

191

"The object of the petition appears to be to protect the life of this chattel. There is no need to draw out these proceedings; respondent stipulates that this chattel will be allowed to die a natural death in the hands of its present custodian and moves that the action be dismissed."

"What do you say to that?" the Court asked Pomfrey.

Pomfrey visibly gathered his toga about him. "We ask not for cold charity from this corporation, but for the justice of the court. We ask that Jerry's humanity be established as a matter of law. Not for him to vote, nor to hold property, nor to be relieved of special police regulations appropriate to his group—but we do ask that he be adjudged at least as human as that aquarium monstrosity just removed from this court room!"

The judge turned to Jerry. "Is that what you want, Jerry?"

Jerry looked uneasily at Pomfrey, then said, "Okay, Boss."

"Come up to the chair."

"One moment—" The opposition chief counsel seemed flurried. "I ask the Court to consider that a ruling in this matter may affect a long established commercial practice necessary to the economic life of—"

"Objection!" Pomfrey was on his feet, bristling. "Never have I heard a more outrageous attempt to prejudice a decision. My esteemed colleague might as well ask the Court to decide a murder case from political considerations. I protest—"

"Never mind," said the court. "The suggestion will be ignored. Proceed with your witness."

Pomfrey bowed. "We are exploring the meaning of this strange thing called 'manhood.' We have seen that it is not a matter of shape, nor race, nor planet of birth, nor of acuteness of mind. Truly, it cannot be defined, yet it may be experienced. It can reach from heart to heart, from spirit to spirit." He turned to Jerry. "Jerry—will you sing your new song for the judge?"

"Sure mike." Jerry looked uneasily up at the whirring cameras, the mikes, and the ikes, then cleared his throat:

"Way down upon de Suwannee Ribber
Far, far away;
Dere's where my heart is turning ebber—"

The applause scared him out of his wits; the banging of the gavel frightened him still more—but it mattered not; the issue was no longer in doubt. Jerry was a man.

THE END